Watershed

Watershed

THE UNDAMMING

OF AMERICA

Elizabeth Grossman

COUNTERPOINT

Library of Congress Cataloging-in-Publication Data
Grossman, Elizabeth, 1957–
Watershed : the undamming of America / Elizabeth Grossman.
p. cm.
ISBN 1-58243-108-6 (alk. paper)
1. Dams—Environmental aspects—United States. I. Title.
TD195.D35 G76   2002
333.91'14'0973—dc21
2002000725

FIRST PRINTING

Jacket and Text design by Jane Raese
Title page photo: Glen Canyon Dam (© Jane Raese)

Printed in the United States of America on acid-free paper
that meets the American National Standards Institute
z39-48 Standard.

COUNTERPOINT
387 Park Avenue South
New York, NY 10016-8810
Counterpoint is a member of the Perseus Books Group

10 9 8 7 6 5 4 3 2 1

For the rivers—
and all those working
to protect and restore them

contents

CONTENTS

watershed *n*

1 a ridge of high land dividing two areas
that are drained by different river systems

2 the region draining into a river,
river system or other body of water

3 a critical point that marks a division or
a change of course; a turning point

—adapted from The American Heritage
Dictionary, *3rd edition, 1996*

prologue

On a hot August day in 1995 a friend who lives in Lewiston, Idaho, took me to Lower Granite Dam on the Snake River. We drove up the steep curves of the Lewiston grade, then wound our way into the rolling grass hills of the Palouse, where my love of landscape overcame my lack of interest in a dam. The road looped through miles of rich farmland toward the river and wall of concrete that form the dam. There we watched the locks fill and empty to allow passage of a huge barge of lentils headed downstream for the Lower Columbia, transport made possible by a feat of engineering that has transformed a river with some of the continent's biggest rapids into a tame navigational corridor. My friend, an enthusiastic angler, insisted we visit the fish-viewing room. I humored him and feigned curiosity.

We stood in front of a huge aquarium-like wall watching for fish through the cloudy aerated water. Sunlight filtered through the murky aqua haze. As a flutter of tail and shimmer of fin came into sight I was immediately fascinated. The fish struggled against the moving water. My friend identified them for me—pike-minnow, steelhead and shad—and showed me the official count posted on a door. We then went upstairs to see a fish ladder, a stainless steel apparatus resembling a hi-tech washboard. It was not the season for climbing fish, and bare of water, to my eyes, it looked treacherous.

Before leaving, we walked through the visitors center, which featured a huge relief map of the Columbia and Snake River watersheds with all the dams marked by neat patches of black tape. Almost no bend of river or tributary was free of such a marker.

I had driven much of that watershed, from Montana, west along the Lochsa River, from the Clark Fork and Blackfoot Rivers, to the Selway, Bitterroot and Clearwater, across the Snake to the Columbia. My friend had taken me fishing on the Wenaha and the Grande Ronde. I have hiked along their headwaters, high in the mountains of northeastern Oregon. I have seen the old fishing piers at The Dalles at the eastern end of the Columbia River Gorge where Celilo Falls tumbled for eons before being submerged by the Dalles Dam in 1957. It is magnificent country and to see it reduced to a series of dams was unsettling. Thinking of that landscape and all it represents, I began to understand the magnitude of what was displayed on that map, sitting under a glass box like a prize-winning science fair project.

Until 1996, I lived in Manhattan, where I was born. The Hudson was my river. It was important to the geography and aesthetics of where I lived, but I never thought about being *on* a river. Then, in 1993, I was handed a paddle and invited to float a river in Utah. In a kayak you learn quickly how much attention a river demands. You consider currents, stream banks, riffles and rapids in a whole new light. Where a river comes from, where it goes, what shapes its flow, what and who lives along its shores take on a new meaning. I began to ask questions, to read about rivers and to meet people who have devoted their lives to the preservation of rivers and the country they flow through. To be on a river is to learn its story.

The Pacific Northwest is now my home. The Willamette River, a tributary of the Columbia, is a minute's walk from my door. The Northwest is a region whose identity and character have been formed by its natural environment—by its tall trees and its salmon. The rain that runs off my roof, off my neighbors' lawns and trickles down the curbside affects the habitat of imperiled fish. Rivers and salmon are with us as we walk to the corner.

At dawn of the summer solstice 1998, I am on the banks of the Columbia River. Mist hangs low over the river and ravens cry out in the blue-green light. We launch our kayaks and cross the shipping channel where huge tankers dwarf our tiny muscle-driven boats. Over the next two days we paddle the island channels of the Lower Columbia. We see a dozen bald eagles and rookeries full of herons. Caspian terns and gulls dive for fish as we slide by. There is low water and surf as tides and wind move in from the ocean.

Near evening we round a point and head toward camp. Our small boats ride swells that catch glints of the setting sun. As our arms work against the water's strength, it is hard to fathom that this mighty river, by most reckoning the most powerful river in North America, does not flow freely, but at the whim of a chain of dams that reaches far into the interior Northwest.

Shortly after that trip, I was asked to write an essay about dam removal for the Patagonia catalogue. As I worked on that piece it became clear that the stories around the issue would make a book. For all over the country, from Maine to Florida, the Carolinas to California, the Midwest to the desert Southwest and Pacific Northwest, serious river restoration is under way, involving the removal of dams that have outlived their usefulness and are, quite simply, harmful.

As Americans, we have a curious relationship with our rivers. We depend on them but often take them for granted. We have used them, abused them and yet we love them dearly. In many communities over the past decade or so, rivers have begun to enjoy a renaissance. Rivers paved over by the progress of cities, suburbs and highways, or sullied by runoff and refuse, are taking on new significance as people recognize the ecological importance of, take pride in and work to reclaim their waterways. Many watersheds are now heralded by decorative road signs and curbside storm drains stenciled with geographically grounded warnings: "Dump No Waste—Drains to [your local] River."

America has spent most of its first two centuries turning its rivers into highways, ditches and power plants. Now, slowly, we are relearning what a river is and how to live with one. We are beginning to confront the damage wrought by decades and generations of despoiling and damming our rivers. Reconsidering the use of our rivers means examining our priorities as a nation. It forces us to rethink our patterns of consumption and growth and may well be key to reclaiming a vital part of America's future.

So many dams have been removed and so many communities are considering restoring free flows to their rivers that I had to choose which I would describe. I selected what I hope will be a representative sampling of geography, scale of undertaking and range of issues involved.

Dam removal does not seem to happen quickly, so several of the efforts I describe are works in progress. Given the reams of scientific and logistical studies that accompany each dam removal, one could write a doctoral dissertation on each dam I visited. But I am not a hydrologist, geomorphologist, civil engineer or fisheries biologist, so I present what I hope will be an informed snapshot. There are many books about the building of this country's large dams—Hoover, Grand Coulee, Glen Canyon and those on the Lower Snake and Columbia among them. This book describes the beginning of the next chapter in river history, in which we try to restore rivers and watersheds fragmented by dams.

In my travels, mindful of what a federal agency spokesperson called "ecology by bumpersticker," I've collected quite a few such souvenirs. "Restore Glen Canyon," "Save Our Wild Salmon," "These Dams Don't Make Sense," "Free the Ocklawaha," "Extinction Is Forever—Dams Are Not," they say. "Clean Water, No Dam," proclaims a T-shirt. And then there's my favorite, the commemorative safety vest from the Department of the Interior's "Dam Busters Tour."

Dams have been removed all over the country for many years, but the thinking prompting current dam removals is new. This reevaluation is also taking place internationally, both at the grassroots level and in government. In November 2000, the World Commission on Dams—an international consortium representing governments, non-governmental organizations (NGOs) and businesses—published a report questioning whether large dams, given their long-term ecological, financial and human costs, are the best tool for managing the world's most valuable resource, its water.

Some people have asked if this book will tell how to remove a dam, as if it might be a kind of monkey-wrenching guide. Others have cautioned against being swept up in a zealous enthusiasm for removing dams just for the sake of knocking a hole in the status quo. Dams have been with us throughout history and they will continue to be with us. We cannot turn back the clock, but where dams have come out, the rivers' natural conditions have begun to return.

A dam can disrupt a river's entire ecosystem, affecting everything from headwaters to delta. So removing a dam, large or small, is not an easy process. Inevitably it means a physical change: from the controlled, still waters of an impoundment to the constant movement that comes with a dynamic, free-flowing river. Dam removal alters the visual contours of a community. It is a very public enterprise and is almost always controversial, involving political decisions and civic debate.

I began this book thinking that the impulse to protect the integrity of our rivers' ecosystems came from an understanding and appreciation of nature—values that rise above politics. I knew how contentious environmental issues can be, but work on this book made me realize the vital role of public policy. What priorities are set for the federal, state and local agencies responsible for water quality and wildlife protection, how funds are allocated for river restoration projects—these are political decisions. Yet political campaigns and administrations are fleeting, while river restoration is for the long haul. With dams, we have tried to mold rivers to suit human purposes. We are learning—at great cost—that rivers don't work that way. Rivers reach farther and last longer than perhaps we can imagine.

Watershed

Introduction

Dams and diversions along America's rivers have transformed the country, and in doing so created environmental problems whose resolution will, in many ways, determine how we live in this new century. The vast enterprise of dam building of the past hundred years paralleled the progress of the very American twentieth century. Jobs were created, farms and ranches irrigated and factories built that helped to win world wars and furnish the American dream. Cities rose in the desert, floodplains were drained and rivers channeled to suit civic vision.

Now, barely three generations later, the cost of this extraordinary engineering is acutely apparent. Species of fish once so numerous as to be legendary are now on the brink of extinction. Seasons of destructive flooding, exacerbated by artificially constricted riverbanks, have prompted a reassessment of the value of wetlands as nature's filter, flood-control and reservoir system.

The efficacy of dams is being scrutinized in new comprehensive analyses of ecology, economics, energy efficiencies, water conservation and public safety. Questioning the value of dams requires a serious readjustment in our notion of progress, a process daunting to all, and frightening and threatening to some. But all across the country, communities are identifying marginal and abandoned dams and questioning the relicensing of dams whose environmental impacts are too costly.

Dams alter and block the natural flow of rivers, obstructing fish migration. They change water temperatures and degrade water quality in ways that damage vegetation and wildlife. Dams hold back silt, gravel, debris and nutrients that create a healthy environment for river species. Dams trap sediment and prevent water from reaching the mouths of rivers, disrupting and destroying the ecology of deltas and estuaries crucial to the development of aquatic species. Many dams, including some of the largest, were built with no fish passage whatsoever. Dams make life especially difficult for anadromous fish, those that are born in the cold water of upland and mountain streams and migrate to the ocean to mature before returning to their native rivers to spawn. Dams have decimated native fish populations and have had a particularly devastating effect on the anadromous fish of the Atlantic and Pacific coasts. On the Colorado River, dams have allowed invasive exotics to thrive, endangering native species. Some dams' reservoirs are now choked with sediment, rendering the dams ineffective and conditions untenable for river species.

When a dam impounds a river, it eliminates the ever changing channels, bends and meanders needed to nurture fish, shellfish and other river species. Dams also disrupt the interaction between a river and its banks, upsetting the habitat of aquatic insects and other organisms on which fish depend for food.[1] Relying on dams for large-scale water storage, and delivering water to places where it does not naturally occur, have long-term effects on the balance between groundwater and surface water and on the quality of the surrounding soil. These ecological costs have economic repercussions. Most large-scale dams built by the government are heavily subsidized, as are the power, irrigation and navigation access they provide. Many end up costing far more than expected, especially when the price of restoration, repair and loss of commercial, tribal and sport fishing is included. And while rarely discussed in this country, large dams may carry another substantial cost, when the land their impoundments flood displaces those who live in the adjacent river valley. Dams, said Clinton administration Secretary of the Interior Bruce Babbitt, voicing a significant change in how government officials view dams, "should be judged by the health of the rivers to which they belong."

Yet we are accustomed to the "benefits" of dams. In the West, cheap, heavily subsidized hydropower, irrigation and shipping passage directed development of the region's economy. From the earliest days of New England's settlement, local industry grew up around sawmills, gristmills and factories powered by dams. The impoundments and slackwater created by dams are often recreational and residential magnets now ingrained in the custom and character of surrounding communities. Dams for drinking water, flood control and the diversion of wetlands stimulated the growth of urban and agricultural centers. Removing dams affects all of this. But a great many dams no longer serve the purpose for which they were built, and their small output of hydropower or irrigation water can be provided by other less destructive means.

There are over 75,000 dams on the Army Corps of Engineers' National Inventory of Dams, and that includes only dams over six feet tall. "That means we have been building, on average, one large dam a day, every single day, since the Declaration of Independence," Babbitt said to the Ecological Society of America in 1998. It's estimated that less than 1 percent of the nation's river miles are protected in their natural state, and approximately 600,000 miles of what were free-flowing rivers now lie stagnant behind dams. Virtually no major river in the United States is without a dam. But the nation's dam building peaked in the 1970s, and since 1998, according to the World Commission on Dams, the rate of decommissioning dams in the United States has overtaken the rate of construction.[2]

When we think about dams, we tend to picture the behemoths of concrete like Grand Coulee and Hoover Dam or the dams of the Tennessee Valley Authority. Most of the dams that block our rivers are far less grandiose. Many are unassuming stretches of mossy cement, masked by a small curtain of falling water. They were built for local enterprises, to water pastures and modest farm fields, to grind grain, turn logs into building boards and sluice small mines. Yet even these smaller dams have seriously detrimental effects on their rivers, especially as many rivers suffer the cumulative effects of multiple dams throughout a watershed. These small dams often become safety hazards as they fall into disrepair and impound deceptively inviting swimming holes.

Dams are so ubiquitous that most of us are utterly unaccustomed to looking at a free-flowing river. It may look like a river, but chances are what you see is a series of impoundments or reservoirs now labeled "lakes." Even the rapids of the Colorado, plunging through the Grand Canyon, apparently the essence of wildness, are subject to flows as tightly controlled as those on a kitchen sink. Because of the controlled flows and the way dams trap sediment, impoundments do not function biologically as a natural lake does. Impoundments develop their own ecology, but it is often at odds with the river's natural ecosystem and can cause trouble for native species. But these "lakes"—whether a small millpond or vast reservoir—often occupy a prominent place in a community. In fact, the stated use or purpose of the largest number of dams—31.3 percent—in the National Inventory of Dams is recreation.

Although the federal government owns and operates most large hydropower dams in the United States, most of the country's other dams are privately owned. The federal government actually owns only 3 percent of the Inventory's 75,000 dams. Local governments own 17 percent, state governments own 5 percent and public utilities just 2 percent. A large number of these dams—over 1,700, or 15 percent—are of undetermined ownership. Since most state regulations require the state to assume financial responsibility for its abandoned dams, they can easily become a burden to their communities.

Of these 75,000 dams, only 2.9 percent have hydroelectric power as their primary purpose. Only 13.7 percent are primarily devoted to irrigation, less than 10 percent to water supply and 0.3 percent to navigation. Of the inventoried dams, 14.6 percent are used for flood control, 17 percent to store water for farm ponds and fire prevention and 8 percent in mining activity.[3]

Ownership and responsibility for operation and regulation vary from dam to dam. Many dams have multiple uses and fall under the jurisdiction of a collage of local, state and federal authorities, their ownership often transferred over the years between private parties, public utilities and local governments. The Army Corps of Engineers and U.S. Bureau of Reclamation built and operate most federal dams, but guidelines and regulations for these and other dams may involve the Bureau of Land Management, Environmental Protection Agency, Department of Energy, National Marine Fisheries Service, National Park Service, U.S. Fish and Wildlife Service and U.S. Forest Service. The navigable waters of the nation's rivers belong to the American public, yet the dams that block their flow are mostly private property, adding an essential complication to considerations of dam removal. In western states, dams are often bound up with the allocation of water rights. Think *Chinatown*, or the Colorado River Compact, which once caused Arizona to send troops to the California border. In the Pacific Northwest, dams' impact on salmon implicates tribal treaty rights as well as international fishing agreements with Canada. Given the complexity of ownership and oversight, dam removal always involves a host of interested parties.

Most hydroelectric dams not owned by the federal government are regulated and licensed by the Federal Energy Regulatory Commission (FERC), part of the Department of Energy.[4] FERC licenses dams for periods of thirty or fifty years, before the end of which the dam owner must apply for a new operating license. Counts by FERC and several nonprofit river-advocacy groups show that as of the year 2000, well over two hundred hydroelectric dams were due to be relicensed. As many as five hundred dam licenses will come up for review by 2010. It cannot be assumed that all those licenses will be renewed.

To be relicensed, a dam must meet current safety and environmental standards, including those of the Clean Water, Endangered Species, Electric Consumers Protection and National Environmental Policy Acts. The dam owner must also show that operation of the dam is in the public interest, which means weighing environmental and recreational as well as power-generating values. This is important because so many older dams lack effective fish passage, are in a hazardous state of disrepair and are increasingly detrimental to water quality and the health of native river species.

It is during the relicensing process that the public has become actively involved in determining the future of many dams. Five years before a dam's current FERC license expires, dam owners must declare their intention to renew. The information submitted to FERC about the dam's physical and operating conditions and the renewal application are available for review by the public and government agencies. At this point, interested parties can file a formal Motion to Intervene with FERC. If granted, the intervenors' comments—often concerns about the health of the river not raised by dam owners—will be officially considered during the relicensing process. The current public reassessment of dams can be seen as an extension of the 1972 Clean Water Act, which gave citizens the legal wherewithal to protect the health of their rivers.

Maintaining and operating an older dam and bringing it up to current safety and environmental standards often cost more than the revenue yielded by its power generation. Dam removal is often less expensive than repair and maintenance—even more so when the environmental benefits of removal are factored into the equation. Thus many dams have become a liability for their owners— some to the extent that they cannot even be given away. "Many dams will be removed for reasons of sheer economic pragmatism," a former staffer at the Department of the Interior told me.

Yet simply taking a substantive inventory of dams can be controversial, as California river advocates learned during their 2000 legislative session, when a bill to determine which of the state's dams might no longer be needed was defeated. Despite FERC's regulatory power over nonfederal hydroelectric dams, no single federal agency is responsible for all the nation's dams and no government agency is charged with tracking dam decommissioning and removal. When I asked the Clinton Department of the Interior about this, it suggested I contact American Rivers, a national, nonprofit conservation group dedicated to river restoration.

According to American Rivers, Friends of the Earth, Trout Unlimited and the World Commission on Dams, close to 500 dams, and perhaps more, have been removed in this country since 1912. Well over 250 dams have been removed in the last twenty years. (In this context, "removal" means actual deconstruction and removal of the dam's structure. "Breaching" a dam usually refers to a partial deconstruction that allows the river to flow through.) As of January 2000, dams had been removed and removals planned in over forty states and the District of Columbia. Since 1990, the most dams have been removed in Wisconsin and Pennsylvania, followed by California, Ohio and Tennessee.[5]

Local river advocates are involved in most dam-removal efforts, but dam removal is by no means an activity dominated by "radical" environmentalists. Government agencies, the military, private energy companies, engineers, irrigation districts, city planners, neighbors who like to canoe and recreational and commercial fishermen are all working on dam removal. The Army Corps of Engineers (which once declared war on nature) and the Bureau of Reclamation (which constructed the country's biggest dams) are now participating in dam removal. Divisions of the Air Force and Marines have helped take out dams on the East Coast. Members of the Clinton administration's Department of the Interior, led by Secretary Babbitt, traveled the country attending ceremonies celebrating dam demolition.

Most of the people I spoke to became involved with dam removal because the river is their neighbor. While this sounds homey and folksy, the process of working toward dam removal is not. There are endless papers to file, hearings and meetings to attend, government documents to review and opinions to deal with. Those who oppose dam removal often do so because they fear the free-flowing river will jeopardize their livelihood or property. Battles are waged on the editorial and letters pages of local newspapers. Very private people end up voicing unpopular views in public. But in a number of cases, people who opposed a dam removal quickly become fans of the newly restored river.

Some of the dam removals I visited have been successfully completed. Some are in process, and still others yet to be decided upon. New studies and policy pronouncements emerge daily, while river conditions change constantly, so this is very much a story in progress. As 2000 ended, bringing with it a presidential administration that campaigned in the Pacific Northwest with lawn signs that read "Save Our Dams," I was asked what this change means for the future of dam removal. When I asked Secretary Babbitt how tied to Clinton administration policies dam removal efforts were, he said, "This movement is on its way. It's no longer dependent on the policies of federal agencies. It's rooted in communities all over the country." What we need, Babbitt has said, is a "new culture in which politicians and the destruction of dams go together." I can only hope that a growing number of people—business leaders in particular—will come to understand that, in the words of former Wisconsin Senator Gaylord Nelson, "The economy is a wholly owned subsidiary of the environment," and realize that healthy rivers, from mountain streams to deltas and estuaries, are something we cannot do without.

The history of this country is inextricable from the history of its rivers. Too much of this country now depends on our manipulation of rivers for these water projects to be entirely undone, but we can try to learn from the damage. We can attempt to make decisions for the long rather than short term and repair some of the fragmentation—especially that caused by dams that no longer make sense.

On March 14, 2000, at the Carl Hayden Visitor Center on the northwest side of Glen Canyon Dam, David Brower, whose career came to national prominence over the fight against a dam, sat at the foot of a makeshift stage set up on the back of Edward Abbey's old truck. As the assembled crowd squinted in the bright sun and the water of the impounded Colorado River reflected a deep indigo against the red rock canyon walls, a songwriter from Austin, Texas,[6] strummed his guitar and with the help of volunteer backup singers calling themselves the "Drain Its!" sang, "Let's act like we know what we didn't know then. Let's take out a couple of dams."

Maine

"HOW LONG DOES IT TAKE FOR
A FISH TO SWIM 17 MILES?"

As I drive north into Maine on a sunny spring morning, the air has a yellow-green light with touches of pink, where buds sprout among the new leaves of maple, oak, birch, dogwood and cherry. It is May 17, 2000, and I have come to the Kennebec River in hopes of witnessing fish history: to see the river's alewives—a native species of river herring—swim up a stretch of river to which they have not had access since the days when Henry David Thoreau wandered the woods of Maine. In July 1999, the Edwards Dam, built across the Kennebec at Augusta in 1837, became the first operating hydroelectric dam in the nation to be removed, opening a new future not just for the Kennebec but for rivers everywhere. Now, with the dam gone, locals are anxious to see if the first upstream migrants of the season, the alewives, will take advantage of the newly freed seventeen-mile stretch of river. A big spring run will be an early indicator of the dam removal's success.

In Augusta, I take a walk near the Kennebec, which flows through the center of downtown. On this mid-May morning, even with sunshine, it's chilly, and there's a steady breeze blowing up-river. Augusta has the look of a small city in transition, of a city beginning to appreciate its old industrial architecture and long-ignored waterfront and to encourage business back to its historic thoroughfares. Away from highway traffic, from the malls sprawl-ing along the interstate and from the busy intersection at the south end of town, Water Street is quiet. Many storefronts are empty or in the process of changing tenants. On the east side of the Kennebec, I notice that Front Street's red-brick and gray-stone buildings were built with their backs to the river. A stretch of the waterfront is now dedicated to parking. I stop for a cup of coffee and read the local papers in a cheerful eatery where people from state offices are meeting over sandwiches and salads. Salmon and water quality are in the headlines.

From its headwaters in Moosehead Lake, the Kennebec flows for over 150 miles through terrain shaped by the ebb and flow of ancient glaciers and ocean water. Before emptying into the At-lantic, the Kennebec threads its way through the rich estuary of Merrymeeting Bay, then past the rocky islands of Casco and Sheepscot Bays. Piping plovers, bald eagles, roseate terns, egrets, ibis, herons and osprey live around the bay's tidal mudflats and salt marshes. This river system is an important nursery ground for the alewives, shad, smelt, sturgeon, striped bass and salmon that migrate up and down the Kennebec. With a watershed that drains nearly a fifth of the state, the Kennebec is Maine's fourth-largest river.

Archaeological evidence suggests that the Kennebec Valley has been inhabited since the retreat of the Ice Age. The river was long known to the Abenaki Indians, who gave the Kennebec its name. American Indians and later European trappers, traders, Colonial soldiers and farmers followed the Kennebec River corridor inland, north into what became Canada. In 1607, a British sea captain named Raleigh Gilbert sailed up the Kennebec to an island the Abenaki called Cushnoc, said to mean where "the tide runs no further up the river," and attempted to settle at the site of present-day Augusta. Gilbert's colony was not successful, but he was followed by others from the Plymouth Colony, who established a trading post at Cushnoc in 1628. French Jesuits sailed up the Kennebec in the early 1600s, as did Dutch, French and Spanish fishermen and fur traders. The Kennebec formed a boundary of the territory disputed in the French and Indian Wars. Fort Western, built by the British in 1754 as a supply base, still stands, complete with its pointed wooden palisades, across the river from downtown Augusta, just downstream of the Edwards Dam site.

What is now Augusta was known as Cushnoc or Koussinoc, named after the Kennebec River island, until the late 1780s, when the city was renamed to honor the daughter of Henry Dearborn, a Revolutionary War soldier who represented Maine in the early days of the United States Congress. Cushnoc Island was inundated when Edwards Dam blocked the Kennebec in 1837 and was not seen again until the river fell back to its natural level after the dam was removed in 1999. Local history buffs are delighted that the gravel bar island is again exposed.

In the late eighteenth century, Maine's coastal shipbuilding industry with its demand for tall mast pines created a boom in the timber business along the Kennebec. The river served as a highway for logs felled upstream and floated down to shipyards and sawmills near the mouth of the river. Between 1842 and 1846, the Edwards Dam powered seven sawmills, a gristmill and a machine shop. So much wood was cut from the forests of Maine, remarked Thoreau in 1848, that it is "No wonder . . . we hear so often of vessels which are becalmed off our coast, being surrounded a week at a time by floating lumber from the Maine woods." Maine's river rapids, wrote Thoreau, supplied "the principal power by which the Maine woods [were] converted to lumber."[1] And the river water itself was commerce, for in the 1800s, the frozen Kennebec was sold in a lucrative ice trade to ships bound for warm climates. In 1894 alone, over a million tons of ice were cut on or near the Kennebec.

"When my forebears arrived in 1629, they used the river to pay off the debt they'd created to come to America," says Steve Brooke, a founder of the Kennebec Coalition, a group formed in

1989 that laid the groundwork for removal of Edwards Dam. "They set up a series of trading posts and the colonies paid off their debts with beaver pelt trading along the Kennebec. The Yankees put the rivers to work, with the assumption that there were unlimited resources."

By the nineteenth century, the Kennebec had long been thought of as a working river. With the coming of the Industrial Revolution, rivers were used throughout New England to turn water-wheels to power mills, factories and machine shops. The legacy of all that industry persists on riverbanks and in river bottoms throughout the Northeast. When a dam was proposed for the Kennebec at Augusta in 1834, the citizens of Maine were already concerned about the decline of local fisheries. But in 1837, the Kennebec River Dam Company—later called the Kennebec Locks & Canal Company—built the dam at Augusta to provide mechanical power to local sawmills and aid upstream navigation through its locks. By the mid-nineteenth century, the railroad overtook the river as the predominant means of local commercial transportation and brought an end to barging on the Kennebec.

For a century and a half, industry poured its effluent into the Kennebec, severely degrading conditions for the river's fish already taxed by overfishing and dams. "I remember the Kennebec as an open sewer," says Steve Brooke of the river he grew up with, "with all the houses along the river dumping into it. Towns, businesses and industry, the chicken-processing plants, they all dumped into it. When you fell into the Kennebec in those days, the first place they took you was the hospital."

When the big trees of the Maine woods were gone, timber companies began cutting smaller trees more useful for pulp and paper than construction lumber. "It was the growth of the pulp industry that ruined the Kennebec as anything but a working river," wrote Louise Dickinson Rich in her 1956 history of coastal Maine. "The sawdust from the mills has covered the feeding grounds of the fish, and the chemicals used in the manufacture of paper have polluted and poisoned the water. There's no more good fishing except way up near the headwaters, and nobody in his right mind would think of swimming in the dirty water."[2]

"By the 1970s, the river was dirty, polluted and dangerous," says

Brooke. "That was mantra of mill-town rivers." Then, in the 1980s, a few fishermen, members of the Kennebec chapter of Trout Unlimited, started wondering what the river would be like without the Edwards Dam. Their conversations led to the formation of the Kennebec Coalition. "People would laugh," recalls Brooke, who now directs the Maine field office for American Rivers. "The image of dams was that they're part of the landscape, one that you don't expect to change."

Brooke credits Maine Senator Edmund Muskie, who grew up nearby along the polluted Androscoggin and was a principal author of the Clean Water Act, with helping the country understand what a river could mean to a community. "The state of the Kennebec didn't really improve until the passage of the Clean Water Act in 1972," says Gordon Russell, Field Supervisor of the Maine office of the U.S. Fish and Wildlife Service. "Government isn't particularly popular today," Brooke says. "But to me, the government has given me back the river."

"What this is all about," he says, "is changing the cultural values surrounding the river." When he used to paddle the river, it was rare to see anyone else out, but since the dam came out, canoes and kayaks are becoming a common sight.

Like many nineteenth-century dams, Edwards Dam was of modest construction. It was a timber and crib structure, a pyramid shape built of logs and rock 917 feet long, rising twenty-four feet above the river. Local history records breaches of Edwards Dam in 1839, 1846, 1855 and 1870. The most recent breach came in 1974, when a winter storm washed out about 150 feet of the dam. Biologists wanted to maintain that breach to improve conditions for fish, but the dam was repaired.

The original construction of Edwards Dam included a fish ladder, but that washed away in the spring flood of 1838 and was never rebuilt. Over the years, attempts were made to install new fish passage, but none was lasting or effective. In the late 1980s, a pump was used to lift migrating alewives over the dam so they could be transported to their spawning grounds above several dams further upstream. Yet long before that, the dam had caused a significant decline in the Kennebec's native fishery. The dam blocked the migration of the Kennebec's anadromous fish—

Atlantic salmon, rainbow smelt, blueback herring, alewife, American shad, striped bass, Atlantic and shortnosed sturgeon—and of the catadromous American eel, which is born and spawns in the ocean, but spends most of its life in the freshwater river. The shortnosed sturgeon are now listed under the Endangered Species Act (ESA), and the Kennebec's salmon are so scarce that they should be.

Until the 1850s, when their numbers plummeted, wild Atlantic salmon were plentiful in the Kennebec. The Indians who lived along the Kennebec moved their camps up and down the river valley following the migration of river herring, shad and salmon. In the early decades of European settlement, Kennebec river salmon were fished in great quantity, sold to markets in Boston and New York and sent to grace dinner tables in Britain and Europe. While we now consider salmon a gustatory treat, they were then so commonplace that ordinances were enacted to prevent salmon from being fed to hired help more than three times a week or being cleaned on public wharves.[3] Shad, alewives, and striped bass were important commerce for communities along the Kennebec and Sebasticook Rivers until the 1930s, when pollution exacerbated the decline begun with Edwards Dam. In fact, according to local history, commerce in striped bass helped fund the first public school in the American colonies.

Small dams were constructed on Kennebec tributaries as early as the 1600s. By the late 1700s, dams so thoroughly blocked alewives from their spawning grounds that local runs began to disappear. In the mid-1800s, technology improved, allowing construction of bigger dams across Maine's largest rivers. Consequently, by the end of the nineteenth century, the Kennebec and Penobscot's commercial anadromous fisheries were effectively gone. By 1872, there were sixty-nine dams on the Kennebec and its tributaries, none with fish passage.[4] In 1887, a half century after Edwards Dam went up, Charles G. Atkins, Maine's first fisheries commissioner, noted that, "The only breeding ground remaining accessible to Kennebec salmon was on the gravel beds within the first half mile below Augusta Dam and to this opportunity is the continuance of the brood in this river doubtlessly due."[5] Today there are probably close to a hundred dams in the watershed.

In 1882, a large textile factory employing over 700 workers was built on the west bank of the Kennebec at Edwards Dam, owned at the time by the Edwards Manufacturing Company. The dam provided mechanical power for the textile mill, which remained in operation until the early 1980s, when the factory closed. The mill buildings were demolished after a fire in 1989.

The dam began generating electrical power in 1913 and continued doing so until the turbines were shut down on January 1, 1999, in preparation for the dam's removal. In its final years, Edwards Dam generated about 3.5 megawatts, less than 0.1 percent of the electricity used in the state. Although Edwards Manufacturing Company sold the power to a state utility, Central Maine Power, at several times the market value, by the 1990s, the dam's future as a profitable enterprise was no longer assured.

Betsy Ham, coordinator for the Kennebec Coalition and river advocate for the Natural Resources Council of Maine, has agreed to take me on a post–Edwards Dam tour of the Kennebec. The nonprofit Natural Resources Council—a conservation group working on environmental issues throughout the state—is housed in a tidy modern building not far from Augusta's State House. The elegantly imposing State House was built in 1832 of local granite by Charles Bulfinch, the architect who designed the Capitol Building in Washington, D.C. It's barely noon and already I've encountered architecture from before the Revolution, the Federal period, the Industrial Revolution and the computer age, all on a visit prompted by some rather revolutionary deconstruction.

Betsy is a native Mainer—something people take seriously around here—and former executive director of Friends of Merrymeeting Bay, a nonprofit group working to protect that sensitive tidal wetland. Her enthusiasm for the estuary is so infectious that I decide not to leave Maine without seeing it for myself. We'd hoped to see the Kennebec by canoe, but a stiff wind is still blowing upstream, and that would make for miserable paddling. Instead, we take Betsy's car to our first stop, the boat launch in the town of Sidney, several miles upstream from the Edwards Dam site. At a glance, the river looks bucolic but unremarkable until Betsy points

out the banks that were exposed when the Edwards's impoundment receded after the dam was breached. The old high-water
mark is clearly visible, a light gray muddy stripe in the foliage, but
the abundance of new growth indicates that by summer, the banks
will be lush and green. In Sidney, Betsy tells me, folks were concerned that removing the dam would cause the river to fall so far
that they'd lose their boat launch and recreational access to the
river. The water level fell but not drastically, and a new boat ramp
was built to accommodate what most agree is a much-improved
river. Not far upstream from Sidney are what are called Six Mile
Falls. Looking carefully I can see the undulation of real river riffles
forming as the river rediscovers its currents and channels.

Before Edwards Dam was removed, this stretch of the Kennebec was in a kind of biological limbo. Like impoundments
everywhere, the slow-moving slack water was really neither river
nor lake. The lack of natural flows created conditions detrimental
to fish and other aquatic species, including the little organisms at
the bottom of the riparian food chain known as macrobenthic invertebrates. Betsy calls them the "canaries of the river system."
Once the dam was out, "We saw an immediate increase in water
quality," Dave Courtemanch of the Maine Department of Environmental Protection later tells me. According to Gordon Russell
of the U.S. Fish and Wildlife Service, "The habitat has made a remarkable recovery. . . . The river bottom is now clean gravel and
small boulders, an excellent environment for aquatic invertebrates
and potential spawning areas for salmon."

Removing Edwards Dam has improved humans' view of the
river as well. Betsy points out undeveloped land along the river
which has increased in value since the dam came out. I stand for
a few moments on the smooth new boat ramp to sketch the river
horizon in my notebook. The newly leafed trees bend toward the
moving water. It astonishes me to think that it has been 162 years
since the springtime Kennebec moved freely to the ocean.

From Sidney we continue upstream to the town of Winslow,
where the Sebasticook River enters the Kennebec. On the Sebasticook, just above the confluence is Fort Halifax Dam, now the
first dam encountered by fish migrating upriver. On this sunny
May afternoon, the shallows below the dam's falls are a piscatorial

amazement. The water is so full of fish that it is hard to tell splashing water from fin. Hundreds of alewives are hurling themselves into the tumbling water trying to leap over the dam in an attempt to reach their spawning grounds. To prevent fish from being trapped in the shallows, workers from Florida Power & Light, the company that owns the dam, have put sandbags around some of the rocky pools, hoping to urge the fish into deeper water. Still, many stray and are becalmed. Many are several fish-layers deep. Walking out on the rocks, Betsy and I begin scooping still-flapping fish up with our hands and tossing them into deep water. A more systematic effort is under way on the far shore, where biologists have set up a pump-and-bucket system, with which they've managed to transport thousands of alewives over the dam. A newspaper account will report that over 7,300 alewives have been lifted over Fort Halifax Dam. Fish are flying up through the air and water. I think of the early accounts describing North American rivers as so full of fish one could walk across the water on their backs. I bend down to rescue a few more of the blue-gray, foot-long, half-pound alewives.

Alewives are one of the most abundant fish in the Kennebec and are found along the Atlantic Coast from Labrador to South Carolina. They can be smoked for eating but are more often used as lobster bait. Their primary role, however, is in the fishy food chain, where they are an important source of food for larger fish like striped bass and for birds, like osprey and eagles, that live along the Kennebec. Alewives also help the development of certain freshwater mussels; when the fish swim through, mussels release their spawn, which alewives then carry upstream on their gills. After hatching in headwater ponds, alewives spend three to five years at sea, before returning to their home tributaries to spawn. Removal of Edwards Dam gets the alewives one step closer to their spawning grounds without artificial transport.

As Betsy and I climb back up the riverbank, several boys on their way home from school jump off their bikes and rush down to the river and begin scooping alewives with their hands. Though it's still early in the season, several older men stand on the rocks casting lines in the water, hoping for striped bass, known locally as stripers. In his *Maine Lore* column of June 21, 2000, Dwayne

Rioux wrote, "At this time, massive schools of forage fish such as blueback herring and alewives are converging to the Kennebec River, providing a major attraction for migrating striped bass fresh from Chesapeake Bay and the Hudson River."[6] A week later, Rioux reported a reader's "trophy catch" of a fifty-two-inch-long striped bass weighing nearly forty pounds and the sighting of "monster fish," later identified as sturgeon, which can be five or more feet long, "surging and swirling with enormous force on the river's surface." That month, for the first time since Martin Van Buren was president, sturgeon were seen jumping in the Kennebec upstream of Augusta.

"The amazing thing really is the kids," says Doug Watts, a former newspaper reporter who lives down the street from the Edwards Dam site and helps run a small nonprofit called Friends of Kennebec Salmon. "The kids went crazy!" he says, describing how they joined the bucket brigade scooping the fish up from the ledges of the river below Fort Halifax Dam. "They were soaked," says Watts, "and having the time of their lives."

"Nobody knew exactly what was going to happen when the dam came out," Watts says. "When we first talked about getting the dam out, people literally thought we were nuts. We were in a tough pickle doing the advocacy because we didn't know what it would look like." One of the biggest hurdles to overcome in the Edwards Dam removal—like removals elsewhere—was that people would look at the river and say, "What do you mean?" Watts tells me. "There were no photographs of what the river was like before the dam went in. They thought the impounded river was the way a river was supposed to be."

Except for a few anglers, people in Augusta had no memory of the Kennebec's fish, says Watts. In the 1930s and 1940s, the river was like an open cesspool, he says. There were big fish kills. "Anyone who grew up here was told early on, 'Do not go near the river,'" he says. Now Watts expresses what the biologist René Dubos might have called despairing optimism about the recovery of Maine's native fish runs. All is far from well, but there is hope.

One of the reasons many Kennebec fish have made such an immediate comeback since Edwards Dam came out, explains Gordon Russell, is that all of the river's fish have been present to some extent in the fertile estuary of Merrymeeting Bay. In addition, an active restoration of the river's native fish began in the late 1980s. Under the 1992 Comprehensive Management Plan for the Kennebec, Maine's Department of Marine Resources began to improve fish passage at Edwards Dam and to stock river herring and alewives. When the dam came out, Russell explains, a healthy number of fish were simply waiting for the opportunity to migrate upstream without the aid of pumps and buckets. The immediate results of removing Edwards Dam—improvements in fish migration and water quality—are enormously encouraging and gratifying, but Russell points out that current fish numbers, even of the prolific alewives, are only a fraction of what they once were.

Historically, the Kennebec probably had 600,000 to 700,000 shad, but there's now no truly fishable shad run in Maine, Doug Watts tells me. American shad spawn in open, free-flowing river water, as do blueback herring, so both benefit greatly from the Edwards removal. The Kennebec's American shad, explains Matt O'Donnell of Maine's Department of Marine Resources, release their eggs into moving water in the river's main stem and in the Sebasticook. The eggs hatch in four to eight days, and the young fish spend their first summer in the river. In the late summer and fall, young shad move downstream into the Gulf of Maine and the ocean, where they'll spend the next four to seven years. There, the Kennebec's shad join those from other Maine, New England and New York rivers, generally moving southward toward the Carolinas. When it comes time for them to spawn, the shad follow the Atlantic's thermal bands north up the coast to their native rivers. A female shad can have as many as half a million offspring, says O'Donnell, but the larval fish have a high mortality rate, so far fewer survive to adulthood. Shad, he says, are a delicate fish, and it's too rough on the fish to tag them, making it hard to get a "good handle on population numbers." Although the Kennebec has only a few hundred shad, with improved conditions, they are slowly coming back.

After leaving the alewives thrashing at the foot of Fort Halifax Dam, Betsy Ham and I drive through Waterville to see the next dam upstream on the mainstem of the Kennebec. In 1987, explains Betsy, the Kennebec Hydro Developers Group, owners of the seven dams upstream of Edwards, signed an agreement with the state of Maine to restore the river's alewife, American shad and Atlantic salmon runs. (Not surprisingly, the owners of the Edwards Dam initially refused to participate.) In exchange for contributing nearly $5 million to the project, these dam owners were allowed to defer some of their restoration responsibilities, specifically fish passage. Bath Ironworks, shipbuilders on the Lower Kennebec, also participated, contributing $2.5 million in exchange for permission to expand its riverside facilities. To add to this kitty of river restoration money, Maine's congressional delegation obtained $1 million in federal funding.

According to Evan Richert, director of State Planning for the state of Maine, who was closely involved with the process, "It became clear to the Department of Marine Resources and the leadership of the state that it was important to restoration of the Kennebec to remove the Edwards Dam, and that the benefits would outweigh the costs." In 1991, Governor John McKernan's State of the State speech called for Edwards's removal, as did a resolution passed by the state legislature.

With the dam's thirty-year hydropower license from the Federal Energy Regulatory Commission (FERC) due to expire in 1993, in 1991 the Edwards's owners applied for a new fifty-year license that would allow them to expand the dam's power-generating capacity to 11.5 megawatts. During the relicensing process, when it was determined that installing viable fish passage at Edwards would cost about three times more than removing the dam, the Kennebec Coalition, along with state and federal agencies, formally intervened in the relicensing process, advocating removal.

Recommendations for dam removal continued to accumulate. "The 1992 Comprehensive Plan for the Kennebec looked at alternatives for restoration and concluded that removal was the best option," says Richert. In early 1992, Richert tells me, Ron Kreisman, counsel for the Kennebec Coalition and a key strategist on the project, suggested the Edwards's owners might be interested in discussing dam removal. But complicating these negotiations was the fact that, in 1992, Augusta became a co-licensee of the dam with Edwards Manufacturing Company in an agreement that gave the city 3 percent of the dam's gross revenues.

As co-licensee, receiving both property taxes and royalties from the dam, the city of Augusta was predisposed to side with the owners and oppose removal, says Bruce Keller, Augusta's city planner. "It was a dream on the part of some in Augusta for the city to become owner of the dam and receive free power," says Keller. Yet once it was clear that resources were available to make up for any financial losses Augusta might incur with decommissioning of the dam, the city manager joined those recommending removal.

"The Edwards' lucrative power contract was due to expire on December 31, 1999, and the owners would have been willing to fight for relicensing if they had to bear the costs of removal and associated liability," reflects Richert. The state, however, suggested that if Maine could acquire the dam as a gift, it would then seek funding to remove it and restore the river's fishery and would assume the liabilities associated with removal. Governor Angus King, elected in 1994, endorsed the concept. Several years of proposals, counterproposals, comments, recommendations and environmental-impact statements followed. Finally in 1997, FERC ruled that the economic and environmental benefits of removing Edwards Dam exceeded those of hydropower generation and ordered the dam removed at the owners' expense. Edwards Manufacturing and the city of Augusta appealed FERC's decision, but in May 1998 an agreement was reached to transfer ownership of Edwards Dam to the state of Maine specifically so the dam could be removed. "Edwards had to come down for anything key to happen on the Kennebec," says Richert. Thus, Edwards Dam became the first dam that FERC would ask to have removed against the owners' wishes, and the first to be ordered removed for the purpose of river restoration.

At the "dam-busting" ceremony, on July 1, 1999, Augusta's church bells pealed and spectators cheered as the first river water rushed through the dam's breach. "This is the beginning of something that is going to affect this entire nation. . . . This is a statement about our capacity to honor and respect God's creation, the sacramental commons, and to live not just in the past, but in a visionary and a different future, in a way of harmony and balance with creation," said Secretary of the Interior Bruce Babbitt in remarks that were reprinted by newspapers from Boston to Seattle.

The Edwards Dam made international news, with reporters coming from as far as Japan to chronicle the event.

"Today, with the power of our pens, we are dismantling several myths: that hydrodams provide clean pollution-free energy; that hydropower is the main source of our electricity; that dams should last as long as the pyramids; and that making them friendlier for fisheries is expensive and time consuming," declared Secretary Babbitt. This is "a challenge to dam owners and operators to defend themselves—to demonstrate by hard facts, not by sentiment or myth, that the continued operation of a dam is in the public interest, economically and environmentally."

In the end, no state or federal funds financed the actual dam removal, which was paid for entirely by the Kennebec Hydro Developers Group in exchange for delaying its implementation of fish passage and by Bath Ironworks as mitigation for its expansion. "The dam came down on time and on budget," Richert tells me. Removal was completed in October 1999 and cost about $3 million, some $6 million less than the price of installing effective fish passage. "We have active participation from the National Marine Fisheries Services, the Army Corps of Engineers and the U.S. Fish and Wildlife Service who are all signatories to the settlement agreement, and Senator Olympia Snowe has been a great champion of all this," says Richter. "With this support, we've been able to fund a ten-year fish restoration plan for the Kennebec, which began in 1999." With Edwards Dam gone, it seems likely that it will not be long until the accounting comes due on at least some of the Kennebec's upstream dams.

The backhoe and earthmoving action took place during the summer and fall of 1999, when a temporary cofferdam was built to ease the river flow as the old dam was breached. Edwards's construction and the nature of the Kennebec made engineering this removal simpler than that of other dams may be. The Kennebec's flows vary greatly so Edwards Dam impounded relatively little sediment. An average Kennebec summer flow is about 4,000 cubic feet per second (cfs), with spring flows as high as 22,000 cfs and flood levels around 70,000 cfs, explains Steve Brooke. Each year's high spring flows flushed sediment through the dam so no special arrangements were required to manage sediment during removal.

What sediment had accumulated was simply allowed to wash down the river.

At the Edwards Dam site, Betsy Ham and I walk out on the point where the old mill buildings stood. The area is surrounded by a protective chain-link fence. The ground has been graded and newly seeded grass is coming up. Plans for the site currently include a garden and park. Looking over the water we notice that the river is regaining its current, islands and sandbars. Mid-river, kingfishers, osprey and cormorants dive for fish. "With the dam gone there's a lot more food for fish-eating birds," says Betsy as we spot a bald eagle on the river islands.

"It's an amazing turnaround for Augusta," says Betsy. "There weren't even signs on the bridges to indicate the Kennebec. Augusta kind of ignored the waterfront at its peril but now they are really thinking of it as an asset."

"What we're doing here is changing a mind-set. We have the opportunity to show that we now have a river that's worth investing in," says Bruce Keller, whom I speak to a few months later. As Governor Angus King told the *Bangor Daily News,* "It's time for the city to face the river instead of turning its back to the river."

What I saw in May 2000 is only the beginning of improvements to come. Removal of the dam has helped kick off plans for Augusta's Capital Riverfront Improvement District, which includes new parks, waterfront trails, boat launches, improved people-friendly transportation corridors and a mix of residential, commercial and professional buildings designed to highlight the city's location on the Kennebec. The city's draft plan completed in the summer of 2000 admits that "in the last century, the Kennebec . . . became an embarrassment, an eyesore," but, the plan continues, "that is all in the past. Today the Kennebec River . . . is once more a source of pride."

"The most important thing that came out of this is a good long-term relationship between the city and state government," says Keller. "The city was clearly skeptical at the outset, then people realized the good it would do Augusta. Everyone took some risks in hopes that nobody would bear an undue share of the cost." The riverfront improvement will be funded in part by community-development grants with some money coming from the dam owners.

"Not only is there the new vision of the Kennebec to become accustomed to," says Keller, "there is a new sense of Augusta's downtown to contend with." Augusta is not a predominantly affluent community, Keller explains, so people were concerned about who would plan these improvements, who would benefit from them and what their impacts would be. Especially, says Keller, because the Riverfront plan involves an urban revitalization that could be described as "something approaching gentrification."

"The strongest ethnic community in Augusta is French Canadian and a lot of those families helped build the dam and run the mill over the years," says Keller. For some in this community, a visible changing of the guard like the removal of Edwards Dam was not necessarily welcome or easy to accept. And as Doug Watts tells me, "It's still a pretty big learning curve." There are still some people who say, "Why would you care to bring back the fishery? This is a foul river. You can't eat them anyway."

Removing Edwards Dam freed one stretch of the Kennebec, but many improvements still need to be made that are not visible from the banks of the river. "Up until the 1980s the Kennebec was a severely polluted river," says Dave Courtemanch, director of Environmental Assessment with the Maine Department of Environmental Protection. The pollution came largely from paper mills, particularly one located in Winslow that closed in the late 1970s and was replaced by one with newer, cleaner technology further upriver in Skowhegan, says Courtemanch, whose specialty is water quality. Maine has been fairly aggressive in tackling "the dioxin problem," requiring its paper manufacturers to use a process that is essentially dioxin-free.* This, says Courtemanch, has taken care of the gross pollution problem, and the Kennebec has "responded pretty well over the last two decades." Yet because it is a persistent and bioaccumulative toxin, even if no new dioxin enters the river, what is there will linger for years. "What we needed to do,"

---

*Dioxin, a persistent toxic, is a common by-product of the pulp and paper manufacturing process.

Courtemanch tells me, "is bring the fish back, give the fish access to the river. Now we need to make them edible."

The state currently warns against eating some Kennebec River fish because of dioxin and PCB (polychlorinated biphenyl) contamination. The PCBs come from electrical transformers and many other now-defunct industrial processes. The production and use of PCBs were banned in the 1970s, but their toxic legacy persists and has proven extremely difficult to clean up.

Another toxic to contend with is mercury, which, says Courtemanch, is a problem for most of Maine's rivers. The effects of mercury poisoning have been detected in Maine's loons and eagles, which eat river fish that have mercury in their body tissue. Some mercury comes from consumer sources (lightbulbs and medical and mechanical instruments), but much of it arrives in vapor form, from waste burners in neighboring states and coal burners in the Midwest and elsewhere around the world. The regional and local sources are coming under control, Courtemanch tells me, but those outside the region are difficult to deal with.

"So many factors work against salmon restoration that with Edwards Dam in place they would have no chance of recovery," says Betsy. "Everything but salmon has improved this year," she says. "2000 has been a poor year in general for salmon, but if the dam wasn't out they wouldn't have a chance in heck. The Edwards removal is an essential piece but is it going to solve all the river's problems? No." Yet it was a literal glimmer of hope when, early in the summer of 2000, a salmon was spotted leaping in the Kennebec near Waterville, nearly twenty miles upstream of Augusta.

To better understand the challenges facing Maine's salmon and get a sense of where the restoration of the Kennebec fits in this picture, I went to see the "Down East" rivers at the heart of the battle to protect Maine's Atlantic salmon: the Machias, Dennys, East Machias, Pleasant, Narraguagus, Ducktrap, Cove Brook and Sheepscot, where as part of the efforts to improve the prospects for their wild salmon, dam removal projects are under way.

Despite their distance from hubs of business and industry, these coastal rivers, which once teemed with wild salmon and have probably fed humans since the Old Stone Age, if not longer, are now disturbingly depleted of their native fish. The Norse saga of Eric the Red recounts the voyage of Leif Ericson and his band of Vikings in about A.D. 1000 to a land lush with salmon larger than any they had ever seen before.[7] In 1999, according to the U.S. Fish and Wildlife Service and National Marine Fisheries Service, only about thirty adult wild Atlantic salmon returned to all of these rivers combined: the Narraguagus, Pleasant, Machias, East Machias, Dennys, Ducktrap, Sheepscot and Cove Brook (a tributary of the Penobscot). It is possible that "the first fish mentioned in the [European] chronicles of North America"[8] will vanish from the planet.

Populations of Atlantic salmon native to the rivers of Maine and northern New England have been dwindling since European settlers began damming the rivers at the end of the Colonial period in the eighteenth century. The decline increased because of aggressive fishing, pollution from mills, factories and power plants, the impacts of development, logging, irrigation, agricultural runoff, and more recently the effects of toxic chemicals percolating out of the air into the state's vast system of wetlands, lakes and streams. There is also concern about diseases transmitted to wild salmon by those raised in aquaculture ponds.

Yet in the early 1970s, some 1.5 million Atlantic salmon still returned to the rivers of eastern North America. That number has now shrunk to about 350,000.[9] Since the early 1990s, Maine's wild salmon numbers have plummeted yet further, says Andy Goode, director of U.S. Programs for the Atlantic Salmon Federation based in Brunswick, Maine. Despite years of active stocking with hatchery fish, there is now no commercial Atlantic salmon fishery in Maine. The numbers are simply too small. According to Goode, over the years, the state's largest rivers—the Kennebec, Penobscot and Androscoggin—have lost more than half their salmon habitat due to dams. Fishing and changes in ocean and climate conditions have contributed to the decline of wild Atlantic salmon, but the major human cause of their decline is attributed to the damming of the salmon's home rivers.[10]

On November 13, 2000, the National Marine Fisheries Service announced the listing of wild Atlantic salmon of these eight "Downeast" rivers as endangered under the federal Endangered Species Act, a move so controversial that the governor of Maine almost immediately appealed the decision. "Less than ten percent of the fish needed for the long-term survival of wild Atlantic salmon are returning to Maine rivers. Without the protection and recovery programs afforded by the Endangered Species Act, chances are this population will die out completely," said Jamie Rappaport Clark, director of the U.S. Fish and Wildlife Service. This listing comes after seven years of lawsuits and petitions filed by a host of conservation groups and despite a state salmon conservation plan designed in hopes of averting such a move. The controversy stems from disagreements over the precise cause of the salmon's decline, questions of fish genetics and fear of ESA regulations. But it's clear that the numbers of wild Atlantic salmon are perilously low.

"The listing is good for the salmon. It will cause everyone to pay more attention to what they're doing," says Courtemanch, who thinks the entire species of Atlantic salmon should be listed, not just those on the eight Maine rivers. "The subpopulations are clearly endangered," he says, and even "the Penobscot, which used to be the flagship run, is nothing compared to what it used to be."

In the early morning before full light, as I drive northeast out of Augusta toward the tiny town of Columbia Falls, spring recedes. The leaves are smaller, the buds tighter, and branches barer. The colors are more sepia and gray than green. This is wet and boggy country. There are tangles of birch, short pines and thickets of berry bushes. Braids of water reflect the gull-colored sky. It reminds me of muskeg I've seen in Alaska, and I think about moose. I pass a sign that says, "Ice Augurs All Makes All Brands."

This is Washington County, the first place in the continental United States to greet the rising sun. The area was once inhabited by the Wabanaki, and before them by the Red Paint People, identified by the ocher dye they used. Europeans settled here in the 1760s, and the first naval battle of the Revolutionary War took place in Washington County. It thrived on timber milling and shipbuilding well into the nineteenth century. Sparsely populated by East Coast standards, Washington County now cultivates about 30 million pounds of blueberries a year—90 percent of the country's entire crop. The town of Cherryfield calls itself "the blueberry capital of the world."

The *Maine Atlas and Gazetteer* shows that I have traveled a stretch of road along something called The Whalesback. The map names countless brooks, ponds, marshes, swamps and bogs. Not far off are the West Barrens and the Great Heath. I pass a few towns and villages, but almost none announce their presence with a sign. In fact, once off the interstate, apart from intersections, I encounter almost no signs whatsoever.

When I reach Columbia Falls at the mouth of the Pleasant River, the sky is gray and the wind blowing in from the coast. There are wide-mouthed river bays and tidal inlets. The glaciers were late to retreat here, and this part of Maine is nearly all coast, with deep fingers of bay stretching inland to meet rivers streaming out of the wet woodlands. I look at the map and realize I am almost 300 miles closer to the Canadian border than I am to Boston.

At the mouth of the Pleasant River, I find the Wild Salmon Resource Center, where I'm to meet Dwayne Shaw, the center's program coordinator. The Wild Salmon Resource Center is part of the Downeast Salmon Federation—a nonprofit formed to coordinate Atlantic salmon conservation efforts and the activities of Maine's Downeast watershed councils—and home to the Pleasant River Hatchery.

The Resource Center is housed in a small wooden building with a deck that extends over the mouth of the river looking seaward across tidal flats and beach grass. In the hour or so I am there, the tide rolls in, erasing the beach. The rising water laps at the small bluffs that separate land from sea. The center teaches local schoolchildren aquatic and marine biology. It occupies the site of a private dam—now dismantled—that was built during the late 1970s. As we stand on the deck, Dwayne points out the smelt shacks on the beach and concrete remains of the dam's fish ladder—a zigzag, L-shaped corridor of cement. "It never worked," says Dwayne, "and now we have kids go through the ladder to see what it was like for the fish. They always bump their noses."

Inside the center are posters illustrating the life cycle of Atlantic salmon and maps showing their migration routes from Maine and eastern Canada to the waters of Labrador and western

Greenland. Fish from the Narraguagus have been found off the coast of Greenland, identification tags indicating that they've swum nearly 2,000 nautical miles.[11] A bulletin board is covered with magic-marker and crayon drawings sent as thank-you notes from an elementary school class's visit to the center. An aquarium is filled with local sea life. Downstairs is the hatchery, where salmon eggs are being nurtured in hopes of jump-starting recovery of the river's severely diminished native salmon runs.

The Narraguagus, Pleasant, Machias and East Machias were once all prolific salmon streams. In the 1780s, fish passage was mandated at the first dams built across the river after Machias was settled in the 1760s. Despite this requirement, two dams were built at Machias in 1841 and 1842 and another at nearby Whitneyville in 1842, all without fish passage. The salmon runs disappeared until a fishway was built at the Whitneyville dam in the 1870s. But by 1872, when a survey of Maine's salmon rivers was taken, memories of large catches of big salmon on the Narraguagus at towns like Cherryfield already belonged to old-timers' lore.[12] Still, in the 1940s people remembered so many big salmon in the river that one could nab a fish by standing on the banks of the Machias with a pitchfork. Until the 1960s, thirty-pound salmon were still seen in the river. In 2000, the returns of wild Atlantic salmon to some of these rivers were the lowest on record.[13]

Before we head out into what has become a raw rain-spitting day to see some local rivers, Dwayne unfurls the original architectural drawings of the East Machias dam that is due to be removed in the summer. The dam, which is now defunct, was built in 1926 on the site of an older one, which powered a gristmill. The meticulous drawings and careful lettering show the location of the old millpond and tailrace, where a lathe and plane once sat, and the exact placement of their gears and pulleys. These drawings will help with the dismantling of the dam. Because it did not generate enough power, the dam was abandoned by Bangor Hydro in 1962 and later sold to the town of East Machias for $1. "Vandals opened the dam gates permanently in 1973," says Dwayne, and the river has been free-flowing ever since. The aging structure is now a safety hazard and impediment to river restoration so there's no reason to preserve it.

In East Machias, we scramble up a small slope to stand on the edge of the dam. The dam is a nasty looking construction of battered concrete and rusted metal. Below, the river rushes through over big mossy rocks. The water runs a rich, reddish coffee brown, the color of the peat bogs. Dwayne tells me the river is favored by paddlers who like to run these rapids. Some of the weathered mill buildings still stand on the riverbank. Tucked into the bank at the base of the dam is an old wooden smokehouse used for smoking alewives. Its blue-gray paint is weathered. A small whisk broom, dustpan and a pair of work gloves hang neatly from nails tacked outside the door. Next to them is a scrap of paper noting the current and past years' prices of smoked alewives, "split" or "round." The owner, Dwayne tells me, is an old-timer who's worried that removing the dam will destroy his smokehouse. The smokehouse owner seems to be one of the very few opposed to the dam's removal. Coastal America—a branch of the U.S. Air Force involved in river and wetland restoration projects all over the country—has been engaged to manage the dam removal. It has agreed to move the smokehouse if that's what will save it. Coastal America's website calls the East Machias dam removal a "military training" exercise. It will be done at no cost to the town. When I check back with Dwayne at the end of the summer after the dam removal, I ask after the smokehouse. It's intact, in its original location, and the owner is happy.

The wind has picked up and rain is falling sideways. Water is coming in from the ocean and flowing out to the sea. There is no escaping that this landscape is shaped by hydrology. Over a sandwich and cup of coffee, Dwayne tells me a bit about what it's like to live in this community and work on conservation issues, about his wife's work with local social services and about the river guiding they do together. Like many in rural communities, especially those struggling to keep up with the evolving economy, Washington County residents are cautious about change. Washington County currently has the lowest average household income and highest unemployment rate in the state. Dwayne says that, often, "Downeast" folks deal with problems by being quiet about them, hoping no one notices and that they'll go away. Unfortunately, in the case of wild Atlantic salmon, the fish—not the problem of their disappearance—are what's vanishing.

Our last stop is a small dam in Cherryfield on the Narraguagus. The dam was built here in the 1960s after an ice jam nearly flooded the town. The dam stopped the flooding but destroyed the best salmon pool in the river. Dwayne points out a wooden frame with sturdy dowels attached standing several yards from the river. It's a rod rack. The salmon ran so consistently here that anglers would take turns, resting their rods until their time came to hook a fish. The dam caused a rift in town, says Dwayne, between those who wanted the dam and those who did not. "Nearly forty years later there are people who still don't speak to each other," he says.

In July and August 2000, the Red Horse Squadron of the Air Force, with funding from Fish America Foundation, removed the East Machias River Dam. "It went much quicker than expected," says Dwayne, when I speak with him in September, and the river is settling back into its natural channel. The town is pleased with the results, reports Dwayne, who says there seems to be only one detractor, a local cranberry grower who has expressed concern about silt washing downstream. Because fish have had free passage on the East Machias for nearly thirty years, it will take some time to assess how this dam removal affects aquatic life.

"The local salmon have endured quite a lot," remarks Doug Watts, but he wonders how much longer they can hold on. "I don't know if we're going to be able to save them. . . . It would be the worst irony if we've given the river back to these fish and they couldn't hold out long enough. It's a real question if they're going to survive."

Watts then waxes philosophic. "This is the price you pay when you lose something so completely it's not a part of your culture anymore. When there's no cultural tradition, you hit a big blind spot. Once you think extinction is okay, you're lost. I was taught at an early age what we did to the bison, the passenger pigeon, the great auk," he says. "What really scare me are kids that spend most of their time indoors playing video games. It doesn't matter to them if things disappear. They can play virtual zoo on their computers. That was what was so extraordinary about the kids up at Fort Halifax. There were seven- and eight-year-olds saying, 'It isn't fair. These fish are trying to get upstream and they can't!'"

"Some of these dam removals offer the best hope for the Atlantic salmon but it's not simply a question of removing one dam on a river," explains Andy Goode. "It's a long process and there's a lot more we could be doing here."

In the pouring rain, I drive toward Boston, looping around the seemingly endless bays. Sky and ocean are the same steel blue. Gulls wheel and screech. Tidal islands and patches of glowing green beach grass are visible through the murky mist. As a child, I spent part of several summers on an island in Casco Bay, mostly in small boats. We pulled mussels off the barnacled rocks and boiled them for dinner. We swam in the icy salt water, baited lobster traps and watched seals bob in the swells. My best friend and I spent hours in all weathers sailing a wooden boat with a single sail out in the middle of the bay. We navigated our way home by setting our sights on the dock of a house where Harriet Beecher Stowe once lived. We learned to tie knots, watch for tides and read a simple nautical chart, but no one ever spoke to us about fish. I wonder now if that was, in part, because it was the late 1960s, and Maine's rivers were dirty. It was then not even a full decade since Rachel Carson had written in *Silent Spring* of the effects of DDT on Atlantic salmon. Whatever the reason, we were not told of these problems. We were simply children and learned to love the water. As a nation, we have come a long way since then in our efforts to repair and curtail some of the damage our use of these waters has wrought, but clearly not far enough.

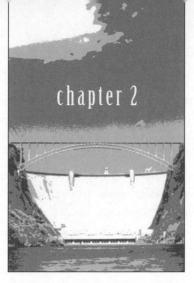

North Carolina

"MARINES BLOW UP DAM TO
IMPROVE FISH HABITAT IN
NEUSE RIVER BASIN"

There's plenty of greenery amid the cities of
Raleigh, Durham and Chapel Hill, but not until the suburban
sprawl recedes does North Carolina's landscape become apparent.
Traveling across the Neuse River Basin and Piedmont coastal
plain on my way to the Outer Banks, I pass brick farm buildings,
tobacco fields and small towns filled with churches. Narrow, unlit,
two-lane roads angle through flat fields that stretch out with an
intense watery green. This lush and flood-prone farmland was
once submerged by ocean, and it's easy to imagine it as an immense tidal flat. On this evening in late May, the air is thick and
humid. The sunset is liquid peach as the light fades and insect
hum begins to rise. I stop for gas near the Trent River. The station's pumps have old mechanical numbers. There is a squeaky

screen door. The woman at the cash register trusts me with the amount I read off when I come in to pay. On the counter is a row of small paper bags, hand-stamped with a local farm's imprint. I am told the peanuts were roasted that day.

Before European settlement began in the sixteenth and seventeenth centuries, the Piedmont plain was covered by longleaf pine. But gradually, the longleaf pine savanna was converted to agriculture and replaced with hardwoods and loblolly pine. Oak, hickory and maple trees mark the edges of fields and homesteads, but the woods still harbor such floral curiosities as the carnivorous Venus flytrap and pitcher plant. In wetland areas closer to the coast grow cypress, ash and tupelo.

The Neuse River is thought to be about two million years old, and there has likely been human settlement in the basin for at least 14,000 years. The Native people who lived in what became North Carolina predated European arrivals by at least a thousand years. Among them were the Coree, Neusiok, Scotan and Tuscarora. They lived near the rivers, grew vegetables in the rich soil, gathered hickory nuts and huckleberries and hunted deer, turkey and bear. European colonization brought disease, war and displacement. After the settlers' 1714 war with the Tuscarora, only a remnant of the Native population remained. Like much of the Eastern Seaboard, now settled for nearly four hundred years, the Neuse Basin has a distinctly cultivated appearance. In the spring of 2000, the scenery looks more like a backdrop for a novel by Reynolds Price or Pat Conroy than it does for an epic about hunters and gatherers.

As I approach the coast, salt air begins to mingle with river moisture. Oncoming headlights blur in the slight fog. When I cross the bridge leading to a spit of the Outer Banks, the crash of surf becomes audible. I follow directions that bring me within yards of the water's edge, to the house where friends have invited me to spend the night. It was a hot day, and the evening has barely cooled, so I sleep with a screen door open to the roar of breaking waves. In the morning, my hair is damp with salty mist.

The next day, my host, his four year-old daughter and I kayak through some of the nearby tidal inlets. The sky is overcast and the marsh grasses seem to vibrate against blue jay–colored water. Great blue herons and egrets flap their pterodactyl-like wings. The white-feathered egrets contrast sharply with the surrounding palette of blues and greens. We beach the boats and wade the warm shallows, watching for hermit crabs. The nooks and crannies of bay seem to go on forever. It's tempting to think of turning the boat inland and taking the river upstream from the coast, to follow the route of North Carolina's migratory fish.

The inlets of the Outer Banks form part of the Albemarle and Pamlico estuary, the second largest estuary system in the country; only the Chesapeake, just north up the coast, is bigger. The whole estuary drains some 30,000 square miles, parts of two states, Virginia and North Carolina, encompassing five major river basins—the Chowan, Roanoke, Pasquotank, Tar-Pamlico and Neuse—and seven sounds. The region contains nearly two million acres of water,[1] where the freshwater rivers meet the salt water of the Atlantic, creating fertile habitat for countless aquatic species. The salt marshes around which we paddle are just such a place.

North Carolina's rich coastal waters have long attracted commercial and recreational fishing. Though the volume is far from what it was, commercial fishing still earns North Carolina about $1 billion annually.[2] The Albemarle-Pamlico estuary nurtures 90 percent of the commercial seafood caught in North Carolina, and sportfishing is a significant factor in attracting tourists to North Carolina's coast. Tourism is the state's second largest source of revenue. The kayaks we rent, the ice cream we buy for four-year-old Hannah, and the families arriving by the carload with beach toys and fishing rods all contribute to the estimated $2 billion a year tourism brings to the coastal economy. This is a powerful incentive for keeping clean water and fish flowing through these rivers toward the Outer Banks.

Until recently, enough fish migrated through the Neuse River and its tributaries to support a thriving commercial fishery that included striped bass, American shad, blue crab, river herring, sturgeon, oysters, clams, catfish and bluefish. In 1896, eight million pounds or more of American shad were caught in North Carolina.

More American shad and striped bass were taken from these waters in the early 1900s than from anywhere else in the United States. But because of pollution and dams, the quality and quantity of habitat declined and the number of fish in these coastal rivers plummeted. While the commercial fishery for striped bass and shad continued until the late 1970s, by 1995 the catch of American shad was less than 3 percent of what it had been a hundred years before.[3] The 1995 catch of shad from the Neuse was only 3 percent of what it had been in 1953.[4] Now, the Environmental Protection Agency (EPA) describes many of the estuaries' marine species as "stressed" and "severely depleted."

The damaging effect of dams on North Carolina's fish was noted as early as 1881.[5] To improve at least some conditions for North Carolina's coastal river fish, several dams have been removed on the Neuse and its tributaries, but it's clear that dam removal alone will not solve the basin's water-quality problems. Releasing some of these rivers' natural flow, however, will help restore habitat for aquatic species, especially those whose survival depends on reaching both ocean and headwaters. So I went to the Neuse to see the river freed by removing Quaker Neck Dam, "the first large dam in the nation to be removed for environmental reasons."[6]

Although North Carolina's dam removals have not generated the controversy that removals have in other parts of the country, it is still a dramatic step. "It's an act of removal, but it's really an act of restoration and renewal," said Secretary of the Interior Bruce Babbitt in December 1997, at a ceremony marking the removal of the Quaker Neck Dam. The following year, the Cherry Hospital Dam on the Little River, a tributary of the Neuse, was removed, followed by removal of the Little River's Rains Mill Dam in December 1999. Removing these three dams opens over a thousand miles of mainstem and tributary spawning grounds for Neuse River anadromous fish.

The Neuse and its tributaries made national news in 1999 when they overflowed their banks so disastrously in the wake of Hurricane Floyd. The flooding exposed and intensified the most serious threat to the health of these rivers, pollution from the state's industrial-scale hog production. When compared to the overflowing lagoons of hog waste and scary bacteria, removing Neuse River dams seems relatively simple.

Having heard about massive fish kills and pfiesteria* in the Neuse, I found it impossible to separate my thoughts about the lower and upper river. I've been struck by our tendency to divorce upper and lower basin issues, so while the upstream dam removals and downstream pollution may seem quite separate, I went to see both parts of the Neuse. Reinforcing the watershed's connection was a little sticker pasted on local sinks and toilet tanks: a blue arrow pointing toward the drain, with the words "The Neuse starts here."

To learn more about the lower Neuse, I travel to New Bern to meet Rick Dove, Riverkeeper with the Neuse River Foundation. Located at the mouth of the river, New Bern was founded in 1710 by the Swiss Baron Christopher de Gaffenreid, who purchased the land from the Tuscarora Indians. The Tuscaroras had a settlement at the confluence of the Trent and Neuse Rivers called Chattawka, or "where the fish are taken out." New Bern was the first permanent Colonial capital of North Carolina. It was home to the state's first public school and its first newspaper and printing press. The city became a major port known for shipping tar, pitch and turpentine, all products of the eastern forests. During the Civil War, New Bern was part of the Union, which accounts for the preservation of many of its old buildings. One of the world's largest Marine Corps air stations is just downriver at Cherry Point. Another claim to fame is the local pharmacist who invented a soft drink later sold as Pepsi Cola. The waterfront streets of New Bern are lined with well-kept historic brick buildings and old-fashioned–looking streetlights.

A sense of civic pride is evident as Rick Dove talks about his work as Riverkeeper. Dove grew up on the Chesapeake and now

---

*Pfiesteria is a dinoflagellate, a microscopic organism that sometimes behaves like a plant and sometimes like an animal. It can produce toxins that produce lesions in fish and has caused fish kills in the lower Neuse, Tar-Pamlico and New River estuaries. Pfiesteria also has seriously detrimental effects on human health. Pfiesteria seems to be a problem only during warmer months, between April and October. (See the North Carolina Department of Environment and Natural Resources and the work of Dr. JoAnn Burkholder.)

lives on the banks of the Neuse. He is a retired Marine colonel, has practiced criminal law and served as a judge at the Marine Corps Base Camp Lejeune. He has also worked locally as a commercial fisher and crabber with his son. "I stepped out of a law practice to do this seven years ago. Friends called me a Don Quixote," says Dove. He clearly relishes the surprise some may find in discovering that one of the Neuse's most outspoken advocates is an ex-military man who describes himself as a political conservative. Dove has put his Marine flying experience to work on behalf of the Neuse and spent hundreds of hours cruising over the watershed, observing and filming river conditions. He patrols the water in his boat and encourages the three hundred volunteers who help the Neuse Riverkeeper keep an eye on the health of the river.

In Dove's shiny red pickup we tow the gleaming Riverkeeper boat to the river, a few minutes' drive from the office. We head out toward the mouth of the Neuse, said to be the widest river mouth in the continental United States, six miles across. The bright sun bounces off the water. "The Neuse is the number-one fish nursery in the country, certainly on the East Coast. It's still a big commercial crab fishery," Dove tells me. "Most East Coast fish have their young here. If we lose this estuary, people in New York, Connecticut, Maine, they're all going to suffer. We've so changed that landscape that we've pushed nature to the point where she's had it with us."

Dove tells me that in the early spring, bull sharks come up to New Bern. In 1994, the last manatees seen locally were spotted at the marina near the Sheraton Hotel in town. As we cruise out into the bay, Dove asks me to keep an eye out for fish, dead or alive. About a billion fish died in and near the Neuse in 1991, and there were other big fish kills in 1995, 1999 and 2000. Scientists began to suspect that an overload of nutrients from agricultural runoff flowing into the Neuse and its tributaries was causing an excessive growth of aquatic vegetation and harming fish. The hog farms that Dove calls "eating machines" are a major source of this problem.

The streams and rivers are the "veins that carry waste through the coastal plain." Wastewater treatment plants for hogs and poultry "leak like a sieve. We've put junkyards in the wetlands. We didn't have to fill these wetlands and put all these roads, homes and bridges in harm's way. Alligators now walk across highways rather than wetlands. Mother Nature makes a river, she does it just right. She took all that time to make it right. Then we come along and upset that balance," says Dove, shaking his head.

Wondering how the downstream pollution might affect the shad and bass that migrate up the Neuse, I later speak with Joseph Hightower, an associate professor of zoology, a member of the North Carolina Cooperative Fish and Wildlife Research Unit at North Carolina State as well as a fisheries biologist with the Department of the Interior's U.S. Geological Survey. Hightower has been studying the migration of American shad and striped bass, and he explains that the shad migrate out of the Neuse in March and April, and by May, when the water warms up, they're out in the ocean. The bass follow closely behind. "In the spring when these fish are in the rivers, the water's cold and dissolved oxygen levels and water flows are high. As far as we know, the water quality is good. It's not until the water heats up that the dissolved oxygen levels are down and you start to have problems."[7]

"When you're trying to fix a river, you don't fix it by trying to make friends. You fix it by getting the respect of the people who need to fix the problem," says Dove. As Riverkeeper, he talks to local politicians and news media and has testified before Congress. Credibility, he tells me, is key. "If I lose credibility in anything, I'm finished." The Neuse River Foundation has a science team and hours of video footage documenting waste spills throughout the watershed. The strategy has been to pressure the state to fix what's wrong with its rivers, beginning with the Neuse. "As long as the river's happy with me, I'm okay," Dove says.

We circle around a buoy marker where an osprey has nested. Dove cuts the motor so we can listen for baby birds. The mother osprey gives a high-pitched squawk. Nearby terns and other osprey dive for fish. Before heading upriver, we circle once more around the osprey on buoy marker #27. Dove speaks of her the way he might a special neighbor. "Osprey are by far my favorite bird," he says.

We follow the river upstream along its tidal flow to Turkey Quarter Creek, a spot Dove is fond of. We pass people fishing from small motorboats. The banks are lined with tupelo and cypress trees. The cypress, with their big comblike fans of knobby roots—called knees—grow right through the water. There's a whole forest of cypress knees, a mysterious world of its own. Some cypress are 500 years old, says Dove. He shows me one that's been identified as 300 years old. Another he points to has clamshells embedded in its bark, "left after a beaver's feast," Dove thinks. The water extends into the streamside woods. Hardwoods and pines grow in the floodplain here. The water-adapted tupelo roots have been used for corks and bobbers. We see osprey, egrets and pelicans. Dove says he sometimes sees alligators here. As we pass close to the trees, Dove reports that this is mating season for snakes. "They can get pretty aggressive," he says, chuckling. This will not be the last time I'll hear about snakes dropping off tree limbs into passing canoes and kayaks. Dove silences the motor for a moment. "If you stop your boat and let nature embrace you. . . ," he says reflectively, before we zip back downriver.

In December 2000, the Neuse River Foundation, the Neuse Riverkeeper and a coalition of conservation groups initiated legal proceedings against North Carolina hog producers, charging them with violations of the federal Clean Water Act. It's going to be a long fight. When I read this news, I think of the osprey and the fish that have so recently regained access to the upstream reaches of the Neuse, swimming the sunlit waters of the river harbor.

Like other East Coast rivers, including Maine's Kennebec, North Carolina's coastal rivers are home to anadromous fish. A handful of these species migrate thousands of stream miles in the Neuse Basin: American shad, hickory shad, alewife, Atlantic and shortnosed sturgeon and striped bass. Dams throughout the watershed have long blocked these fish from their spawning grounds. Dams have also hampered survival of the dwarf wedge mussel and Tar River spinymussel. In their larval stage (when they are called glochidia), these shellfish attach themselves to the gills or fins of certain fish and hitch a ride to a new part of the river to begin the next stage of their development. Blocked by dams, the glochidia become marooned. This situation, along with toxic runoff from farms, lawns, golf courses and industry as well as acid rain, has caused populations of these mussels to plummet. They are now listed as endangered under the federal Endangered Species Act.

Long and snout-nosed with rows of platelike bony protrusions, sturgeon have a dinosaur-era look. *Peterson's Field Guide to Freshwater Fishes* describes them as "large ancient fishes." Shortnose sturgeon are usually about three-and-a-half feet long, but the Atlantic sturgeon, which were once plentiful in the Neuse, can grow to as long as fourteen feet and live for sixty years. Sturgeon live in the downstream reaches of larger rivers and Atlantic coastal waters from southern Canada to northeastern Florida and spend most of the year in salt water. Their eggs are served as the salty delicacy called caviar. Because of dams, pollution and overfishing, the Neuse River shortnose sturgeon are now a federally listed endangered species. Atlantic sturgeon, once the "cash crop" of the Jamestown Colony, are now so scarce that fishing for them is no longer permitted along the Atlantic Coast of the United States.

As an indication of how much river issues, despite many similarities, can vary from region to region, in North Carolina all inquiries about dam removal lead me to the U.S. Fish and Wildlife Service rather than a grassroots conservation group. Mike Wicker, a biologist with the U.S. Fish and Wildlife Service in Raleigh and the coordinator of the Albemarle-Pamlico Coastal Program, is kind enough to spend an afternoon showing me the Neuse River dam removal sites. Wicker has a jovial air and is enthusiastic about these projects. He seems genuinely delighted to spend time with an inquiring visitor.

It's a hot, bright day as we set off from the U.S. Fish and Wildlife Service offices on the poetically named Pylon Drive. Our first stop is the Quaker Neck Dam site near Goldsboro, about fifty miles southeast of Raleigh. In American landscape terms, the drive is unremarkable. Small strip malls with gas stations, fast-food restaurants and convenience stores dominate the foreground. There are mobile-home parks and "manufactured home" dealers, some advertising replacements for hurricane-damaged homes. Old trees with wide trunks and green farm fields lie beyond, in a patchwork of rural and encroaching suburban.

From its headwaters at the confluence of the Flat and Eno Rivers near Durham and Chapel Hill, the Neuse flows about two hundred miles to the ocean at Pamlico Sound. Over a million people, nearly 15 percent of North Carolina's residents, live within the 6,000-square-mile Neuse Basin, which drains about twenty counties. On its way to the coast, the Neuse picks up runoff from six fast-growing cities, two military bases, a major pulp mill, sprawling suburbs and farms. About a third of the watershed is devoted to agriculture. Many of the farms that make North Carolina the country's second-largest hog-producing state are located here, contributing to the water-quality problems I heard about from Rick Dove.

Near the dam site we take a short walk through some oak, pine, hickory, river birch and alder trees. On this late spring day, the woods feel similar to those of southern New England. Yet the air is just moist enough to hint of a southern coastal climate without deep freezes or long stretches of snow. The riverbanks are shallow and the river looks gentle. We walk down on the banks where the dam once stood. Unless you knew that a 260-foot-wide, seven-foot-high dam was here for forty-five years, creating a 360-acre impoundment, you'd never be able to tell.

Quaker Neck Dam was built in 1952 to supply water to cool turbines at a local coal-fired, steam-generating electrical plant. Before the dam was built, American shad and striped bass migrated far enough upstream to support commercial fishing near Raleigh. Discussions about removal began in 1989, when the U.S. Fish and Wildlife Service formally identified the dam as an obstruction to the river's migratory fish. What Wicker calls "a whole hodge-podge" of local, state and federal agencies and conservation groups subsequently became involved in the project, but the Fish and Wildlife Service has been the lead player throughout the process.

In 1991, the Coastal America Foundation* proposed improving the dam's fish passage, but when it was determined that a cost-

---

*Coastal America Foundation is a partnership of federal agencies established in 1991 that includes the Air Force, Army, Navy, Departments of Agriculture, Commerce, Defense, Housing and Urban Development, Interior and Transportation, the Environmental Protection Agency and the President's office.

effective alternative to the dam could be built, the dam's owners, the Carolina Power & Light Company, agreed to work with state and federal agencies to remove the dam. To replace the old dam, which blocked the whole river, the U.S. Army Corps of Engineers built a small weir dam on an inside channel to provide cooling water to the electrical plant. Deconstruction of Quaker Neck Dam, accomplished with a five-thousand-pound wrecking ball and hydraulic hammer, was completed between December 1997 and September 1998.

I ask about the sediment behind Quaker Neck and the other Neuse dams that have been removed. Wicker explains that the sediment was a problem only for a brief period. The sediment wasn't contaminated; it was only a question of how much would enter the river and when. As with the Edwards Dam, accumulated sediment was left to wash downstream naturally. Rick Dove thinks the sediment in the Neuse remains a problem, if only because so much of it enters the river from the Raleigh-Durham area.

The removal cost $205,000, paid for by the National Fish and Wildlife Foundation, the North Carolina Marine Fisheries Resource Grant Program and the EPA. American Rivers calls Quaker Neck Dam's removal one of the most cost-effective river restoration projects in the country. Because there were complicated legal, financial, safety and engineering problems, the whole process, Wicker tells me, took nearly six years. Yet, says Wicker, addressing the problems on a technical basis created a lot of common ground for everyone on all sides of the project. And, he adds, there was "absolute consensus that what's good for the fish in this river is good for the economy." Due to the mutual respect of all those working on the Neuse River dam removals, Wicker says these projects have "not been contentious at all."

Wicker explains that North Carolina's rivers benefit from the National Estuary Program's work in the region. That EPA program has funded millions of dollars' worth of research, including an inventory of wildlife in the Neuse Basin, and has been "tremendously useful in getting different groups talking to each other." Program scientists take advantage of North Carolina's university system, working with university scientists to conduct inventories of aquatic species throughout the watershed and monitor the effects of dam removal. "People think it's kind of a dim-witted place where people talk slow," says Wicker, "but North Carolina has always been really committed to education. Academia is really respected and has always been very influential here." We've long been aware of the problems in these rivers, Wicker says, but awareness that something could be done about them is kind of new.

The American Sport Fishing Association greeted Quaker Neck's demolition with enthusiasm, estimating that enhanced fish runs could add several million dollars annually to North Carolina's economy. "The net effect of the dam removal is that the 40,000 full-time jobs sportfishing supports in the state will grow significantly," said American Sportfishing Association President Mike Hayden when the dam removal was announced.

A look at a map of North Carolina rivers reveals the impact of removing a dam as apparently modest as Quaker Neck. Because of what Mike Wicker calls the "dendritic pattern of all those twisty little tributaries," with the obstacle of Quaker Neck removed, 75 more miles of the mainstem and 925 more miles of streams that feed into the Neuse are now available to fish. A map of these newly freed tributaries makes these streams look like capillaries, and the analogy of rescuing a body from a blocked artery comes quickly to mind.

Another major fish obstacle identified in the 1989 Fish and Wildlife Service study was Cherry Hospital Dam on the Little River in Goldsboro. It was built in 1949 to impound water for the Cherry Hospital, a state psychiatric hospital. Because the hospital now gets water from the city of Goldsboro, the dam is no longer needed. While the dam site's modest hardwood trees and stream bank vegetation seem to lack drama, the restoration's potential is significant. Removing the dam freed up an additional seventy-six miles of spawning habitat for Neuse River alewives, shad, sturgeon and striped bass.

Still more Neuse River habitat—an additional forty-nine miles —was opened up when the Rains Mill Dam was removed from the Little River near the town of New Princeton in 1999. Built in 1928 by a local farmer, Rains Mill Dam powered a gristmill and later a sawmill and cotton gin, blocking mportant spawning grounds for alewives, American shad, hickory shad, shortnose sturgeon and striped bass, as well as for the endangered Tar spiny and dwarf wedge mussels. In addition to improving conditions for aquatic life, restoring the river to natural flow levels will help prevent flooding upstream of the dam. Like Quaker Neck and Cherry Hospital Dam, Rains Mill Dam was removed with the voluntary cooperation of the dam owners and was a restoration project undertaken by Coastal America and the North Carolina Department of Environment and Natural Resources' Division of Water Resources.

"This is an act of restoration and re-creation for our rivers. Through the violence of destruction, we undertake the healing act of creation," said Secretary Babbitt as he gave the signal to light the fuse for the explosion that leveled the dam on December 1, 1999. "Today, the Marines are saving a few good species, from eight tiny freshwater mussels to the rare, ancient shortnose sturgeon. Dam owners, fishermen and public officials are working together to permanently restore what was once thought lost forever. And we have only begun."

It was the military's involvement that helped garner local support for the dam removals, Wicker says. "Most of the rural people don't like the federal government, but love the military," he tells me. The headline on the press release that announced the Rains Mill Dam removal was "Marines Blow Up Dam to Improve Fish Habitat in Neuse River Basin."

"With Rains," says Wicker, "the Marines needed some practice blowing stuff up." Blowing it up is a lot cheaper than doing it any other way, he explains,[8] "even if you have to fix people's homes afterwards. Our military is good at blowing stuff up, but not as good at minimizing collateral damage. They almost blew it up too good. A lot of people had photographs fall off the wall and break. But there were no lawsuits." The only real damage occurred a mile-and-a-quarter away from the dam, where the edge of a house sat on a rock ledge. The house's floor joists were substandard and vibrations from the explosion jammed a bathroom door shut while the owner sat on the toilet. "Coastal America went in and fixed it up. The thing about explosives," Wicker adds, chuckling some more, "is people really enjoy them."

Shad are now back in the Neuse Basin, where they haven't

been since these dams were built. The Department of the Interior estimates the additional spawning and nursery habitat above Rains Mill Dam alone could produce some 50,000 alewives and 5,000 American shad each year. The habitat opened by all three dam removals should produce from hundreds of thousands to several million of these fish each year.

To determine the location of important spawning grounds in the Neuse, Joseph Hightower, at North Carolina State, has been studying the migration of American shad and striped bass. When I first looked at Hightower's website it showed a video clip of the wrecking ball flailing away at Quaker Neck Dam. Since 1996, his research team has tracked fish by tagging them with sonic transmitters. The information they've gathered will be used to protect fish habitat from degradation. He's already providing evidence of these dam removals' success. In addition to the good prospects of restoring shad and bass runs, Mike Wicker is optimistic about the opportunity for sturgeon restoration, citing the opinion of Boyd Kynard, of the U.S. Geological Survey, whom Wicker calls Mr. Sturgeon.

Removing these three dams has opened the Neuse all the way to Raleigh, as far upstream as Millburnie Dam and Lassiter's Mill Dam on Crabtree Creek, which Wicker takes me to see. It's an old dam located in a park about 218 miles from the mouth of the river. Picturesque white clapboard houses overlook the impoundment and the dam's little waterfall. We walk out on the mossy rocks of the dam and talk above the rushing water. Wicker tells me that fish passage will be installed on this dam to preserve the surrounding historic buildings.

"The mainstem is in pretty good shape," he says. "Now we're opening up some of the tributaries. We're marching up the tributaries all the way to near Zebulon," a town just southeast of Raleigh. "One dam out on the mainstem. Two dams out on the Little River, and we're working on another. Whole dams have been removed. Others may not have to be." He tells me that, overall, these dam removals have been accomplished "pretty inexpensively," all with partnered funding. It's been important to the progress of these projects that no single entity has had to bear all the costs of removal.

Much of the press on dam removal emphasizes the disputes between the competing interests of the environmental, business, industrial and agricultural communities, generally giving the
impression that dam removals are all instigated by radical mon-
key-wrenchers. In the Neuse River Basin, nothing could be further from the case. "We've learned a lot from The National
Estuary program," says Wicker. "They went through a grueling
process where it seemed like everybody was at each other. Now
they go drink beer together," he says, smiling.

Wicker says that it's important that dam removals be a joint decision, and "to talk to the dam owners first, and address the concerns up front. We looked at Cherry Hospital and Quaker Neck,
and once we were convinced of the environmental benefit, we lis-
tened to the neighbors." He stresses the importance of credit
sharing and that there be "no fighting about how to have a winner
and a loser. There's a real tendency on this type of project to splin-
ter disciplines: biologists, engineers, attorneys. If you get into
that, it's a death knell. And it's important to approach the individuals involved with a solution, not with a problem."

"People want to know how something like a dam removal will
affect business and property," Wicker tells me. If people in the
community believe in the benefits, and there's some compensa-
tion for any loss, they'll be amenable to the restoration, he says.
Besides, he adds, around here "most people would rather do stuff
than talk about it.

"I don't consider myself an environmentalist, I consider myself
a scientist," says Wicker. Still, in 1997, he was one of three who received North Carolina's Governor's Award for Water Conserva-
tionist of the Year, for their work in removing Quaker Neck Dam.

On a system as big and complex as the Neuse, "really fixing the
river will probably take a century," says Rick Dove. But Dove,
Wicker and others working on restoration of the Neuse seem completely prepared to keep doing what needs to be done. "Open a
river and it has an ability to heal itself," Wicker says. "It will bring
a real sigh of relief to those little animals and fish, too. A lot of
those fish will now survive to live normal fishy lives."

Florida

THE CROOKED CREEK
AND THE CANAL

From North Carolina, where dam removal seems a generally apolitical activity, I drive to Florida, where a fight to remove the Rodman Dam on the Ocklawaha River has been going on for almost forty years. The Ocklawaha is the largest tributary of Florida's longest river, the St. Johns, and Rodman Dam, built in 1968 by the Army Corps of Engineers to control water for the Cross Florida Barge Canal, has been opposed from the moment it was proposed. In July 2000, Jeb Bush became the fifth Florida governor to support the breaching of Rodman Dam, but complexities of ecology and competing local interests continue to make it uncertain how this restoration project will progress.

As I drive south, the heat and humidity increase. I cross rivers whose names evoke the lush vegetation that obscures their water.

I cross the Lumber River, the Little Pee Dee River, then the Great Pee Dee. A great blue heron flaps its huge wings and flies low over the road. I stop in a convenience store that sells catfish bait, fireworks, pickled hard-boiled eggs and pig's feet in brine. All around are grass-green swamps broken by ribbons of water with short trees and leafless trunks protruding from the soggy ground. When the American naturalist William Bartram* traveled this stretch of coast in the 1770s, he wondered if these coastal wetlands represented an eastward advance of the American continent or an inland march of the ocean. It is comforting to realize that the essence of this landscape remains as Bartram described it over two hundred years ago.

I cross the Edisto, Ogeechee, Salkehatchie, Coosawatchie and Altamaha Rivers. Egrets, looking far too elegant to be standing by the side of a highway, are so numerous along these southern roads that from a distance they look like handkerchiefs littering the grass. It would have been exciting to see a live armadillo, but alas, all those I spotted were in the unfortunate roadkill phase. Huge vultures circle over the Little Satilla River. Just north of the Florida border I begin to see palm trees and saw palmettos.

Leaving the interstate, I head southwest toward Gainesville and the Ocklawaha. Small roadside stands with handwritten signs announce "original green fresh boiled peanuts," Georgia peaches and Vidalia onions. Near the Lawtey State Prison is a thrift shop with a sign saying, "Come Worship With Us." There are signs for strawberries, shelled peas, butter beans, pecans and silver queen corn. Near Starke, I pass "R. T. Whiskers Taxidermy Studio" and cross Alligator Creek.

To glimpse a bit more of rural Florida before heading into the sprawl of Gainesville, I take a detour through Paynes Prairie—a low wetland expanse, a remnant of ancient savanna—to Micanopy, a few miles from Cross Creek, where Marjorie Kinnan Rawlings wrote *The Yearling*. The town's tall trees are festooned with Spanish moss. The old brick houses have tin roofs and

*For a detailed description of the southeastern coast, I highly recommend *Travels* by William Bartram, an account of his travels there in 1773.

screen porches. I stop in a used-book store where a ceiling fan rattles and there is the dense scent of warm, aging paper. The hot, almost yellow air is full of insect hum. I have the sense that if I listen hard enough, I will hear things growing.

There is a raw, wild feeling about this landscape. As I walk around part of the Paynes Prairie preserve, I find myself looking over my shoulders, between palmetto fronds, listening to the unfamiliar insect and bird sounds. Later, I read an essay by Florida naturalist and zoologist the late Archie Carr, whose wife, Marjorie Harris Carr, became one of the Ocklawaha's staunchest champions. "Through millions of years Florida was spread with veld or tree savanna. Right there in the middle of Payne's Prairie itself," Carr writes, "there used to be creatures that would stand your hair on end. Pachyderms vaster than any now alive . . . there were llamas and camels . . . and bisons and sloths . . . bands of ancestral horses; and grazing tortoises."[1]

This part of Florida was formed by the remains of ancient sea and riverbeds. "When the oceans fell millions of years ago, it was probably the first part of Florida to rise out of the water," writes Al Burt, a longtime chronicler of north-central Florida. "The scrub landscape looks like a backsliding desert. Scraggly growth anchored by stunted trees. . . . Beautiful oases come in clusters and streaks. On deeply greened land islands, giant live oaks and toweringly tall canopies of pines give dimension to the horizon."[2] As I wander through Paynes Prairie and surrounds, ponds come into view, ringed by brushy palmettos, dry yellow grasses, plants with shiny leaves I don't recognize, interspersed with taller deciduous trees and the occasional pine. Since 1936, Florida has lost nearly 80 percent of these ancient scrub communities and at least 40 percent of its original marshlands.[3] Restoring the Ocklawaha will help repair some of that loss.

The Ocklawaha flows north through central Florida toward the Atlantic, through a region underlain with layers of limestone. The temperate and subtropical zones coincide here, fostering a great density and diversity of flora and fauna. A shallow and slow-moving river, the seventy-eight-mile-long Ocklawaha is fed by nearly two dozen artesian springs. It rises in a series of lakes whose names sound like a family reunion—Lake Apopka, Lake

Dora, Lake Eustis, Lake Griffin, Lake Harris. The Ocklawaha is fed by water from Silver Springs and the Silver River and gains additional headwaters from swamps and prairie wetlands as it flows past Ocala, a prosperous community known for the racehorses bred in its lush pastures. The Ocklawaha joins the St. Johns near the towns of Palatka and Welaka; the name *Welaka* is thought to come from a Seminole word meaning "river of lakes" or "big water."[4] Altogether the Ocklawaha basin drains about 2,800 square miles, encompassing parts of five counties. Much of the watershed is water and marshland, although many of its wetlands have been drained to accommodate suburban development.

The name *Ocklawaha* is said to come from the Indian words "Okli-Waha," which mean great river, or "ak-lowahe," meaning creek or crooked creek.[5] It is thought that the St. Johns River valley was first settled after the end of the last Ice Age. Before the Spanish arrived in the sixteenth century, the area was inhabited by the Timucua, and later the Creek and Seminole Indians. And before the Timucua, "there was a succession of even earlier peoples, stretching all the way back to the Paleo-Indians," writes Bill Belleville in his book about St. Johns River, "who briefly shared the river valley with huge Pleistocene megafauna like the . . . saber-toothed cat and the glyptodont, an armadillo-like animal the size of a Barco-lounger."[6] No wonder I look over my shoulders as I wander alone through the basin shrubbery.

The Ocklawaha now harbors alligators and turtles, cypress and palm, a great variety of birds and other floodplain-forest flora and fauna. It sustains 110 species of fish, including at least one that exists nowhere else, the isolated, endemic Lake Eustis pupfish. At least three species of salamanders and four species of turtles live here, as do ten species of plants listed by the state or federal government as threatened or endangered. The Ocklawaha once provided a home for black bears, wolves, panthers, bobcats, gray fox and river otters. For many species, the Ocklawaha is the southern end of their range, while for others it is an important stop on their migration route. Some live in this river's floodplain and nowhere else. The Ocklawaha's water has been noted for its clear tea color. An oft-quoted nineteenth-century description of the Ocklawaha calls it "the sweetest water-lane in the world."[7]

From the 1860s through the 1920s, paddlewheels and steam-boats sailed up the Ocklawaha to Silver Springs on what were called "jungle cruises." To peer at the underwater rock formations and aquatic creatures, tourists have ridden glass-bottom boats on the river at Silver Springs since before the turn of the twentieth century. Later the Ocklawaha's dense vegetation provided the backdrop for Tarzan movies. Today, Silver Springs has a multimil-lion-dollar theme park.

Farmers began moving into the Ocklawaha basin in the late 1800s. They grew row crops in the muck of drained lakes and wet-lands. At the same time, steady commercial harvest of the river's old cypress trees began to destabilize the banks, sending sediment into the river, degrading riparian habitat and decreasing the river's navigability. Farming further eroded the soil, and pesticides and fertilizers washed quickly into the surrounding waters. The water became overloaded with nutrients and depleted of oxygen, so that beginning in the 1940s, the source lakes of the Ocklawaha became eutrophic, setting the stage for the problems that now plague the river. As modern-day settlers moved in, draining swamplands, straightening and dredging the river channel, the Ocklawaha's wildlife began to disappear.

Since Europeans first explored the Florida coast, there have been schemes for an inland water route across Florida from the Atlantic to the Gulf of Mexico. In the sixteenth century, King Philip II of Spain and Pedro Menéndez, the Spanish colonizer who founded the city of St. Augustine, dreamed of such a route. John Quincy Adams and Andrew Jackson contemplated the build-ing of this waterway, which was thought to be the solution to the dangers of rounding the southern tip of Florida. The Cross Florida Barge Canal, as this inland waterway came to be called, was for-mally proposed during the Depression as a Roosevelt administra-tion works project. According to a 1939 history of Florida commissioned by the federal government's Works Progress Ad-ministration, the canal was designed to "aid national defense and facilitate shipping between the Gulf States and the Atlantic seaboard . . . provide a sea-level, toll-free waterway 195 miles long . . . [following] the channel of the St. Johns River from its mouth through Jacksonville to Palatka, thence southwest along the

Ocklawaha River to a point 8 miles south of Ocala." President Franklin Roosevelt inaugurated work on the canal by setting off a charge of dynamite from the White House on September 19, 1935. By the next summer, when the project was suspended for lack of funding, 13 million cubic yards of earth had been excavated and 4,700 acres of right-of-way cleared.[8]

The Army Corps of Engineers next considered the canal during World War II. It was to be part of an extensive system of inner coastal waterways and promoted as an American alternative to the Panama Canal. Boosters hailed it as a boon to business and national security. As Joe Bakker, of the Florida Department of Environmental Protection, described it to me, "The United States thought it would be a brilliant idea to have a canal that would connect the Gulf of Mexico with the Atlantic Ocean coming across the peninsula of Florida. They wanted to do it using existing waterways as much as possible and with a minimum of excavation." But to use the Ocklawaha, it would have to be dammed.

Congress narrowly approved construction of the canal in 1942, but another twenty years passed before federal funding was made available. Work on the canal began in 1964, celebrated by a chicken barbecue in Palatka[9] attended by President Lyndon B. Johnson. But opposition to the canal had already begun in 1962, when Marjorie Carr and Gainesville's Alachua Audubon Society initiated their "Save the Ocklawaha" campaign.

Opposition to the Cross Florida Barge Canal is credited by many with galvanizing the Florida conservation movement. In 1969, Marjorie Carr—whom U.S. Senator Bob Graham called "the environmental conscience for Florida's leaders"[10]—helped found Florida Defenders of the Environment expressly to protect the Ocklawaha from canal construction. Carr's dedication to the cause was so staunch that, at her funeral in 1997, friends and supporters draped her hearse with a banner reading "Free the Ocklawaha."

The canal was to operate with a series of locks and dams, including Rodman Dam, which blocks the Ocklawaha eight miles from its confluence with the St. Johns. The impoundment flooded sixteen miles of river. What became Rodman Reservoir covers 9,000 acres of river corridor and surrounding floodplain forest.

The dam generates no hydropower and stores no drinking water. Its sole purpose was to serve the lock that would facilitate ship passage on the canal. Since cancellation of the canal-building project in 1971, the only thing the dam does is retain the reservoir favored for its bass fishing.

Undaunted by their failure to stop initial dredging of the canal, Florida environmentalists continued their fight against the project. Using the National Environmental Policy Act of 1969—the law requiring environmental impact statements to be prepared for all federal projects—Florida Defenders of the Environment published a report assessing the environmental impact of the barge canal. Because of this report, presented to the Florida Senate in 1970, that body asked the Army Corps of Engineers to reevaluate the project. A year later, the Florida Game and Fresh Water Fish Commission called for the restoration of the Ocklawaha. The Commission felt obligated to examine the canal project "in terms of its ecological impact . . . specifically the destruction of a rare and rapidly decreasing aspect of the Florida scene—the periodically inundated hardwood swamp with its unique wildlife and aesthetic value—in exchange for a lake with which central Florida is abundantly blessed." This declaration outlined the terms of the debate that continues to this day. Which has greater merit: restoring the Ocklawaha or maintaining the Rodman Reservoir?

In 1970, Florida Defenders of the Environment and other conservation groups filed for an injunction in Federal District Court in Washington, D.C., to stop construction of the Barge Canal. A preliminary injunction was granted, and in January 1971, President Richard Nixon, acting on the recommendation of the recently established Council on Environmental Quality, halted construction of the Cross Florida Barge Canal. Nixon said work on the canal was being stopped "to prevent potentially serious environmental damages" and called the Ocklawaha a "uniquely beautiful semitropical stream, one of a very few of its kind in the United States." The presidential order to stop work on the canal was unprecedented. Never before had a congressionally authorized project to which federal funds were already committed been canceled.

Canal supporters then challenged the presidential order, launching what has become a thirty-year legal and administrative wrangle. The federal court agreed that the president lacked authority to stop work on the canal but granted a permanent extension of its injunction while a new environmental and economic evaluation was prepared.

An injunction against work on the canal—to last until filing of an Environmental Impact Statement by the Army Corps of Engineers—was issued in February 1974. That statement was not completed until 1977. Meanwhile, in 1976, as part of plans to restore the Ocklawaha, Florida Governor Reubin Askew asked Congress to formally de-authorize the Barge Canal, a move supported by Florida's U.S. senators and later by President Jimmy Carter. After assessing the Environmental Impact Statement, the Council on Environmental Quality, the EPA, the Departments of Agriculture and the Interior, the Army, the governor of Florida, and the majority of the state's congressional delegation and legislature all called for a plan to restore the Ocklawaha.

Before any real restoration could proceed, however, Congress would have to officially de-authorize the canal, but this was delayed by local supporters of the canal who wanted to preserve the reservoir for recreation. It wasn't until 1991 that President George Bush signed the bill completing de-authorization, which transferred the canal, locks, dam and surrounding lands to the state of Florida. The following year, Governor Lawton Chiles approved the removal of Rodman Dam, but as of the fall of 1999, the Florida legislature had not appropriated any money to accomplish this task.

It would be an understatement to say that both sides in the debate over Rodman Dam have stalwart supporters. Those who favor a natural ecosystem and free-flowing river over the man-made describe the Rodman Reservoir as a "drowned river channel." Anglers who favor the reservoir say its submerged snags, stumps and floating vegetation create an ideal habitat for bass and other game fish. Reservoir supporters say the sportfishing brings welcome business to surrounding communities. Those who support dam removal say the buildup of aquatic vegetation in the reservoir harms river species. Those who would maintain the reservoir contest this. Now there are serious water-quality problems on the Ocklawaha to be dealt with before removal of Rodman Dam can progress. The one point on which both sides agree is that breaching Rodman Dam must not harm the water quality of the St. Johns River.

To get better acquainted with the story, I visit Florida Defenders of the Environment and speak with their restoration specialist and Ocklawaha Project Coordinator Kristina Jackson and executive director Leslie Straub in their Gainesville offices. One of the first things to understand about the ecology of Florida, Straub tells me, unfurling maps and photographs, is that anything involving water is a statewide issue. "Florida is a water state. A drop of water falls on Tallahassee and it affects the Keys," she says. Because of the extent of Florida's porous soils, the interaction between surfacewater and groundwater is extremely important, particularly when most of Florida's drinking water comes from groundwater aquifers. Florida's lakes are relatively shallow, so under natural conditions, there's a high rate of evaporation and constant turnover in their water content. Straub points to a map of the lakes and springs that feed the Ocklawaha. Block this flow somewhere in the cycle and water would begin to slow, stop flushing itself through the system and eventually stagnate. I begin to picture a constantly percolating spring-fed fountain, continually renewing the water in its pools.

This fountain is the Florida Aquifer, which extends from southern South Carolina[11] across southern Georgia, southeastern Alabama and throughout Florida. The spring-fed Ocklawaha is part of this watery system. Much of the Ocklawaha's natural streambed and floodplain are made up of freshwater marl, a crumbly substrate containing a lot of lime. Beneath much of this layer is the Ocala limestone of the Florida Aquifer. The aquifer, limestone layers and areas of clay create a rich combination of springs and water-absorbing wetlands, through which surfacewater and groundwater circulate.

Straub shows me a photograph of an enormous machine, a giant combine-like vehicle she calls "a huge three-story tree crusher" used when Rodman Reservoir was created. It drove around "squashing trees and pushing them into the mud," she says. About five thousand acres of red maple, tupelo, cypress, cabbage palm and longleaf pine forest were leveled for the canal.

Crushed trees and logs still occasionally float to the surface of the reservoir, Straub tells me. As in North Carolina, Florida's native longleaf and loblolly pine have been cut and replaced for rapid harvest with quick-growing slash pine. "We've sacrificed many of our native species for those we can make money with," says Straub. The loblolly pine and giant cypress that grow in and around the Ocklawaha tolerate and thrive on wet conditions, which water diversions and development have altered. These bottomland wetland forests are not just an important wildlife habitat. They help control flooding and act as a natural filter and recycling system for the surrounding water. When these forests are clear-cut—that is, when all the trees have been removed—this system is destroyed, allowing sediments and nutrients to accumulate to harmful levels. This is more or less what has happened on the Ocklawaha. The flooding of Rodman Reservoir also submerged some twenty natural springs that used to feed the river, stifling the natural recirculation of water through the Ocklawaha's whole ecosystem.

To figure out how to manage Rodman Dam and Reservoir as well as the land around the canal once the project was canceled, Florida formed the Canal Lands Advisory Committee. And the Cross Florida Greenbelt State Recreation and Conservation Area, or Cross Florida Greenway, was created from what were to have been canal lands. The plan for the Greenway, explains Kristina Jackson, also included a recommendation for restoration of the Ocklawaha. But in a move that sounds like "déjà vu all over again," north Florida legislators who favored the reservoir convinced the state legislature to revisit the issue of restoration yet again.

So in 1993, the state of Florida undertook another study to compare the advantages of restoring the Ocklawaha versus those of maintaining Rodman Dam and Reservoir. By the time it was completed in 1995, the study weighed in at twenty volumes and had cost almost a million dollars. Its conclusion: that the Ocklawaha should be restored. So in 1995, Governor Chiles, who supported restoration, asked the Florida Department of Environmental Protection to begin securing the required state and federal permits for restoration of the Ocklawaha that would include a drawdown of the Rodman Reservoir. In 1997 Florida received over half a million dollars from the EPA to support wetlands and river restoration and cover permit fees.

Yet while plans for river restoration and reservoir drawdown were moving ahead with support from the governor's office and federal agencies, opposition, led by state Senator George Kirkpatrick, was once again rallying in the state legislature. Kirkpatrick's support for preserving the dam was so strong that in 1998, the legislature passed a bill renaming the dam in his honor. So Rodman Dam, as it continues to be known, is now officially Kirkpatrick Dam. Term limits ended Kirkpatrick's tenure in the state Senate in 2000, but preservation of the dam and reservoir was an issue in the campaigns of candidates running to fill his seat, and the debate continues.

Supporters of Rodman Dam and Reservoir propose a "Lake Ocklawaha Recreation Area" that would preserve the impoundment for sportfishing and introduced a bill in the 1999–2000 legislature that would have created a state park around the reservoir. It failed, but a similar bill was introduced in 2001 and after much debate on both sides, the fate of funding for Ocklawaha restoration remains in limbo. Ed Taylor, president of Save Rodman Reservoir, is optimistic about its prospects. "We've convinced a lot of legislators in Tallahassee to see our side," Taylor tells me. And indeed in 2001, legislative maneuvering around the dam included a sizable budget for building recreational facilities that would increase the value of the reservoir.

Despite its renown, Leslie Straub tells me that "the term *microscopic* can be used for the economic benefit the state derives" from bass fishing on Rodman Reservoir. According to Ed Taylor, the fishing and associated tourism bring Putnam and Marion Counties about $6–$7 million each year. But a 1995 Florida Department of Environmental Protection study showed the reservoir contributing less than 3 percent to either of these counties' income.

Some of the land around the canal and reservoir belongs to the U.S. Forest Service. The Forest Service permit allowing Rodman Dam to occupy its land expired in July 2000, a deadline that pushed Governor Jeb Bush toward making a decision on the fate of the dam. The permit was up for renewal and if the state didn't submit its plans on time, the dam would be taken over by the

Forest Service. Both the Forest Service and the EPA had clearly voiced their support for full river restoration, including dam removal. The implication seemed to be that if the state of Florida did not move in that direction, the federal government would.

Jackson and Straub explain that the dam and its lock, Buckman Lock, are an obstacle for the anadromous fish that migrate up the St. Johns River and for manatees, which are now protected under the federal Endangered Species Act. Sometimes called sea cows, manatees are large marine mammals that feed on aquatic vegetation. Resembling a snub-nosed, two-flippered, tuskless walrus, they are definitely a charismatic megafauna, and the Internet is full of "Save the Manatee" sites. Although they are the size of a small boat—about ten feet long and weighing a thousand pounds and more—manatees have been killed trying to get into the dam's spillway at the lock and crushed by its gates. Rodman Dam and Buckman Lock, I am told, are the main cause of death for the area's manatees.

After hearing this complex tale of political maneuvering and manipulated water, I am more than ready to see the river that has caused such controversy. So Leslie Straub, her colleague Leah Cohen and I head out for an afternoon's canoe trip on the Ocklawaha. Our destination is Eureka, near the unfinished Eureka Dam, which partially impounds the Ocklawaha upstream from Rodman Dam into what is called Lake Ocklawaha.

On the way, we stop at Rodman Dam. The reservoir stretches out beyond the dam's wide shallow arc of concrete. Drowned tree trunks, gray and branchless, stand in the water pilings from an abandoned pier. At the base of the dam a few midweek fishermen have cast their lines over the chain-link fence. Egrets and cormorants are fishing too. If there's a place that big-spending bass fishermen go, it doesn't seem to be this part of Rodman Reservoir. Given my prejudice for a moving river, even with the allowance that my Florida Defenders of the Environment hosts may have shown me one of the reservoir's ugliest spots, it's hard for me to see its aesthetic appeal.

From the dam we drive south through part of the Ocala National Forest toward the small town of Eureka. I'm used to roads that wind through forests; this one is very straight. The *National*

Audubon Society Field Guide to Florida says that the Ocala National Forest is the oldest national forest east of the Mississippi and one of the country's most visited. But there is little evidence of tourist activity as we pass through.

We rent canoes at the Eureka Outpost, a small outfitting shop where guinea hens, chickens and tiny peeping chicks peck, chirp and coo their way around the yard. There are palms and palmettos. Spanish moss hangs from the live oaks and ash trees. Owners Larry and Gloria Reiche's house, built out of what look like small logs, sits up on stilts several hundred yards back from the shop. Its wood is weathered a soft gray, and its screen porches make it seem, to my northern eyes, exotic and tropical. The day is slightly overcast after a morning rain. The overwhelming color is a thick avocado green. Inside the shop are a couple of glass-fronted cases housing various sizes of taxidermied alligators and gator parts.

Larry Reiche loads a canoe on the trailer and drives us about eight river miles south, upstream to Gore's Landing. The river is narrow and shallow here. Red maple, live oak, ash, palm, saw palmetto and cypress with their feathery arms of leaves and big buttressed fans of roots line the banks. Spanish moss and layers of epiphytes, or air plants—both members of the pineapple family—hang by slender vegetal filaments from overhead branches. The knobby cypress knees are an impressive aspect of river architecture. They also have an important biological function, as they allow the trees to breathe, giving them access to oxygen even when the lower roots are underwater. There are rafts of milky yellow water lilies and purple pickerel plants that bloom upright like bright bottlebrushes. In a few places, we see delicate white lilies of the amaryllis family. Where we are floating is clearly floodplain forest and river swamp, an ecosystem where water and land intermingle. There are tupelo, cabbage palm, sweetgum, water oak, hickory and loblolly pine. The variation of leaf shapes and sizes and subtle variations of green create a mesmerizing collage. It seems as if it would be easy for just about anything or anyone to be absorbed by that vegetation and simply disappear.

Ahead of us, deep slate-colored great blue herons loft out of the banks and flap slowly under the canopy of trees. Smaller, more lavender-colored, little blue herons, white ibis, snowy egret, yellow-throated warblers and a hawk interrupt the dense foliage. There are wood ducks and a rustle of wild turkey in the brush. Had we been lucky we might also have seen an anhinga, some prothonotary warblers, a swallow-tailed kite or hairy woodpecker. To my delight, we spot an astonishingly large pileated woodpecker with a bright red crest working its beak on a trunk. Further along, a limpkin, an imposing bird (which looks like it might confer with Owl in a children's storybook) over two feet tall, with brown feathers and a light orange beak, stands on a floating log.

It is quiet except for the splash of our paddles and our conversation. In the shallow clear water, bass and a couple of prehistoric-looking gar with long pointed heads slide by. Swimming somewhere in the Ocklawaha are endangered sturgeon. Small turtles sun themselves on downed branches, some with one hind leg extended like a reptilian ballerina. Every so often there is a rustle in the shrubbery as a disconcertingly large alligator launches itself into the slow-moving water and glides beneath the bow of the canoe. I am assured that unless provoked or in mating mode, these toothy creatures are not aggressive. But they are very large, both long and hefty, and numerous. They pass so close to the canoe I am surprised we don't bump or get jostled in their wake. We spot some baby alligators, miniatures of their imposing parents but with narrow yellow stripes banding the length of their bodies, apparently resting by the side of the water.

The landscape of the stretch of the Ocklawaha we float practically oozes with textures. Its wild fecundity is particularly impressive when compared to the suburban sprawl that seems to be reaching its blacktop fingers ever further into the swampy river prairies. Many places I've been, the contours of the natural landscape, even when covered with shopping centers and housing development, are still visible. In north-central Florida, development seems to utterly erase them.

With a high annual rainfall—about fifty-four inches a year—and a great volume of water coming from Silver Springs and the Silver River, the Ocklawaha carries a lot of water. Undammed, water moved swiftly down the river channel. With Rodman Dam impeding its flow, it now takes about eight times longer for river water to flow from the Ocklawaha's headwaters to the river's confluence with the St. Johns. The dam has degraded the water quality of both rivers, and nobody wants to further impair the St. Johns with poor-quality water from the Ocklawaha. The water Rodman Dam impounds is warmer than the natural river and contains less oxygen. Consequently, where the reservoir now is, the Ocklawaha's native striped bass, shad, channel catfish, mullet and American eels have almost entirely been replaced by warm-water species and stocked game fish.

The reservoir's oxygen-depleted water is also thick with nutrients from farm runoff. These eutrophic conditions create a fertile environment for fast-growing aquatic weeds like hydrilla. During the 1980s, these conditions contributed to two huge fish kills totaling at least ten million fish. Another such fish kill occurred in September and October 2000, when a long dry season created shallow water conditions in Rodman Reservoir. The shallow water allowed an unusual amount of sunlight to penetrate, encouraging the growth of hydrilla, coontail and other aquatic weeds. When the vegetation began to die, it choked off oxygen in the water, killing as many as two million fish.

"The reservoir is going to stay," Ed Taylor, president of Save Rodman Reservoir, Inc., tells me confidently. "We've got to clean up the backwaters—the headwater tributaries of the Ocklawaha, the streams coming out of the Harris chain of lakes," he explains. "But the aquatic growth in Rodman Reservoir acts as a filter for this nutrient content, partially cleaning the water before it flows into the St. Johns River. We're not going to try and restore one river at the expense of another."

"The Rodman Reservoir is a fish factory," says Taylor when I speak to him in October 2000. He says that despite the past month's fish kill, "The fishing's been absolutely great." What were killed, he says, were just small fish, "under legal-sized sport fish," small fish that get stuck in shallow water. "We need to clean the water but we're opposed to restoration," says Taylor. Restoration appears to be code for dam removal. "We've always said that creating the barge canal and flooding the river for the reservoir was the wrong thing to do. But the reservoir's been here for thirty-five years and people enjoy it."

There is now $500,000 in the Florida Department of Environmental Protection budget to complete the Ocklawaha restoration plan. Gaps need to be filled in, says Kristina Jackson, particularly regarding water quality. The groundwater in the Ocklawaha basin is showing elevated levels of nitrates. These come from several sources: row crops, the region's small unincorporated towns that use septic rather than sewage treatment plants and the area's cows and horses. Because of the Ocklawaha's quickly percolating sand, sinkholes, wetlands and underlying karst limestone, nitrate runoff makes its way into groundwater much faster than it might in other river systems. These excess nutrients could move directly and swiftly to the St. Johns if normal flows were restored to the Ocklawaha under current conditions. There is also concern about water quality because of the low water in some of the feeder creeks, says Leslie Straub. There's so little water in some of them, she says, that they don't even look like flowing water systems.

In addition to the money for the restoration plan and water-quality study, $600,000 has been made available to install steel grating and other devices to keep manatees out of the dam's locks. Because manatees are listed under the federal Endangered Species and Marine Protected Mammal Acts, as owner and operator of the dam and locks, the state of Florida is liable for any harm those structures cause the species.

According to the Florida Department of Environmental Protection, the nitrogen pollution behind Rodman Dam and in the Ocklawaha and Silver Rivers now flows at an estimated 15 million tons a year. This problem, says Straub, will have to be addressed before the state tackles any further restoration of the Ocklawaha. Lucia Ross, communications director for the Florida DEP, confirms that the dam will not be removed without the water being cleaned. Much of the damaging nutrients come from non-point sources, so with the Ocklawaha's geology, curbing this pollution will entail a solution far more complex than shutting off a pipe. It may take four to six years to solve these water-quality problems, postponing dam removal by at least five years.

Having been told that Rodman Reservoir's aquatic vegetation was both a source and a solution to water-quality problems, I sought further information. Hoping to speak with someone knowledgeable and not allied with either the pro-reservoir or dam-breaching faction, I was directed to Douglas Robison. Robison is program manager for ecological science with the engineering firm PBS & J, a large national firm with corporate headquarters in Miami that's been hired by the Florida Department of Environmental Protection to work on the Ocklawaha restoration project.

The current thinking, says Robison, is that the Rodman Reservoir is now acting as something of a treatment plant for excess nitrogen but only on a seasonal basis. During the spring, from April and July, when the aquatic plants in the reservoir are growing, they absorb the excess nitrogen flowing into the reservoir. In winter, when cold fronts move in, these plants grow dormant, die off and decay. When the plants decay and die they release nutrients into the water that, in excess, cause problems that can include fish kills. Robison is concerned that the St. Johns Water Management District—the state agency that monitors the St. Johns River—is not looking at the nitrogen load on an annual basis. Because the reservoir now acts as both a nitrogen sink and source, the challenge of restoration, Robison says, will be to re-create wetlands to mitigate the loss of the reservoir's sink while the impoundment is being drawn down and natural river flow restored.

The goal, as Robison describes it, is to restore natural floodplain function to over two thousand acres in the Ocklawaha watershed. Vegetation will help stabilize and restore biological function to the river channel and improve water quality. "The trick," Robison tells me, "is to get the system of natural flows back to one that works as a whole on an annual basis." He acknowledges that the project is very polarized, but as an ecological restoration, he feels it stands on its own.

One of the biggest challenges in restoring the Ocklawaha is not scientific at all: it is getting people to imagine what the river will look like after the reservoir's gone. People simply have a fear of the unknown, Straub says. "We have to explain that restoration is not a four-letter word," Jackson jokes. She cites a common misperception of what happens when an impoundment is drained: "The reservoir's not going to be a big mud hole."

Marjorie Carr believed in bringing accurate science to laypeople, Jackson and Straub tell me. Now they fear the science is being held hostage by politics. They also worry that the Ocklawaha and Rodman Dam will be "studied to death." Dam removal is never quick or simple, but it seems clear that on developed rivers like the Ocklawaha, the longer restoration waits, the more complex it becomes.

"If you give them the truth and do it in a way they understand, then people will make the right decision," Jackson says with assurance. Defenders of the reservoir are equally passionate about their view of the river. In 2001, the Florida legislature once again failed to include funding for restoration of the Ocklawaha in the state's annual budget. Meanwhile, in March 2001, the U.S. Forest Service issued a report supporting restoration. And so the river waits.

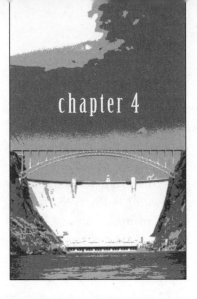

Wisconsin

"MOST DAMS REMOVED"

I't's a joke around here that if you want to give someone you don't like a gift, you give them a dam," says Stephanie Lindloff,[1] Small Dams Program manager for the River Alliance of Wisconsin, as we sip coffee in the shadow of the capitol dome in downtown Madison.

Wisconsin may sit smack dab in the middle of the continent, but it is also an intensely watery place. Wisconsin has over 40,000 miles of rivers, streams, lakes, ponds and wetlands. There are ponds and wetlands. There are rivers wide enough to have bays, islands and water passages called flowages. There are small wriggling creeks and streams. When Europeans and Americans settled Wisconsin in the nineteenth century, they put these waterways to work with dams, dikes and water diversions, so there are now an estimated 3,600 impoundments on Wisconsin's rivers and streams. As in the East, dams were built to harness hydropower to run grain or gristmills, power sawmills, impound fishponds, retain local water supplies and help transport logs.

Most of Wisconsin's smaller dams* were built between the mid-1880s and early 1900s. As older dams outlived their original purposes, many were converted to generate hydroelectric power for local neighborhoods and industry, but the advent of cheap fossil fuels rendered some unprofitable. "Many of the old dams had their turbines pulled out. Maintenance and operation stopped. As the dams fell into disrepair, they became safety hazards and economic burdens," Stephanie explains.

"It's the Department of Natural Resources policy to ensure the safety of dams," says Stephanie. In Wisconsin, dam repair typically costs three to five times more than removal, so "removal is often a more cost-effective way of ensuring dam safety," she explains. Wisconsin "doesn't have a policy to remove dams per se, but it's been deemed fiscally responsible to remove dams for reasons of public safety, and how can you argue against public safety?" Stephanie asks rhetorically. With this history, Wisconsin has become the state that's removed the most dams. Over the past forty years, sixty dams have been removed from its rivers and the total is higher than that. Among the rivers that have lost dams are the Milwaukee and Manitowoc Rivers in eastern Wisconsin, the Prairie and Baraboo Rivers in central Wisconsin, the Kickapoo and Yahara Rivers and Turtle Creek in the south, the Flambeau River in northern Wisconsin and the Willow River, a tributary of the St. Croix in western Wisconsin.

My July 2000 tour of Wisconsin dam removals takes me from Turtle Creek and the Yahara to the Baraboo, Prairie and Milwaukee Rivers. Like other water-filled northern landscapes, Wisconsin was shaped by glaciers and its history by rivers. The glacial ebb and flow sculpted the landfall of what became Wisconsin to create a sort of statewide Continental Divide. Rivers on the west side of this divide flow into the Mississippi and the Gulf of Mexico. On the east side, rivers flow into Lake Michigan, which flows into the

---

*Most are privately and municipally owned, some are state owned and a very few, located in Wisconsin's national forests, are federally owned.

St. Lawrence Seaway and the North Atlantic. Some rivers in northern Wisconsin flow into Lake Superior, which, like Lake Michigan, sends its waters to the Atlantic by way of the St. Lawrence seaway.

My first stop is the Shopiere Dam on Turtle Creek, which is at the southern end of the basin also drained by the Yahara, Rock, Bark and Crawfish Rivers. These rivers, my guidebook tells me, "drain a vast area of glacial debris" and "rise in marshes amid drumlins and eskers—hills and narrow ridges of sand, gravel and boulders deposited by streams flowing beneath the glaciers."[2] What we see today among the tidy towns, sprawling suburbs, farmland and cities of south-central Wisconsin are the watery remains of retreating glaciers. The low-lying land rolls and swoops with an undulating rise and fall so that it's possible to imagine the push and pull of a giant slab of melting ice. Tucked amid these landforms, especially along the Fox and Wisconsin Rivers, are mounds left by the people known as Mound Builders, who, with the Woodland People, lived here about 5,000 years ago.

When the French explorer Jean Nicolet sailed across Lake Michigan toward Wisconsin in 1634, the journey was so long that he thought he would be in Asia when he reached shore. Wisconsin's woods and riverbanks were then filled with deer, muskrat, beaver, raccoon, mink and bear. The Menominee, Potawatomi, Fox, Sauk, Winnebago, Chippewa, Ojibwa and others hunted, fished and gathered wild rice, but, as elsewhere, they fared badly after the arrival of white settlers. The federal government relocated entire tribes to west of the Mississippi. Many others left their original homelands after the disastrous Black Hawk War of 1832.

The non-native settlers made their living from trapping, mining, farming and lumber. Trees felled in Wisconsin woods in the early years of statehood helped fuel the west-bound railroad construction boom. Great log drives went down the rivers to be processed at water- and steam-powered mills. As in Maine, Wisconsin's woodsy and watery landscape gave rise to its industry. Similarly, when Wisconsin's big timber was exhausted, papermaking, which can use smaller trees, grew prominent in the state's industrial economy. In the nineteenth century, many of the state's river cities became industrial centers, manufacturing brick, lumber and other household goods.[3]

It's a warm, overcast July afternoon when I make my way to the site of the Shopiere Dam. Outside Madison, miles of pillow-shaped fields swell with tall corn and bright green soybean plants. Silver metal silos and rectangular grain elevators rise by neat red barns trimmed in white. Perusing the offerings at a convenience store and on a lunch menu, I am quickly introduced to Wisconsin culture: the walleye sandwich and plastic sacks of Bucky Badger's Cheese Curds—"Kids like them," a helpful ten-year-old boy tells me. "They squeak."

Despite the right-angled grid that makes the map of Wisconsin look like the template for a patchwork quilt, these narrow two-lane roads wind like ribbons through the orderly towns and farm communities. Wisconsin's system of assigning letters to county roads makes the map look like it's littered with Scrabble tiles. More than once, older men out checking their mailboxes wave a hand in greeting even though I am a passing stranger in an out-of-state rental car.

Shopiere Dam was constructed in the 1840s to power a grist-mill. It was rebuilt in the early 1900s, but the timber, crib and concrete structure failed safety inspections in 1943 and again in 1973, 1983 and 1993. The ten-foot-high dam leaked continually and deteriorated steadily. Over the years, water coming down the creek over the dam had scoured away a pool that had become a local swimming hole. People, especially kids, liked to jump off the defunct dam and swim through holes in its foundation. Between the disrepair and recent drownings, the dam was a well-documented safety hazard. It also had an adverse impact on the water quality of Turtle Creek. This was of particular concern because upstream from Shopiere is a state-designated "Exceptional Resource Water," meaning that the water quality is good and riparian habitat is in excellent condition.

Stephanie Lindloff tells me that Shopiere Dam was, for all practical purposes, an abandoned dam. Shopiere Dam's owner had moved away from the area and was delinquent in paying taxes on it, so since 1973 the dam had been considered ownerless. Under Wisconsin state regulations, if a dam is to be repaired, there must be a responsible owner. If none can be found, the Department of Natural Resources can opt to remove the dam, paying for removal with the state's Abandoned Dam Fund. If, however, there is a responsible owner and money is available for repair, the state cannot force removal of a dam. Reinforcing the neutrality of official policy, Wisconsin has municipal grants available to fund both dam repair and dam removal. Still, given the costs and liability associated with old dams, "some have been sold for a dollar just to get rid of them," Stephanie says.

Turtle Creek flows southwest along a park with picnic tables and neatly mowed ball fields. A small footpath runs through the shrubbery above the banks behind neighboring backyards. When I arrive at the park, two large yellow pieces of earthmoving equipment are removing the last of the embankments that had anchored the dam. Dam removal began by breaching the dam during the winter when cold weather helped stabilize the banks and sediment. This allowed the pond behind the dam to drain down to a river channel. By July, workers had removed the dam, but work is still very much in progress. A low fence of black plastic shields the shallow banks from the deconstruction. Some backyard lawns run all the way down to the creek, and the lower, natural river level will expose about sixteen more acres of streamside land. Clover is blooming purple-pink. Willows and oaks bend low over the water. With the dam gone, gravel bars are emerging, and Turtle Creek riffles freely downstream.

The community of Shopiere considered the water falling over the dam a visual asset to their stretch of Turtle Creek. Because the dam had been in place for 150 years, "It was difficult for people to see it differently, and that became a factor in the discussion about removal," Stephanie tells me. But given the obvious safety concerns, when no owner could be found and neither town nor county wanted to assume ownership, Shopiere decided in favor of removal. It was also persuasive that removal would cost about half as much as repair and maintenance and would be paid for by the state's Abandoned Dam Fund. The final cost of removing the dam and stabilizing the exposed land was about $84,000.

Turtle Creek is considered one of the best smallmouth bass fisheries in southern Wisconsin. It's home to catfish, northern

pike and walleye, the imperiled Ozark minnow, greater redhorse*
and gravel chub. These fish may have less dramatic life cycles
than the coastal salmon, but they are equally important indicators
of the health of their home waters. The gravel chub, a three-inch
fish that lives in the lower Rock River drainage and lower reaches
of Turtle Creek, needs swiftly moving water and small gravel for
spawning. Slow-water impoundments and accumulated silt and
agricultural runoff have caused declines in gravel chub and Ozark
minnow populations so that both are listed as state endangered
species. Removal of Shopiere Dam eliminates the warm-water,
low-oxygen impoundment behind the dam, allowing the accumulated sediment to dissipate as it would naturally, improving conditions for aquatic species.

"There are fears and basic misconceptions about how rivers operate, about how dams operate and the relationship between
wildlife and rivers," says Stephanie over coffee in Madison.
"Rivers aren't just about water. You have a whole terrestrial ecosystem that goes along with them. Rivers are corridors or highways
for many species. When you're a species living in the water and
come up against a log and concrete structure, you don't have a lot
of choice."

When dams disrupt the flow of rivers, they can also change the
composition of surrounding wetlands. Wetlands are nature's way
of absorbing overflowing water, and communities in the Midwest
have learned from experience that manipulating river flow with artificially hardened riverbanks, dams, dikes and levees can actually
exacerbate flooding. Restoring a river system and riparian corridor
involves more than simply taking out a dam. It means restoring a
natural configuration of stream banks and vegetation. "We're just
beginning to figure out how to deal with this, especially with one-
hundred-and-fifty-year-old dams and associated wetlands," says
Stephanie.

Curious to see more of Turtle Creek, I follow the road that par-
allels the creek upstream to a small bridge, where children from a

---

*The greater redhorse has been listed in Wisconsin since 1989 as a threatened species. Be-
fore that it was listed as endangered. A much bigger fish than the Ozark minnow or gravel
chub, it can grow to eighteen inches.

nearby Boys and Girls Club are fishing. Supervising them are two grandfatherly men who dispense advice, help untangle lines and hook bait from the comfort of their lawn chairs. The kids scramble excitedly along the banks in the hazy sun. There is rumor of a fish on a line and one in a bucket. With Shopiere Dam gone and thirty miles of Turtle Creek open to fish passage, these young anglers are casting their lines in a bend of creek that is flowing freely for the first summer since Wisconsin first became a state in 1848.

The next stop on my tour is Baraboo, the site of what Stephanie Lindloff calls "some of the most intense dam removal monitoring in the country."[4] The Baraboo River flows through south-central Wisconsin,[5] taking in a watershed of about 650 square miles. It winds through the hills of the Baraboo Range to its confluence with the Wisconsin River near the city of Portage. Where the Baraboo meets the Wisconsin, the Wisconsin River makes a forty-mile looping curve created by the melting of enormous ice jams during the Great Ice Age. "When the glacier came down out of the north, crunching hills and gouging valleys, some adventuring rampart of the ice climbed the Baraboo Hills and fell back into the outlet gorge of the Wisconsin River. The swollen waters backed up and formed a lake half as long as the state, bordered on the east by cliffs of ice, and fed by the torrents that fell from melting mountains. . . . The lake rose through centuries, finally spilling over the east of the Baraboo range. There it cut a new channel for the river, and thus drained itself,"[6] wrote Aldo Leopold in A Sand County Almanac.

On its way to the Wisconsin, the Baraboo flows through the tidy small city of Baraboo, where the Waterworks Dam was removed in 1998, followed by the Oak Street Dam in the winter of 1999–2000. The Linen Mills Dam, which sits on the Baraboo just outside of town, will be removed by the end of 2001. A fourth dam upstream in the town of La Valle is also being removed. With these dams gone, all 120 miles of the river's mainstem and an additional 350–400 miles of tributary streams will be open to migratory fish and other aquatic species.[7]

As I approach Baraboo, I see signs that say, "Save our Baraboo Hills—Stop the National Landmark." The Baraboo range is a low series of quartzite hills that were the furthest reach of the Wisconsin glacier, what's called its terminal moraine.[8] These hills contain Precambrian sandstone estimated to be half a billion years old, as well as some of the continent's most ancient rock, where evidence of prehistoric humans has been found. The Baraboo Hills range from high, dry and rocky to wet prairie and low-lying marshes and now harbor one of the largest, mostly unfragmented deciduous forests in the Upper Midwest. Over 18,000 species of plants and animals live here, about a hundred of which are listed as either state or federal threatened or endangered species. The National Park Service has expressed interest in making the area a national natural landmark, a move opposed by a small group of local property rights defenders.

"The Baraboo bluffs are an important breeding and migratory bird area," explains John Exo, of the University of Wisconsin's Extension Service. John, whose work centers on natural resources issues and river basin education, has generously offered to show me around the Baraboo dam removals. I meet John in downtown Baraboo, where large trees shade its tidy town center. The residential streets are filled with pretty nineteenth-century houses that remind me of New England. Among the Baraboo area points of interest noted by tourist guides are the Circus World Museum, Time Travel Geological Tours, Dairyland Expeditions and the Mid-Continent Railway Museum.

The first dam building on the Baraboo began in the 1830s. The dams were located to take advantage of the steepest drop of the river, then called Baraboo Rapids. According to some local lore (and theories abound), the name Baraboo comes from "barbeau" or "barbu," the French word used for the river's fish. Old newspaper stories tell of hundred-pound sturgeon caught in the Baraboo up until the turn of the twentieth century. The Native American name for the river was said to be "Ocoochery," meaning "plenty of fish." An Indian village once stood on the banks of the Baraboo, where the Circus World Museum now sits.

Historically, the Baraboo was an important breeding ground for such Wisconsin River fish as smallmouth bass, lake sturgeon, paddlefish, walleye, catfish, sucker, redhorse, sauger, burbot and a diversity of minnows, shiners and darters. The Baraboo also has mussels that, like those in the Neuse River, need free-flowing water and fish to reach the habitat they need for successful development. Dams hamper the survival of fish that rely on cool, swift-moving water and create conditions favoring warm-water fish like carp and black crappie.

Before the Depression, John Exo tells me, Baraboo was a regional agricultural center. Since then farming has been overtaken by manufacturing, plastics, printing, food canning, tourism and a two-year college program of the University of Wisconsin. The Baraboo runs right through town and the property of its major tourist attraction, the Circus World Museum, site of the Ringling Brothers Barnum & Bailey Circus's original winter home. The museum's one-story red and white buildings and striped tents line the lawns that slope down to the river.

At one time there were eleven dams on the mainstem of the Baraboo. The impoundments of the dams in and around Baraboo, John says, turned the Baraboo Rapids reach of the river "from a fast-moving stream with healthy fish populations to a series of sluggish impoundments."[9] The slow moving water allowed silt that washed into the river from surrounding farms to accumulate, smothering what had been a healthy environment for aquatic invertebrates. The dams also blocked access to this section of the river, which had been an important spawning ground for Baraboo River fish.

The Waterworks and Oak Street Dams were built on this reach in the 1840s as grist and lumber mills. Sometime between 1900 and 1910, the city of Baraboo bought the Waterworks Dam to power a well and to pump water for the city water system while the Oak Street Dam generated a small amount of hydroelectric power that was fed into the general Wisconsin state grid, as did the Linen Mills Dam. These dams provided no flood control and did not retain storage reservoirs. The impoundments were not used recreationally, and although there isn't much private property along their banks, "there is always a lot of emotional attachment to a dam and to the serene water conditions of the impoundment," says John.

A 1994 Wisconsin Department of Natural Resources fish survey revealed that the diversity of fish species in the free-flowing reaches of the Baraboo was far greater than in those that were impounded. At the same time, inspections of the Waterworks Dam—which had a concrete structure on top of the old timber and crib dam—showed that to meet current safety and environmental standards, it would need major repairs. As hydroelectric dams, the Linen Mills and Oak Street Dams fell under the jurisdiction of the Federal Energy Regulatory Commission. They had never been properly licensed, and to be licensed, they would have to meet current environmental and safety standards, an expensive proposition for the dams' private owners. Investigating what repairs and maintenance would be required, the city and the Wisconsin Department of Natural Resources discovered it would make better financial and environmental sense to remove all three dams.

As Karl Frantz, Baraboo's city administrator, tells it, "The first dam that came out, Waterworks Dam, was the hardest, and faced the most resistance and generated the most public concern. The city took all the initial criticism and forged the path. Yet there was hardly any public discussion or criticism about the second two, Oak Street and Linen Mills." Some of the strongest opposition to removal of Waterworks Dam came from Circus World Museum, which felt the loss of the impoundment would be aesthetically offensive and damaging to a national historic landmark. Being just upstream from the dam, Circus World Museum was concerned about the future use of the river. But when plans were announced to landscape newly exposed riverbanks on its property, the museum changed its position. It now enjoys its new access to the river. In fact, as I pass by on my way out of town, I see an elephant being led down to the river for a bath.

Fish restoration was a powerful catalyst toward persuading the community that dam removal would be a positive move, says Frantz. And with the dam gone, the city does not have to pay thousands of dollars each year to insure it, nor does it have to pay for dam maintenance. In the end, removal of the Waterworks Dam cost about a third as much as it would have to keep the dam in place. "Some electricity production was lost with these dams, but that was pretty marginal," says Frantz. "Since we've tied dam removal to the creation of river walks and parks, it's been a re-birthing for the river." A community's response to dam removal depends very much on the rivers involved, Frantz remarks. "I'd been involved in a dam removal in Jefferson, Wisconsin, where I was labeled a dam buster," he adds, laughing.

John Exo takes me to see the reach of river downstream from Circus World that has been freed by removal of Waterworks Dam. The dam has been out for two years now, and there's no trace of the structure. We walk down the shallow banks to the muddy shoreline. There's a graceful curve to the river here. Full-leafed maple, ash and oak trees shade the water. There are some mussel and clam shells in the dark river sand. "It's been amazing how quickly sand and silt scoured out," John says, and even more will wash away if there are big summer rains. Before the impoundment came out, about eleven fish species were found in the water here, he tells me. Shortly after the dam was removed, twenty-four species were found in the same location. And there are nearly thirty times as many smallmouth bass here as there were when the dam was in.

After looking at the site of Waterworks Dam, we go to the more urban setting of the Oak Street Dam site. There are light-industry buildings on either side the river and a small traffic bridge just upstream. Apart from the now-defunct power generation, "very little or virtually none of the surrounding businesses depended on the river in its impounded condition," which eased negotiations about removing the dam, John explains. There was a coal gasification plant across the river from Oak Street Dam that lit the town's gaslights in the late 1800s. The power generation created coal tar that ended up in the river at the bottom of the impoundment. The company that now owns the plant paid for the removal and disposal of these contaminated sediments, a process that made removal of Oak Street Dam more difficult than that of Waterworks Dam.

John tells me that the power company that owned that property donated about $5,000 for native wetland plantings to revegetate the newly exposed riverbanks, which are just starting to green up. There's still rubble on the shore, and it's clear that not all the post–dam removal landscaping has been done. Before removal, the Wisconsin Department of Natural Resources bought the dam, and the city of Baraboo acquired the adjacent land, where a waterfront trail and park will be developed. "It's a pipe dream now," says John, "but it's nice to see that the city is trying to connect people back to the river." He tells me that in the winter after the dam came out, eagles were seen nesting along the river.

We then go to the Linen Mills Dam, which crosses the Baraboo just outside of town. A couple of people are fishing downstream from the concrete building housing the dam's works. Box elder, silver maple, white ash and cottonwood bend over the water. John tells me that sturgeon still spawn in the rocky cobbled bottoms below the rapids downstream from the dam. There are northern walleye, redhorse, sucker, smallmouth bass, sauger and muskee in this stretch of river, as well as freshwater drum, white bass and sheephead. "Fish biologists fully expect sturgeon to spawn again throughout the Baraboo when these dams are gone, but it will take a while," he says.

"So many people of the older generation are still attracted to the paradigm of the control and harnessing of nature," John says, as we look at the dam. "A lot of younger people don't quite understand that. A lot of people in town didn't care one way or another whether the dams came out. Those opposed were almost exclusively of the older generation. For them, removing the dams was analogous to a mourning process of anger and denial. For some people it was like losing a family member. The dam's always been there."

One of Baraboo's connections with the river is the very active Baraboo River Canoe Club. Members have participated in discussions about dam removal, helped with riverside cleanups and played a part in shaping local public opinion of river restoration efforts. City Administrator Karl Frantz describes the Baraboo community as "fairly conservative but supportive of natural things" and says that having "an active canoe club helped a lot" in garnering acceptance for dam removal.

While I'm in Baraboo, I get to witness the Canoe Club in action, for I've arrived on the day "Pass the Paddle," an event organized by the American Rivers Management Council, is due at the Baraboo. At the grassy park, where a group of paddlers have assembled, John Exo and I unload a big metal canoe from atop his vehicle. Todd Ambs, executive director of the River Alliance of Wisconsin, arrives with the paddle that has traveled across the United States. Karl Frantz is there in a suit and tie. In his official capacity, Frantz makes some heartfelt remarks about the restoration of the river, then agrees to roll up his shirtsleeves and trouser cuffs and jumps in a canoe.

It's very clear that these folks are passionate about their river. About a dozen or more of us—including a local TV reporter toting her video camera and a couple in sit-upon kayaks whose dog perches on one of their boats—launch from the rocky banks for a short paddle to just downstream of the Oak Street Dam site. The current is swift but gentle, and the river is midsummer shallow and rocky. It's kind of exciting to think that this is the first summer in over 150 years since anyone's been able to paddle this stretch of river.

The final stop on my Baraboo dam removal tour is upriver in the town of La Valle. The road to La Valle—population 446— winds along the river, past farms and some former farms where the barns are now antique shops. We pass signs for the Norman Rockwell Museum of Art and the Carr Valley Cheese Company. La Valle's tiny town center is situated on a bend in the road that crosses the river. Storefronts have been spruced up to attract tourists coming through on the rails-to-trails system and on country antiquing trips. We stop and look over the edge of the bridge where a millpond, which John describes as a stagnant carp factory, is being drawn down. On the upstream side of the dam the pond has become a large mudflat. Channels are beginning to reappear in the newly exposed wetland.

Downstream from the dam, where the water is still deep, in the shadow of the old mill building, an older man sits in a rowboat, a fishing line cast in the water. Northern walleye and pike might be among his catch. John and I look at what's left of the impounded stretch of the river and wonder where in the pond where the fisherman now floats will the original river channel reemerge. John explains that an environmental group based in Madison called the Sand County Foundation purchased the dam with the intention of removing it. He's been working with the advisory team facilitating discussions about dam removal and says the organization underestimated local opposition to this dam removal.

A local farm family has purchased the mill building and turned it into an antiques mall. We tour the big airy building. Upstairs are cabinets, sideboards, trunks and needlework made by local Amish families. The wife of the family who's bought the mill building tells us that they are making a leap into this new business and selling the bulk of their dairy herd. "My husband's counting the number of milkings left. He says he hasn't counted anything like that since 'Nam," she says. "Thirty-four milkings to go," says her husband who shows us around the millworks in the basement. Down a steep flight of wooden stairs the huge iron gears and handles sit on an uneven earthen floor. They can still be turned by hand. Nearby, there's a little water closet. A small window looks out onto the river. As I lean toward the view, I see that the old cast-iron toilet bowl opens directly on the river, where a turtle sits on a rock, and think again about how our treatment of rivers has changed.

Further confirming this notion, I read a September 28, 2000, press release from U.S. Senator Herbert Kohl of Wisconsin, announcing $100,000 in federal funding for a comprehensive study of the Baraboo River Basin. "The more we learn about how best to protect our natural resources and native species, the better equipped we are to preserve ecosystems for generations to come. This study will help us discover what steps we should take to help reverse any man-made damage to the Baraboo River," wrote Kohl. Whether this is a bold move for conservation or simply bringing home the bacon, I remember that Wisconsin sent environmental champion and founder of Earth Day Gaylord Nelson to the U.S. Senate and was Aldo Leopold's home when he made his eloquent call for a "land ethic."

From the Baraboo, I drive north toward the small city of Merrill, where the Ward Paper Mill Dam was removed from the Prairie River in 1999, causing a stir and some unhappiness in town. On my way, I traverse the part of Wisconsin known as the Central Sands. These are the remains of ancient lake bottoms, a sandy moraine filled with bogs and the occasional rocky butte. Farther north there is granite, and there are gravel pits amid the farmland. This is the eastern portion of the glacial moraine that separates the Wisconsin River watershed and basins to the west from those that flow into the Milwaukee and Lake Michigan. West of the Wisconsin River here are marshlands, cranberry bogs and forests. To the east are sandy plains where enough potatoes are grown to make Wisconsin the third largest potato-producing state in the nation.

I pass much evidence of Wisconsin's standing as a dairy state. "The Cheese Chalet," "The Dairy Shrine" and others beckon with signs that say "Visit the Cheese Factory." Over dinner in Stevens Point I read the local free weekly. An ad for "St. Florian's Millennium Picnic" catches my eye. The picnic, says the ad, will feature "outdoor polka masses and an all new Polish buffet." Intrigued, I ask my hostess in Merrill about the polka masses. "I grew up with polka bands at weddings and things but I can never get used to the beer tents at Mass," she replies, laughing.

My route north closely follows the Wisconsin River. Along the river I pass cheese and paper factories, dams and power plants. In Wausau there are signs for the Rib Mountain ski area that rises above the wetlands. The back roads through the farmland cross many creeks. The land slopes toward the Wisconsin River. Ducks, geese and the occasional great blue heron rise out of the wet spots, flapping toward the big river. This is sandhill crane country, and I try to imagine what it would be like to see a flock of these elegant birds in one of these orderly fields.

The directions I was given to Merrill are so good that I arrive early enough to take a walk under the shade of large hardwood trees in one of the city's seventeen parks. In front of the nearby public library I stop to read the bronze plaque commemorating the Prairie River's "River Rats":

> During the latter years of the 1800s, lumbering drove the economy here at Jenny Bull Falls and throughout northern Wisconsin, providing work for thousands of men. Many workers were needed to cut trees, haul them to water, float them to mills, cut them into lumber and raft them to downstream markets. Many men were lumberjacks in winter, river rats in spring and sawmill workers in summer.

The river rat, or log driver, was responsible for getting logs from forests to mills. During the drive, river rats rode the logs. Using peavey, or pike poles, they pushed, pulled and pried logs free. Townspeople often lined the banks to watch them at work. The drives ended when the logs arrived at the mill booms.

Located where the Prairie and Wisconsin Rivers meet, Merrill has a population of about 10,000. It was originally called Jenny Bull Falls and began as a trading post and mill town in the 1840s. In 1848, a dam was constructed across the Wisconsin River to power a sawmill that, in the 1880s and 1890s, produced tens of millions of board feet and shingles a year. In 1892, there were eight mills operating in Merrill producing 150 million board feet of lumber a year. When the pine forests were decimated, the mills began processing hardwood, and in the 1880s and early 1890s, there were twenty mills in the area producing hardwood timber. Today milled wood products like windows and doors are Merrill's largest manufacturing and employing industry.

The Ward Paper Mill Dam was built in 1905 and its location made it the last dam on the Prairie River before it joins the Wisconsin. The dam originally provided power for the Ward Lumber Mill and later for the Ward Paper Mill. The dam created a shallow impoundment—twelve to fifteen feet at its deepest—of about 118 acres that was about two miles long. In 1989, the mill and dam were sold to the International Paper Company, which shut down the dam in 1991 before closing the mill in 1995. Like many small privately owned dams, by the 1990s, Ward Mill Dam was no longer properly licensed or up to current Federal Energy Regulatory Commission safety and environmental standards. By the mid-1990s, the wooden sections of the dam were badly deteriorated, and the concrete had cracked. So International Paper quickly discovered that the dam was a serious liability, rendering the sale of the Ward Paper Mill property difficult, if not impossible. Adding to this liability was improper operation of the dam's gates during the 1996 spring snowmelt season, which caused upstream homeowners, people living around the impoundment, some $100,000 worth of flood damage. Given a "high hazard" rating by FERC, it was clear the dam would have to be repaired or removed.

To learn more about Merrill's dilemmas with the Ward Mill Dam, I contacted Jeff Moore, a doctor who works at the local hospital, one of the few people in town who spoke publicly in favor of a free-flowing river. Jeff and his wife Carla invited me to visit with them over a Saturday lunch and offered to take me canoeing on the newly opened stretch of river. The Moores' trim and comfortable home is located right on the Wisconsin River. The grassy lawn of their backyard slopes down to the river, where a short path leads to a wooden dock. We talk in the kitchen then over lunch on the sunny back deck with their sons, Bradley and Fred.

Jeff explains to me that, historically, the white pine forests of northern Wisconsin supplied mills like those in Merrill. The Ward Paper Company, he tells me, was a small but profitable company specializing in bright-colored paper. When the mill closed, about 140 workers lost their jobs, creating resentment in the community toward International Paper. "To sell the mill with the adjacent dam would have meant bringing the dam up to standard," Jeff says. Given the estimated high costs of repair—which would include construction of fish passage—and the difficulty of finding a new owner who wanted a dam, in 1998 International Paper applied to the Wisconsin Department of Natural Resources for a permit to abandon and remove the dam.

Part of this application process was a formal Environmental Assessment involving a public comment period. "The Department of Natural Resources received twenty-two letters from residents. Only one was in favor of dam removal and that was mine," Jeff tells me. "I originally spoke out because I wanted to see the river run free."

There are homes around what was the millpond, almost all year-round residences, Jeff explains, and homeowners were worried about what would happen to the aesthetics and value of their property if the millpond was drained. The impoundment was considered a scenic feature of the north part of the city, and residents feared they'd be left with an unsightly mudflat. Millpond homeowners formed the Prairie Lake Association, and those who wished to save Ward Mill Pond—as the impoundment had always been called—began referring to it as Prairie Lake. "Letters to the editor and editorials started popping up in the local papers, saying

'Save Prairie Lake,'" Jeff says. "Save Ward Dam" lawn signs appeared around town. Jeff Moore's was the lone letter to the Merrill paper favoring removal.

The state's Environmental Assessment determined that the dam was indeed unsafe and structurally at risk for failing and that the repairs required to facilitate sale of the dam were prohibitively expensive. The Department of Natural Resources explained to the community that, under Wisconsin law, owners of a dam could not be compelled to maintain it if they chose to remove it. Unless a financially capable new owner came forward with plans to purchase, repair and assume long-term liability of the dam, International Paper's application for removal would continue.

Even though Ward Mill Pond was not connected to the community's source of groundwater, some Merrill residents worried that lowering the millpond would cause the adjacent water table to fall and render their wells unusable. Questions were raised about a fungal infection called blastomycosis related to rotting tree stumps, a virus that comes from bacteria that live in sediment. "Blastomycosis occurs in the county but it cannot definitely be traced to exposed pond sediment, nor can draining a pond definitely increase its risk," says Jeff, an explanation confirmed by the Wisconsin Division of Health. Still, opposition to draining Ward Mill Pond remained high. I ask Jeff about the response to his public comments. "I got some letters and a couple of patients said things to me," he says, "but no one's stopped seeing me." Carla adds that no one said anything about it to their sons in school, either.

When International Paper was granted permission to remove the dam, several citizens, Merrill's mayor and the city government objected to the permit. After a hearing in the spring of 1999 before an administrative law judge, the permit was approved. Lowering of the millpond began in August 1999. The discussion put forth by Judge Jeffrey D. Boldt, who issued the findings of fact in the appeal, provides an interesting perspective on the case. "There is no question that many area residents love Prairie Lake passionately and will be very sorry to see it gone," he writes in his decision.

Unlike many people who urged saving Prairie Lake, the law does not state a preference for a river or an impoundment. [The] Wisconsin Supreme Court has made it clear that the public interest in navigable waters focuses on impacts to and of the water itself rather than indirect, upland socioeconomic impacts. . . . While the changes along this section of the Prairie River will be difficult for many to accept, the long-term interests of the river will be protected.[10]

After lunch we load the Moores' canoe on top of their car and drive upriver a few miles on the Prairie to the home of friends who've agreed to let us launch from their backyard. The Prairie River flows from a chain of natural lakes northeast of Merrill. It runs through what is called "undulating terminal and recessional moraine," an area filled with marshes and small lakes.[11] Water quality is good throughout the watershed. Jeff Moore tells me that the Prairie River has "first-class trout fishing." Removing Ward Mill Dam makes Merrill one of the few sizable cities in Wisconsin with a free-flowing trout stream running through its urban area and allows all 223 miles of the Prairie River to flow freely.

Native to the Prairie are smallmouth bass, northern pike, white sucker, hog sucker, mottled sculpin, common shiner, log perch, rainbow darter, longnose dace, brook and chestnut lamprey. The list of mussel species that live in this stretch of the river reads like a poem: elktoe, mucket, fat mucket, cylinder, spike, pigtoe, common pocketbook, fluted shell, black sandshell, strange floater and floater. Wisconsin has one of the greatest diversity of freshwater mussel species of any state, but 70 percent of these mollusks—which are an indicator of aquatic ecosystem health—are now threatened, endangered or otherwise imperiled. Many of the same species were found up and downstream of Ward Mill Dam, but the dam blocked their passage and created harmful warm water and low oxygen conditions. Draining the millpond allows the river channel and about forty acres of riparian surrounding wetlands to be restored, improving habitat for native fish, frogs, turtles, mollusks and aquatic insects.

The water is very low, and with three of us in the canoe, we're often in danger of scraping bottom. Carla points out Turk's head lilies, black-eyed Susans, blooming milkweed and joe-pye weed. There are sedges, grasses and bullrushes. The light is dappled under the canopy of burr oak, birch, northern hemlock, white pine and mountain ash. We see several great blue herons, lots of kingfishers, goldfinches and song sparrows, and spot a bald eagle perched on a tree. There are redwinged blackbirds and a harrier. As we paddle through a particularly shady spot, a horned owl flaps out of the foliage. Sometimes you can see beaver and otter here, Carla tells me. Mink and muskrat also frequent these riverbanks.

We paddle past the drained millpond, which has been seeded with perennial ryegrass and is starting to green up. The grass will help stabilize the exposed sediment but not interfere with the return of natural vegetation. Houses along this stretch of river have newly extended, still-bare riverfront backyards. Since the pond draining, some 120 acres of land belonging to International Paper have been exposed. Since my visit, International Paper has deeded ninety-nine acres of this land to the city for $1. The remaining acreage has gone to adjacent private landowners. The new city land will be developed into a park with hiking trails and access to the river.

I realize that in two days I've paddled stretches of two rivers that have until now not been free flowing in at least a hundred years. We paddle under the traffic bridge that crosses the Prairie River just downstream from where the dam was and arrive at the confluence with the Wisconsin. The Wisconsin is much broader and has greater currents than the Prairie, and it almost seems as if we've arrived at an ocean. It's late afternoon now and the sun is turning golden. The dark blue water is swimmably warm and has a gentle chop to it. We cross the river and dock at the foot of the Moores' backyard. Being on the river here, I feel as if I've been let in on a secret of the landscape—a sly, subtly ever-changing world quite different from what the orderly streets of Merrill imply.

After leaving the Moores', I head southeast on my way to the Milwaukee River. I pass a sign for Fremont, Wisconsin, which calls itself the "White Bass Capital of the World," and a sign announcing "Fish Fry and Catfish Races" on July 28. When I see a sign for Pigeon Lake, I think of Aldo Leopold's lament for the passing of the passenger pigeon flocks that once darkened the Wisconsin skies.

I drive south along the west shore of Lake Winnebago and pass through Oshkosh, Fond du Lac and townships called Black Wolf and Friendship, where suburbs seem to be eating steadily at the farmland. The road makes a sharp turn in the town of Eden, not far from the headwaters of the Milwaukee River. To the east is the Kettle Moraine State Forest and Ice Age National Scientific Reserve. There are conical hills called kames, bowl-shaped depressions called kettles, ridges formed by sand and gravel called eskers and hills called drumlins and moraines. During the Ice Age, caribou, elk, woolly mammoths, musk ox, mastodons and 500-pound beavers roamed this country. Now there are white-tailed deer, gray fox, coyotes, modern-day beaver, badger and muskrat. On a hot, mosquito-biting, fly-buzzing hike, I hear a deer bounding through the woods and spot a hawk circling above. Lakes nestled in the Kettle Moraine feed streams that flow into the Milwaukee, a river that is slowly but steadily being restored.

In West Bend I meet Rick Emanuel, a local Riverkeeper. His van doubles as a mobile office, has a canoe strapped on top and is filled with paddling and camping gear. Rick has agreed to show me the site of the Woolen Mills and other Milwaukee River dam removals. "I've been canoeing here on and off since I was a kid," he tells me. "In 1995, I started really noticing the success of the Woolen Mills Dam removal and began doing water quality monitoring work as a volunteer." Now he works for a local land trust organization that's preserving shoreline along the Milwaukee River.

The 1988 removal of Woolen Mills Dam is a visually astonishing success. Where the dam and the sixty-one-acre stagnant millpond once sat, the river winds through a park lush with prairie wildflowers and meandering foot and bicycle paths. There are pretty footbridges and places to launch canoes. The West Bend Park Department is developing a canoe program and has six new canoes, Rick tells me. Fishing is encouraged. In mid-July the water is too low to launch a canoe, but the clear water riffles over the gravel and rocky river bottom. It's hot in the sun, and Little League games are going on in the adjacent ball fields.

I remark on the beauty of the flowers and footpaths, and Rick tells me this used to be a carp pond. "It stank," he says, gesturing toward a house at the downstream end of the park. "Guys used to live there who watched TV and fished for carp out of the kitchen window. I have nothing against the carp personally. I come from Mississippi River people and carp fed my people during the Depression."

We walk through tall stands of chicory, cattail, thistle and Queen Anne's lace. There are prairie cone flowers, hawkweed, bergamot, cup plant, angelica, cow parsnip, giant blue hyssop, blue bellflower, willows and oaks and, by the side of a pond area, pickerel weed. There are turtles here as well as perch and brook and rainbow trout. The restored river is really good smallmouth bass habitat, Rick tells me. "The willows and dogwoods are coming up like crazy." Since the river's been restored, greater red-horse, a Wisconsin state threatened fish species, have been found in this stretch of the Milwaukee.[12]

Soon after white settlers arrived here in the 1840s, they began damming the Milwaukee to power grist and lumber mills. Manufacturing and light industry have been the mainstay of the city's economy since the railroad came to West Bend in the 1870s. Known for making farm equipment, pots and pans and a special kind of popcorn popper, West Bend does not conform to the stereotype of a community that's accomplished some landmark river restoration. Rick tells me that West Bend's Rotary Club played a big part in the restoration, as did University of Wisconsin architects and scientists.

Woolen Mills Dam was built in 1870 to power a sawmill and later a woolen mill. The dam was rebuilt in 1919, when Wisconsin Power and Electric converted it for hydroelectric generation, but by 1959 the dam was no longer profitable and its ownership was transferred to the city of West Bend. Found to have serious structural flaws, in 1980 the dam was cited as a public safety hazard, which would require repair or removal. The dam's shallow impoundment was filled with sediment, some of which was contaminated with heavy metals and seeping in from a nearby landfill. The warm water was deprived of oxygen, eutrophic and, in summer months, covered with algae.

Despite the poor conditions, the community initially opted to replace the old dam with a new one. Local homeowners, like those in Merrill, feared their property values would drop if the impoundment disappeared. The 1981 price tag for a new dam was $3.3 million, and funds were not available, so no action was taken. When a solution was sought to the problems caused by the contaminated sediment accumulating in the impoundment, the Wisconsin Department of Natural Resources recommended dam removal. So in 1988, West Bend and the Department of Natural Resources signed an agreement to remove Woolen Mills Dam. The costs of the restoration would be shared by the state and the city of West Bend. The total cost of removing the dam, restoring the river and developing the park came to less than $2 million.

As I marvel at the transformation of the dam impoundment, Rick dampens my enthusiasm a bit by pointing out that "everywhere they put in a footbridge, they threw in a bit of riprap. If you want to be friends with the river, you've got to learn to get out of its way once in a while. Many people don't understand the natural cycles of ecology." Still, the restoration is so pretty, I think it might serve as the poster child for dam removals. "There are a lot of things we should be proud of here, but there is still some sitting on the fence," Rick says. "But the old guard is changing."

Thinking about the glaciers that carved this watershed, I contemplate where on a geologic timeline something like the Woolen Mills Dam would fit. It would be less than a pin dot. "Rivers are the lifeblood of ecosystems. Rivers are energetic systems," I remember Stephanie Lindloff saying. "They're great metaphors for life. They're constantly changing." She paused. "And the saying that you can never step in the same river twice—it's really true."

After leaving West Bend, I drive along the lower Milwaukee River in the town of Grafton to see the Chair Factory Dam, which is due to be removed in the winter of 2001 (and was indeed gone when this book went to press). Intrigued by the number of dams slated for removal in Wisconsin, I make one more stop, Fredonia, where the aging Waubeka Dam will soon go the way of dams like Woolen Mills, Oak Street, Waterworks and Shopiere.

After winding past red barns and silos, I find the dam. It is another modest, mossy old cement structure with a glassy impoundment stretching a ways upstream. I walk out on a small bridge downstream from the dam. An older man wearing a plaid shirt and khaki hat has his tackle box open on the sidewalk and is fishing over the railing. "What do you catch here?" I ask him. "Oh, just about anything," he says contentedly.

Later I reread the "Wisconsin" section of *A Sand County Almanac* and think about Carla and Jeff Moore and their sons, the Baraboo Canoe Club and the new canoes on the Milwaukee in West Bend. "It . . . seems likely that the remaining canoe-water on the Flambeau, as well as every other stretch of wild river in the state, will ultimately be harnessed for power," wrote Aldo Leopold in the mid-1940s. "Perhaps our grandsons, having never seen a wild river, will never miss the chance to set a canoe in singing waters."[13] Wouldn't he be gratified to know that some of these rivers are now being set free.

Glen Canyon Dam
and the
Colorado River

"Polite conservationists leave no mark, save
scars upon the Earth that could have been
prevented, had they stood their ground."
—*David Brower*[1]

On the evening of March 13, 2000, the auditorium at Northern Arizona University in Flagstaff is standing room only. David Brower, eighty-eight years old and made frail by illness, slowly makes his way to the stage and with considerable effort begins to speak. The student sitting next to me whispers to his neighbor, "Who's that guy?" then turns to me for help. "The archdruid," I find myself saying. "Have you read *Encounters with the*

Archdruid by John McPhee?" I ask. "It's David Brower. He used to run the Sierra Club. He stopped dams in the Grand Canyon."

"If we get Glen Canyon back," Brower says, "we'll get back one of the most beautiful pieces of natural architecture in the world. That's what I want to do before I go . . ."

Of all the dam removals being contemplated, the one with the greatest sense of romantic crusade about it is Glen Canyon Dam. Perhaps it's the mesmerizing beauty of the red rock canyons of the Colorado Plateau. Perhaps it's the knowledge of what was lost beneath the waters of Lake Powell and the grandeur of what might be recovered. Perhaps David Brower's valiant yet unsuccessful efforts to prevent that loss capture the imagination. Or it may simply be the audacity of suggesting that such an edifice, itself audacious in what it imposes on nature, be dismantled—but the very notion of considering removal of Glen Canyon Dam has a rousing and emotional effect. And it may not be entirely a case of tilting at windmills.

I'm in Flagstaff to meet with Pam Hyde, executive director of the Glen Canyon Institute—a nonprofit dedicated to restoring a free-flowing Colorado River—and for a conference about Glen Canyon hosted by a brand new environmental group called Glen Canyon Action Network.

Flagstaff has the feel of a western university town not yet spoiled by an influx of tourism. But development is sprouting like mushrooms around the city's perimeter, and there's road construction everywhere. While I wait for Hyde in the front room of the white clapboard house that's home to the Institute, I leaf through *The Place No One Knew*, Eliot Porter's photo book about Glen Canyon, and eavesdrop on a couple who have dropped in to visit with the staff. It's Monday morning, "my first day in the office after being on the river," says a staff member, smiling. Her visitors smile. I smile. That phrase makes people's faces glow. It speaks of sculpted sandstone, riffles and rapids, the fluting sound of the canyon wren, the exhilaration of moving water and ancient rock.

In 1963, I read, the gates of Glen Canyon Dam closed and the waters of the dammed Colorado River rose, inundating miles of twisting canyons shaped by eons of wind and water. "Glen Canyon died in 1963 and I was partly responsible for its needless death. So were you. Neither you nor I, nor anyone else knew it well enough to insist that at all costs it should endure. When we began to find out it was too late," wrote David Brower in his introduction to *The Place No One Knew*.[2]

Thirty-seven years later, March 14, 2000, it's a sunny spring day on the north side of Glen Canyon Dam. The cedar-colored canyon walls contrast sharply with the cobalt sky and equally blue water of the dammed Colorado River below. The 710-foot dam towers across the canyon. The dam's pale gray cement throws back the light, making me squint. The sun will grow hot toward noon, but there's a chill in the shade. People mill about expectantly. A respectful hush falls as people strain to listen. Brower is clearly invigorated by the effort of speaking to a crowd, some of whom may, for the sake of momentum, throw scientific caution and incremental political realism to the wind. They are relishing the possible: that someday this canyon might be restored. There are signs that say, "Drain it!" "Save the Humpback Chub" and "Silt Happens!" There's an undercurrent of tree sitting and monkey-wrenching that is probably only bluster, but the Utah and Arizona police are clearly, though politely, taking no chances. Yet behind the exuberance there is serious ecological science. Given what is known about the physics of delivering water through Glen Canyon's plumbing, this dam may not make that much sense. From the engineering perspective and the biological, there are sound reasons for reconsidering the wisdom of Glen Canyon Dam.

The story of the damming of the Colorado River and flooding of Glen Canyon is now a classic in the annals of contemporary American history. In the 1950s, the Sierra Club—then led by David Brower—launched a successful fight to prevent construction of a dam at Dinosaur National Monument near the confluence of the Green and Yampa Rivers in Colorado and Utah. But the price of that victory was the loss of Glen Canyon. So in 1960, the U.S. Bureau of Reclamation began pouring concrete to build the $272 million, ten-million-ton dam on the Colorado River at the Arizona-Utah border, submerging nearly 200 miles of river canyon under what would be called Lake Powell. "To grasp the nature of the crime that was committed," wrote Edward Abbey of the loss of Glen Canyon, "imagine the Taj Mahal or Chartres Cathedral buried in mud until only the spires remain visible."[3]

The Colorado River's headwaters rise in the glaciers of the Rocky Mountains. Its watershed drains some 244,000 square miles, taking in portions of seven states in the United States and two in Mexico. While ferocious rapids still plunge through the spectacular gorges of the Grand Canyon, the Colorado has become what one assessment calls "a vast complex plumbing system, with Glen and Hoover dams the controlling faucets."[4] Bruce Babbitt describes the Colorado River as being manipulated like a giant toilet bowl. There are now twenty large Colorado River dams, all built since 1913, and many smaller ones. So much water is siphoned off the Colorado River before it reaches the ocean at the Gulf of California in Mexico that the river delta's ecosystem has virtually collapsed. An important stopping place for migratory birds, the delta has been a vital nursery ground for diverse and endemic riparian and marine life, but dams and diversions have starved the Colorado of water, nutrients and natural sediments so that many native species in the delta and throughout the river corridor are now in trouble. The smallest known marine mammal, a kind of porpoise called a vaquita, which lives in the waters off the delta, is threatened with extinction, and at least one native fish, the totoaba, is thought to be extinct.[5] If Glen Canyon were gone, the water stored in Lake Powell would return to the river and help restore Colorado River delta wetlands.

"What's natural to the Colorado, what makes it so unusual," explains Pam Hyde, is its high turbidity and wide temperature fluctuations: "The water can be eighty-five degrees in the summer and below freezing in winter." The natural Colorado River ecosystem depends on a free flow of warm silty water and high spring flows. Glen Canyon Dam causes most of the river's sediment to settle at the bottom of Lake Powell. With the sediment trapped, instead of warm, silt-laden water, which would naturally course through the downstream canyons, water flowing out of Glen Canyon is cold, clear and deprived of nutrients—the opposite of the river canyon's natural environment. Consequently, many native fish, birds and other species that live in the river corridor downstream of Glen Canyon are declining while non-natives thrive.

Damming Glen Canyon affects not just the canyons lost beneath Lake Powell but the whole river corridor through the Grand Canyon. The Colorado's natural floods created and maintained riverbank beaches where native plants and wildlife flourished. Because of these changes in water temperature and chemistry, the Colorado's native humpback chub are now listed as endangered under the Endangered Species Act. The chub have suffered from competition with non-native fish, and the manipulated water levels have eliminated most of the backwaters where the chub spawn and rear their young.

Sediment trapped behind the dam has also depleted the river's sandbars and beaches, eliminating habitat for aquatic and terrestrial species. The Grand Canyon's native species, including the southwest willow flycatcher, razorback sucker, pikeminnow, bonytail and Kanab amber snail, have all suffered because of the dam, some—the pikeminnow, bonytail and humpback chub and razorback sucker—to such an extent that they have disappeared from the Grand Canyon. To make matters worse for the Colorado's native fish, in the early 1960s, the U.S. Fish and Wildlife Service deliberately eliminated all the native fish in hundreds of miles of upstream tributaries so that they might safely introduce non-natives favored for sportfishing.

There is also concern about the downstream effects of toxic sediment accumulating at the bottom of Lake Powell that is exacerbated by oil from the motorboats that ply the lake. The other, more serious source of persistent toxic sediment is from uranium tailings, for all over this part of southern Utah were uranium mines. Some of their leavings are now at the bottom of the Colorado, its tributaries and Lake Powell. This sediment would have to be dealt with exceptionally carefully were Lake Powell ever to be drained.

When I ask if there are problems with surface water pollution at Glen Canyon Dam, Hyde tells me that it's a question more of water quantity than quality. Still, many people comment on what the heavy use of motorized watercraft has done to the quality of water in Lake Powell. "Lake Foul," its detractors sometimes call it, reflecting their feelings more than specific scientific knowledge of the reservoir's water column. "The whole aquatic riparian system of the Grand Canyon has shifted," says Hyde. There's more biomass, more biodiversity, she explains, but it's non-native and not sustainable. "If you keep tweaking one factor after another, how do you restore natural processes?" she asks.

Anyone who has explored the side canyons of the Grand Canyon, San Juan or the Escalante can imagine what Glen Canyon must have been like, with narrow twisting corridors of deep orange sandstone carved into arches and pinnacles. On the canyon shoulders grow prickly pear and datura, paintbrush, lupine, penstemon, globe mallow, mule's ear sunflower and sego lily. There is sage, pinyon, juniper, cottonwood, salt brush and black brush. There are bighorn sheep and lizards. Cliff swallows, violet green swallows, lazuli buntings, burrowing owls and bluebirds dart among the shrubbery. Nestled in clefts and crooks of the rockery are the ruins of ancient cliff dwellings and stick houses. Their inhabitants decorated the rock walls with handprints, petroglyphs and pictographs. If Lake Powell was drained, not only would the reservoir gradually disappear, and these canyons reemerge, but the forty or more years' worth of water soaked into Glen Canyon's walls would slowly return. "It would take 378 days to draw down Lake Powell," says engineer and attorney Steve Hannon. But there is so much sediment now backed up by Glen Canyon that it extends all the way into the San Juan River and is changing that river's flow so it would take a long time for that load to dissipate.

Glen Canyon Dam sits on the Arizona-Utah border just north of the line drawn by the 1922 Colorado River Compact, which divides the seven states of the Colorado River Basin into Upper and Lower but unequal halves. (Colorado, New Mexico, Utah and Wyoming are the states of the Upper Colorado River Basin. Arizona, California and Nevada are the Lower Basin states.) The details of western water law as they've developed since the Colorado River Compact could easily occupy a whole book, but Glen Canyon Dam's location means that water from Lake Powell goes almost entirely to sprawling cities and farmlands hundreds of miles away. Water from the Colorado stored in Lake Powell and Lake Mead—the huge impoundment of Hoover Dam—travels south by river, then is pumped westward toward San Diego and Los Angeles in the Colorado River Aqueduct across the California desert north of Palm Springs. Thus the Colorado waters some of the country's fastest growing cities, Phoenix, Tucson, Las Vegas, Albuquerque, San Diego and Los Angeles among them. At the same time, irrigated agriculture in Arizona and in California's Imperial Valley claims much of those states' allotment of Colorado River water.

"At the time of the Colorado River Compact, water that went to the sea was considered a waste," says Hank Lacey, an attorney and former professor of law at Lewis and Clark College. "Consumptive uses of water were favored. Leaving water in the river for the fish is not considered exercising a water right; this is considered a non-consumptive, non-economic use of the water," says Lacey. "The Lower Basin states cannot demand water for nonconsumptive uses. And there's always been a heavy preference for agricultural uses."

It sounds like putting the cart before the horse, but Lake Powell is the main reason for Glen Canyon Dam, for the dam was built to store water for the states of the Upper Colorado River Basin so that they could deliver water to the Lower Basin states, as required by the Colorado River Compact. "It's illusory in a way because so much water is lost to evaporation," says Pam Hyde. In fact, the enormous impoundment, which took about seventeen years to fill, loses over half a million acre-feet each year to evaporation (an acre-foot covers one acre of land one foot deep). With additional water lost to seepage into the reservoir's sandstone walls, Lake Powell causes roughly a million acre-feet of Colorado River water to be lost each year.[6] This means that each year Lake Powell loses enough water to evaporation and seepage to supply a city the size of Los Angeles. Since its construction in 1963, the reservoir has thus lost more water than the 27,000 acre-feet it was designed to store.

"The Navajo sandstone is a sponge," says Robert Lippman, an attorney and professor of environmental law at Northern Arizona University. "It's been soaking up water for forty years now." Without the reservoir of Lake Powell, water delivery to the Upper Basin states would not change from current levels, and since Glen Canyon Dam was built on the assumption that it would store and deliver far more water than it actually ever has, draining Lake Powell would reduce Lower Colorado Basin water deliveries by only 1 percent.[7]

The only direct users of water from Lake Powell are the nearby coal-burning Navajo Generating Station and the town of Page, Arizona. Studies done by the Glen Canyon Institute indicate this water could be obtained directly from the river or from a small off-channel reservoir. They also point out that the dam was designed to produce maximum power efficiently only at high water levels, which pose safety hazards to Glen Canyon Dam in flood season. Those who oppose altering Glen Canyon Dam or Lake Powell dispute these findings.

Given the ways that water has been diverted from the river and various states' claims to that water, the Colorado Compact has been the subject of intense competition and legal disagreement ever since it was enacted. Add to these complications the fact that Mexico—home to the mouth of the Colorado—was not included in the 1922 compact and not guaranteed legal right to Colorado River water until the signing of a treaty between the United States and Mexico in 1944. As U.S. agricultural use of this water expanded in the 1950s and 1960s, the quantity and quality of the water reaching Mexico became a problem. There have been summer months when the Colorado dries up before reaching the Gulf of California, and agricultural runoff in the United States has caused water reaching Mexico to be so saline, it cannot be used without extensive treatment.

And then there are the questions of where the Navajo and Hopi nations (whose reservations occupy a great deal of land in the Lower Colorado River Basin) fit into the western water allocation scheme. "The Navajo and Hopi never entered into a water rights compact with the United States government," explains Lacey, "and their claims may exceed the entire allotment of the whole basin."

Glen Canyon Dam was built where it was so the states of the Upper Basin would not have to give any water away in a dry year under the delivery requirements of the Colorado Compact, notes Pam Hyde. Compounding the inefficiencies of Glen Canyon, Steve Hannon explains, is that when the Colorado River Compact was established, "Colorado River water was measured at its wettest period since Elizabeth the First." These conditions set up unrealistic expectations of what that water could do, and Glen Canyon Dam is, in many ways, the product of those expectations.

"The whole thing is driven by the water needs and demands of California," says Hannon. "There's got to be some rethinking about how water is used. Not just the numbers. As long as we've got this policy of more and more people, they've got to be served." Later in the year, when I'm in California, I ask if the question of environmental carrying capacity enters any conversations in the state about water delivery. An agribusiness farmer, a representative of the Central Valley Irrigation Project and an academic working on water issues all say no and look at me as if I've uttered a dirty word.

To the casual observer, the great cement arch of Glen Canyon Dam, spanning 1,560 feet across the canyon, looks inviolable. The dam is the fourth highest in the country and contains almost five million yards of concrete. It looks as if the people who built it knew exactly what they were doing. No doubt they did, but Glen Canyon Dam has been fraught with problems since before the first holes were drilled in the river canyon walls. The Navajo sandstone into which it is built is soft and porous, and engineers question how long Glen Canyon Dam's cementing agent will hold. Studies done before construction indicated the sandstone was so porous that some 15 million gallons of water a day would flow around the dam's abutments.

To prove how risky the dam was, an early congressional skeptic put a piece of the Chinle shale that lies under Glen Canyon's sandstone, into a glass of water. It quickly turned to mud. In response, one of the project's boosters, Stewart Udall, then a first-term congressman from Arizona, did the same with a core sample of sandstone; the water remained clear.[8] "Soft sandstone erodes quickly with a horrendous amount of water running down the spillways," says Steve Hannon. This, he explains, creates the concern that erosion might allow water to back up into the reservoir. This is what happened in 1983, when a spring flood almost took out the dam. Hannon explains that if Glen Canyon Dam failed, so much water would be released that it would almost surely breach Hoover Dam and cause catastrophic destruction.

Glen Canyon Dam was designed to generate far more power than it now does. Lake Powell has been filling steadily with sediment, diminishing its water storage and power-generating capacities. Current river flow requirements have also reduced the dam's power generation. According to the Glen Canyon Institute, the dam now generates approximately 5,000 gigawatt-hours of power each year, about 3 percent of the power currently generated in Arizona, Colorado, New Mexico and Utah. This is not an insignificant amount but its production has been heavily subsidized, and, says Pam Hyde, "It's generally acknowledged that this amount could be made up by way of energy conservation." She talks about the need for energy conservation and the potential for alternative sources of power in the Southwest. "This area, the Arizona Republic," she says, only partly joking, "could be the Saudi Arabia of Solar Power." If Glen Canyon Dam were no longer present as a source of power, rates could increase for some customers. But given the current energy situation in the West, rates are likely to increase with or without dam decommissioning.

"I think the decision to drain Lake Powell will be made by folks in the Los Angeles Basin," opines Hannon. "They'll be the ones to say whether Lake Powell is necessary or not, then they'll latch onto the environmental reasons. And Page would have a transformation they wouldn't believe with a restoration of the canyon. People are wanting to see nature on the mend," he adds.

"Everything's grown up on the shoulders of the 1922 compact," says Hyde, but realities have changed since then. The ever-growing demand for water from the Colorado and the reality of the supply, even if environmental considerations were ignored, simply don't balance.

The Glen Canyon Institute was established to do something about that imbalance. The institute began in 1995, the founder, Dr. Richard Ingebretsen, tells me, as a repository of information.

"There was hidden resentment against Glen Canyon Dam but never any organized resistance," he says. So, in October 1996, Glen Canyon Institute held a meeting in Salt Lake City and decided to begin investigating the decommissioning of Glen Canyon Dam.

"We brought together Bureau of Reclamation people, scientists, environmentalists and laypeople," says Ingebretsen. "We needed to present logical arguments and plausible alternatives. We needed to have credibility with the water users, the farmers and the power people. Our approach has been to get credible science and take it to laypeople as well as to our representatives in Congress."

As Ingebretsen wrote in the *Stanford Environmental Law Journal* in January 2000, "What emerged from that meeting was astonishing. Data presented by the Bureau suggested that replacing the reservoir with a free-flowing Colorado—uncovering Glen Canyon—would make water delivery more efficient downstream."[9] Two weeks after the meeting, in recognition of the enormous environmental costs of the dam, the Sierra Club's national board of directors voted unanimously to restore Glen Canyon by draining Lake Powell. With support from the Sierra Club and other environmental groups, Glen Canyon Institute embarked on what it calls a "citizen-led environmental assessment" to collect scientific evidence to support the decommissioning of Glen Canyon Dam with the hopes of someday restoring the canyon and the Colorado River to natural flows. "In my view and in medicine—which is my profession—trends mean everything," Ingebretsen tells me. "And the trend now is dam decommissioning. The trend now is to discuss it."

The Institute's work has coincided with development of a new federal management plan that aims to lessen the negative impacts of the Colorado's manipulated flows on the Grand Canyon ecosystem. One result of this effort was an experimental release of water through the Grand Canyon designed to mimic natural flows. In March 1996, in what Secretary of the Interior Bruce Babbitt called a "sea change" in dam operation and "a new beginning," the government—for the first time ever—released water from a dam for the purpose of environmental restoration. The hope was that the increased water would re-create beaches and restore essential habitat along the riverbanks. "We are at last coming to grips with the American landscape," said Babbitt, who was there when 120 million gallons of water were let loose from Lake Powell.

Following this experiment, in 1997, the House of Representatives held a hearing on the Sierra Club's proposal to remove Glen Canyon Dam. The intention of Utah and Arizona representatives on the panel was clearly to "embarrass those who support restoration of the canyon," Daniel Beard of the Audubon Society and former director of the U.S. Bureau of Reclamation wrote in a *New York Times* op-ed piece. Instead of being met with ridicule, the dam removal testimony was so persuasive that the hearing rallied support for restoration of the Colorado River and legitimized debate on the issue of Glen Canyon Dam.

"When we started this thing, it was met with absolute skepticism," says Dr. Ingebretsen. "Now we have politicians in Utah campaigning on saving Lake Powell, claiming that their opponents are going to drain Lake Powell. I had a little girl come up to me today and say, 'Now that we're going to drain Lake Powell, what's going to happen?'" Ingebretsen tells me in the fall of 2000. "In a couple of weeks I'll be debating a U.S. congressman at Brigham Young University in Salt Lake City and I'll be speaking at a Western Water Users meeting. That's pretty incredible."

It pleases me no end that there's a movement to let the water flow again," says longtime Colorado River runner, guide and writer Ken Sleight to the group assembled at Northern Arizona University in March 2000. "Are we going to let the dam stand as a monument to stupidity or are we going to let the river go around it? At the very beginning when they started promoting this thing, that monstrosity they got down there now, there were demonstrations. Mostly river people walking back and forth with signs. Crazy-looking signs. I hope we can be more effective today." Sleight was one of the first to challenge Glen Canyon Dam. In the mid-1950s, he founded Friends of Glen Canyon and later with Friends of the Earth and others sued the federal government to stop the filling of Lake Powell and the consequent partial inundation of Rainbow

Bridge National Monument—a large sandstone arch that graces the canyon. The Colorado River Storage Project Act, which authorized creation of Glen Canyon Dam, contains a provision that prohibits its projects from impairing national monuments. Today, there is water under Rainbow Bridge.

"Of all the trips I took over the years, Glen Canyon to me was the greatest," says Sleight, waxing lyrical in his dry way. "A big wide meandering river. Great big stately cathedrals, monoliths. To me, one of the greatest tragedies of all time is the flooding of Glen Canyon. I've pledged to myself, this is an ongoing battle. This is where I want to be. Saying what went under: thousands and thousands of Indian sites. Ruins, petroglyphs, pictographs. All that's gone. Gone are Hidden Passage, Cathedral and Music Temple. But I'm going to get my boating job back. I'm going to get my boat back in Glen Canyon to run Dominy Falls. One day we'll do that."

"They call Glen Canyon the place no one knew," says Sleight. "But a lot of us knew it. There was lots of talk on the riverbank. A lot of grandiose plans. . . . But at that time we didn't know how to speak out. We really didn't know how to fight. . . . If the Utah environmental community had been together it would have been different. Now it's a sink-or-swim thing. . . . Never compromise when you have a thing like this."

Salty old river runners and determined ecologists are not the only ones who have questioned the wisdom of Glen Canyon Dam. As senator from Arizona, Barry Goldwater had voted for the Colorado River Storage Project and construction of Glen Canyon Dam, but he later said it was the one vote in all of his career that he regretted the most. "While Glen Canyon has created the most beautiful lake in the world," Goldwater said in 1986, "and has brought millions of dollars into my state and the state of Utah, nevertheless, I think of that river as it was when I was a boy. And that is the way I would like to see it again."[10]

Glen Canyon Dam and the Colorado River Storage Project were created to deliver ever increasing amounts of water and power. "When will we get over this habit of more and more and bigger and bigger, and more and more and more people, more appetites and more stuff?" says David Brower to the group in

Flagstaff. "We don't have to have more and more and more to be joyful. I know, I just came in from Phoenix!"

Pam Hyde describes Glen Canyon Institute's task as one of "trying to get people to ask questions. Think about what you really need. I don't think anyone can look at Lake Powell and say this is the only answer to the problem," she says, smiling and shaking her head.

"We didn't know what we were losing," Brower tells us later. "What the Bureau of Reclamation didn't want us to talk about was the environmental threat Glen Canyon creates. It's built in the wrong place on the wrong kind of rock. That Navajo sandstone still leaks," he says. "The waste of water, the pollution, the destruction of one of the most beautiful canyons on earth. There was pain when it was inundated and there will be pain when it's restored. This is a singular opportunity to remember Glen Canyon as it was and as it can be."

At the March 14, 2000, demonstration at Glen Canyon Dam, those who would like to see a free-flowing Colorado River restored and Glen Canyon Dam gone are assembled on the Utah side of the dam. Across the Arizona state line on the south side of the dam, the Friends of Lake Powell are staging a counter-demonstration. Page, Arizona, thrives on the business generated by Lake Powell and the Navajo Generating Station, so members of Page's Chamber of Commerce consider the reservoir the lifeblood of their town and have come out to support the Friends of Lake Powell. "Let's stop futile environmentalists from destroying our beautiful Lake," reads one sign. "Save Lake Powell" read others.

Touting the benefits of the altered ecosystem in the river corridor, the Friends of Lake Powell question the scientific facts about the dam broadcast by Glen Canyon Institute and other dam detractors. Friends of Lake Powell point to the benefits of the cold clear water as opposed to those of the silt-laden natural river. They point to the loss of business and jobs the community would suffer without Lake Powell.

Glen Canyon Institute is not a supporter of the March 14 dam removal rally; its members consider themselves information activists rather than agitators and have taken pains to separate themselves from the activist Glen Canyon Action Network. "Our approach doesn't always sit well with activists," says Dr. Ingebretsen. "To stand up in front of a bunch of protesters and say, 'Let's study draining Lake Powell,' that doesn't always go over well. But we welcome them to the fray. I welcome the activists. We also have more conservative people saying we should be looking at this."

At the "Drain It" rally on the Utah side of the dam, I talk to a resident of Page who is there with his wife and two children. "It's interesting to watch the process and there are powerful arguments on both sides," he says. "It will be interesting to see if we can live within our means. That would be a big wake-up call to California. It's a cool place the way it is and it would be a cool place without the dam. I've lived in Page for fifteen years but I'm from California so everybody thinks I'm a radical," he adds, smiling. Referring to the eventual demise of Glen Canyon Dam, he says, "It will take years to happen but it's inevitable that it will happen in someone's lifetime. We came to watch, not necessarily to express an opinion."

I walk downstream a few hundred yards to get a fuller view of the immense wall of the dam. There I find Robert Hass, a former U.S. Poet Laureate, peering over the edge. He has been doing some work with International Rivers Network and explains that the organization's goal is the preservation and restoration of biologically living rivers all over the world. One of the things Hass did as Poet Laureate was to invite environmental educators and writers from all over the country to Washington, D.C., to work with local schoolchildren and participate in restoration work on D.C.-area waterways.

"We spent two centuries exploring and a century exploiting this country," says Hass. "The exploiting has been brilliant, heroic and incredibly destructive. And our example has become a model for economic development for the entire world. It's pretty clear that in the next stage of history, that our task is to use our science and our love of the land to restore it. Our task is to undo the mistakes of the twentieth century in the twenty-first. We have to give people a decent possibility of life without destroying the land."

"We're very realistic, but restoring Glen Canyon could be on a time frame that takes generations," says Pam Hyde. "The next step is trying to move into the federal realm and get Congress to authorize an Environmental Impact Statement [EIS]. It will take some time. We've got to get people thinking past protection to restoration—to go the next step in the sequence past protection to restoration. Patience is difficult, but patience is what it's going to take. As a country we're not set up to think about all this."

"We have an interim draft environmental assessment with hardcore data and it's very impressive," Dr. Ingebretsen tells me. "Our next step is to finish the citizens' environmental assessment, take it to the public, then force the U.S. government to do an Environmental Impact Statement, then act on that. There's no question in my mind that an EIS will favor draining. I think we can make this happen. We have time and right on our side.

"That dam is an evil structure. Glen Canyon is an icon. We're starting to set a precedent, and federal dams will have to start coming down," he says with almost surprising vehemence. "We need patience. It may take the next fifteen to twenty years. As for the endangered species, we're hoping adaptive management will keep the species alive. These creatures are protected by law, and if necessary we could force an EIS in order to take care of them. We'll fight for them," he says emphatically.

The Friends of Lake Powell have posted on their website the transcript of a local radio station interview with Secretary Babbitt from July 2000. He assures them that Lake Powell will not be drained. In the interview Babbitt calls Glen Canyon Dam an asset and points out that removing it would require altering the Colorado Compact, which is highly unlikely to happen. A few months later, when I ask him about the future of Glen Canyon Dam, he says, "We've learned a lot about the use of prescribed floods at the Glen Canyon Dam and the possibility of moving water management to better fit with the natural scheme of a river. That's real."

"It's a matter of when, not if," says Ingebretsen. "We have time and sediment on our side. Ultimately the U.S. government will have to perform an Environmental Impact Statement that includes draining the reservoir as one of its alternatives. From an environmental standpoint the native ecosystem is of primary importance. From a western water system point of view, it's that Lake Powell loses more water each year than the entire Nevada water system. The West is not going to come up with more water, so alternatives will have to be found."

Glen Canyon Institute released its latest Citizens' Environmental Assessment on the decommissioning of Glen Canyon Dam in the fall of 2000. Its numbers showed that conditions for the Colorado's native species continue to deteriorate along with the dam's efficiency. It had been a dry year in the West, and drought conditions would persist throughout 2001, so that power generators and irrigators found themselves in fierce competition with fish and wildlife for reduced supplies of water.

David Brower died on November 5, 2000, having inspired two generations of environmental activists to challenge the status quo. A Republican administration that favors business development is now in the White House. While it seems extremely unlikely that Glen Canyon Dam is going anywhere anytime soon, the terms of how we consider such massive ecosystem-altering, water-engineering projects have significantly changed. But perhaps reassessing Glen Canyon Dam will compel us to think clearly about how long places like Phoenix, San Diego and Las Vegas can continue to grow. "By talking about removing Glen Canyon Dam, we've made some other things seem more reasonable," says Jeri Ledbetter of the Glen Canyon Institute.

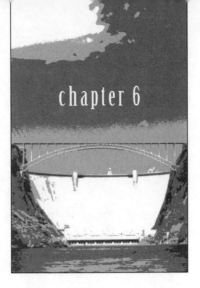

Montana

THE DAM AND THE

SUPERFUND SITE

The Clark Fork and Blackfoot Rivers flow through the forested mountains of western Montana. The slopes are steep, the fir and pine trees tall. The elevation is high enough that there is often new snow in May, then again in August and September, with some snowfields persisting all year-round. The Clark Fork is the largest river in the northern Rockies. It gathers water from the Flathead, Bitterroot, Blackfoot and other tributaries and flows over 300 miles into Idaho and Lake Pend Oreille. The Blackfoot rises on the west side of the Continental Divide near Rogers Pass, where a sign proclaims "Coldest Recorded Temperature." I have driven east along the Blackfoot in a summer dawn so cool the river made long fingers of frosty mist above the sage filled fields. I have traveled along the Clark Fork in the valley of the dense blue Cabinet Mountains, where a pair of towns call themselves Hope and Beyond Hope. Nearby is a town that declares itself the "Huckleberry Capital of Montana." I have camped by a lake full of kokanee salmon and hiked up to a snow-covered ridge on the northern edge of the Missions. From spots on the high slopes you can look out across a seemingly endless succession of peaks and imagine that nothing has changed in two or three hundred years.

These mountain drainages, the snowmelt and trickling streams that form the Clark Fork and Blackfoot Rivers, are the legacy of the immense glacial Lake Missoula. So large was this Ice Age lake that its melting, draining, flooding and carving of valleys and riverbeds shaped not only the rivers in Montana west of the Continental Divide but virtually all the waterways and landforms from the Blackfoot to the Pacific Ocean.[1]

These Montana river valleys were important pathways for the Native people of the region and for the Europeans and Americans who came after. The forests were full of animals to be hunted and trapped and trees to be felled, and the mountainsides were full of ore to be mined. In many ways, this landscape represents the essence of the American West. There are large roadless expanses. Bear and cougar still roam the woods. Herds of deer and elk browse the shrubbery. But the valleys and hills are filling with people.

First settled by European Americans in the 1850s, the city of Missoula now sprawls into the surrounding countryside, the cement of roadside development following the paths the glacial floods once took. The Blackfoot and Clark Fork Rivers bear the burden of what has been taken from these hillsides. Sediment from logging and mining is now joined by runoff from urban, suburban and agricultural development. Evidence of more than a century's worth of extraction can be found in these rivers. Still, up high, the headwater streams run clear over rocks rounded by eons of moving water. Fish jump from shady pools and river otters scamper along the banks.

People come to this country for its beautiful and remote landscape, so it is startling to learn that these picturesque rivers are suffering from the legacy of their upstream mines. At the confluence of the Clark Fork and Blackfoot Rivers sits the Milltown Dam, which holds back a toxic soup of river water and mine waste that has been harming fish and seeping into the adjacent aquifer. Many in the community feel that removing this dam will begin the long needed process of cleaning these wastes from the river. Cleaning toxic waste is a problem for rivers all over the country, and dam removal always involves coping with sediment that has built up behind the dam. The Milltown Dam and Reservoir, however, may present a unique challenge, as the toxins they retain come from what is now the country's largest Superfund site.

"It's a big public issue and not just for the folks in Birkenstocks," says Tracy Stone-Manning, executive director of the Clark Fork Coalition, an environmental group based in Missoula. Yet conservation groups like the Clark Fork Coalition and Trout Unlimited are not the only ones calling for the removal of Milltown Dam. The Missoula County commissioners, the Missoula City County Health Department and the local Rotary Club have all said they think the dam should go.

The 180-acre Milltown Reservoir impounded by the dam on the Clark Fork is the downstream terminus of the heavily polluted 140-mile stretch of the Clark Fork that runs between Butte and Missoula. For nearly a century, toxic waste from the Butte and Anaconda mines has flowed into the reservoir. In 1983, the Environmental Protection Agency declared the reservoir itself a Superfund site. Under the reservoir's still waters now lie over 6.5 million cubic yards of contaminated sediment. In some places the sediments containing arsenic, cadmium, copper, iron, manganese and zinc measure thirty feet deep. Current estimates say the sediment holds some 2,000 tons of arsenic, 13,000 tons of copper, nearly 15,000 tons of iron, over 9,000 tons of manganese and 19,000 tons of zinc. Classified by the EPA as persistent toxic metals, all of these substances are known to have seriously adverse affects on human and aquatic health. There is now so much sediment in the reservoir that it is nearly full.

The dam holding back this immense volume of toxic sludge is ninety-five years old. Milltown Dam is a timber structure filled with rocks and coated with three feet of concrete. It stands twenty-eight feet above the river and is about 600 feet wide. When the rivers run high, it is in danger of flooding, and cracks have been found in the dam's foundation. The reservoir is also what's called a "losing system," meaning that arsenic, copper and manganese are continually lost into groundwater. There are modest houses not far from the reservoir. It is no longer safe for the people who live in these homes to drink water from their own wells.

Milltown Dam and Reservoir sit sheltered in the cleft of hillside where two valleys intersect, near the towns of Bonner and Milltown. Anyone traveling east from Missoula along the interstate toward Anaconda and Butte along the Clark Fork—or northeast along the Blackfoot toward the Continental Divide—will pass this point. Unless you have stopped to look at the hillsides outside of Butte that seem to have whole chunks missing—as if some huge creature had taken enormous bites of the mountain—or peered at the unnaturally blue-green waters of the tailings ponds, you would remain visually innocent of what lurks at the bottom of the rivers.

Railroad tracks follow these rivers. Along the Blackfoot, the tracks stop at its confluence with the Clearwater, but the rails follow the Clark Fork to Butte and beyond. In the second half of the nineteenth century, with the railway easement, the federal government granted railroad companies a sixty-acre-wide swath of land around the tracks. This land was parceled out in square mile sections, alternating with federally held land to create what is now referred to as "the checkerboard." A great deal of this land has been logged, much of it entirely clearcut. Today if you go into these hills, climb high and look down, what you see is a disheartening patchwork of forest and bare slope. How to deal with the remains of that exploitation, and Montana's ongoing debate over whether to allow timber cutting, mining and oil extraction at the expense of wildlife, is very much part of that history, whose legacy will influence the future of Milltown Dam.

To supply lumber to the copper mines at Butte in the 1870s, trees around the railroad lands were cut and milled at Bonner. In the 1880s, Bonner boasted what was reputed to be the world's largest lumber mill. So many trees were cut and floated down the river to the mills that stretches of the Blackfoot and Clark Fork often became choked with logs. The Milltown Dam was built in 1906 by copper-mining magnate William Clark, who later became a U.S. senator, to power sawmills in Bonner, Milltown and Missoula. Electricity from the dam later powered a local trolley, and still later was fed into the general power grid.

Late in the afternoon, on a blustery day in early May 2000, I walk on a ridge high above the dam and reservoir with Tracy Stone-Manning. Snow squalls whip through the blowing clouds as we make our way along a muddy, brushy path. From this vantage point, the confluence of the two rivers is clearly visible, as is the low, wide dam that blocks their free flow and retains the reservoir. The light is fading to blue, the trees are mostly bare. The reservoir looks almost like an innocent mountain lake. The Clark Fork Coalition is working hard to help find a solution to the contaminated sediment at the bottom of Milltown Reservoir. But the sediments are only part of the problem. The dam itself poses its own threats to the river. One solution would be to remove the sediments and then the dam. How and if this can be done is an enormous challenge, technically, legally and politically.

According to the regulations of the Federal Energy Regulatory Commission, which oversees hydropower dams like Milltown, dam owners must announce their intention to apply for a license renewal five years before the current one expires. When Milltown's deadline came in December 1999, its owners, the Montana Power Company, asked for a two-year extension. It was the company's third request as its original license was set to expire in 1993. Montana Power hoped, before announcing its ultimate intentions, to divest itself of the dam or discover the extent of its responsibility for reservoir cleanup. A curious wrinkle of Superfund law written specifically to accommodate Montana Power and Milltown Dam absolves Montana Power of liability regarding reservoir cleanup. If the dam is not licensed or in operation, some argue, Montana Power could become responsible for the cleanup —hence a strong incentive to keep the dam running.

Milltown Dam is far from infallible. In 1908, a major flood on the Clark Fork washed quantities of contaminated mine waste into the reservoir. Some flowed over the top of the dam and waste has been piling up in the reservoir ever since. In February 1996, a potential disaster loomed, when a ten-mile-long, ten-foot-high ice jam on the Blackfoot River began to move downstream toward the dam. Hoping to slow or stop the ice floe, dam operators quickly lowered the water level in Milltown Reservoir. Collision was avoided, but the rapid downstream release of reservoir water scoured out huge amounts of contaminated sediment and an enormous load of toxics. Metal concentrations in the surrounding surface water skyrocketed. Yet when the ice subsided, the community could only breathe a partial sigh of relief.

After the ice jam, Montana Department of Fish, Wildlife and Parks biologists found that the juvenile rainbow trout population had decreased by 71 percent from previous years' populations, juvenile brown trout by 86 percent, full-size rainbow trout by 62 percent and full-size brown trout by 56 percent. Fish that survived were much smaller than normal. The water contained levels of toxic chemicals so high that they were in extreme violation of state standards. Some metal concentrations were found to be as high as forty-two times what is allowed by law.

While the dam held, the accumulating toxics have been steadily seeping into adjacent groundwater. Huge volumes of arsenic-contaminated groundwater flow continually into the aquifer that supplies water to the community of Milltown. In fact, residential wells in Bonner and Milltown that use this groundwater were found to be contaminated with arsenic back in 1981. According to current estimates, nineteen tons of arsenic are discharged annually into the Bonner-Milltown aquifer along with quantities of iron and manganese. The resulting underground arsenic plume now extends about 110 acres. "Without effective removal of the source of the discharge, this huge volume of contaminated water will persist at least for hundreds of years," says Peter Nielsen, the environmental health supervisor with the Missoula City County Health Department. "If the source is removed, it will be gone in several years."

People who use this aquifer have now been supplied with alternative sources of water, but many in the community say this is not an adequate or long-term solution. "No one is drinking contaminated drinking water at this point," says Nielsen. "But under Superfund law," he explains, "if we can keep people away from the contamination rather than clean it up, that's what's done."

The problems with the reservoir don't stop there. In the winter, when its banks are filled with rain and snow, the river runs high. Chunks of ice floating the swollen river regularly push toxic sediments downstream. The flush of toxics seriously degrades water quality, often harming and killing fish.

Adding to the difficulties at Milltown Dam is the absence of fish passage. Consequently, the dam blocks migration of bull trout, which are listed as a threatened species under the Endangered Species Act, and of the Clark Fork's rainbow trout and westslope cutthroat trout, the latter being a candidate for listing under the ESA. "Over the course of a year, the migrations of tens of thousands of fish are interrupted by Milltown Dam," Dave Schmetterling, a Montana state fisheries biologist, told the *Missoulian* newspaper. "Basically everything that's in the river wants to get past the dam. Fish still respond to the river as though it were a connected system. After nearly 100 years, they're still trying to get upstream." Every year the U.S. Fish and Wildlife Service traps and hauls some of these fish around the dam, but with the other problems the dam causes, that's far from an adequate solution.

The reservoir's warm water lakelike environment allows introduced pike, which prey on the native fish, to thrive. The Montana Department of Fish, Wildlife and Parks has recently found pike with bull trout in their bellies, definitive evidence that the Milltown Dam is harming a species listed under the ESA. "The pike problem at the dam certainly presents a taking of some sort," says Keith Large of the Montana Department of Environmental Quality. (In the language of the ESA, a "taking" means an action that harms a listed species.) "They're pretty much eating everything in the reservoir." Peter Nielsen describes pike as being a lot like knapweed—one of Montanans' least favorite invasive plant species—with fins and teeth. "With some forty thousand fish banging their noses against the dam, that's easy pickings for the pike," says Geoff Smith, who spent six years working as staff scientist for the Clark Fork Coalition. Bull trout is serious business here. The story of the trout-eating pike makes the local news.

Since the mid-1980s, if a dam is to be relicensed, its owners must prove to the Federal Energy Regulatory Commission that its adverse environmental impacts do not exceed the benefits of the dam's hydropower generation. Vulnerable to flooding and with a reservoir full of toxics, Milltown Dam relicensing seemed ripe for a challenge. So when the time came for renewal, the Missoula City and County Health Boards, Missoula County, the City of Missoula, Trout Unlimited and the Clark Fork Coalition, among others, became formal intervenors in the process, compelling FERC to consider their concerns.

Extending the period before license renewal would give the dam's owners additional time to make any repairs needed to bring Milltown Dam up to current safety and environmental standards. Given the dam's extensive problems, it seemed unlikely that this work could be done before the original permit expired. Milltown's opponents expected that the cost of these repairs would almost certainly outweigh the benefits of the dam, so if FERC denied the license renewal, the decommissioning process would have to begin.

Any consideration of decommission would entail determining how to clean the reservoir's toxic sediments and the debate over who would pay for what. In the fall of 1999, the Environmental Protection Agency—which oversees the federal Superfund program—indicated that it favored dam removal but had not yet released its cleanup plan. Under the existing Superfund plan, the Atlantic Richfield Company (often called ARCO), which now owns the defunct Butte and Anaconda mines, is responsible for cleanup of Milltown Reservoir. However, any strategy for dealing with the toxic sediments has to be coordinated with the fate of the dam, and ARCO has said it wants the dam to stay. Yet the Environmental Protection Agency, U.S. Fish and Wildlife Service and Army Corps of Engineers, among other federal agencies, and the public must review ARCO's cleanup plan, so ARCO's word is not necessarily the last one.

Until October 2000, Milltown Dam was owned by the Montana Power Company. In a transition emblematic of the changing West, Montana Power is in the process of getting out of energy production and into the telecommunications business. In its evolution into an information-age company, Montana Power sought to divest itself of its hydroelectric plants. The Milltown Dam proved to be a nasty white elephant. The small, two-megawatt facility had become a liability. The dam's operating and maintenance costs—

even with less than a handful of employees—now exceed what it earns by generating hydropower. For safety reasons and because of the contaminated sediments, in the summer of 1999, the Federal Energy Regulatory Commission raised the dam's "hazard rating" to "high." That fall, when Montana Power tried to give the dam to the state of Montana, its offer was declined. But the following year the South Dakota–based NorthWestern Corporation agreed to buy the dam along with Montana Power's energy and transmission lines. Over a year later, the sale is still pending.

Like many of the communities I visited where dam removal is under consideration, what happens to Milltown Dam is very much a backyard issue. Perhaps even more so, given the hazards posed by the reservoir's toxic sediments and the fact that they've already invaded the lives of some who live nearby. If your home's well has been contaminated with arsenic, chances are good that you'll show up at a meeting when the source of that poison is being discussed.

On the day I visit the dam, a regional representative of the Environmental Protection Agency is due to present the latest report on the risks posed by the toxic sediments in the Milltown Reservoir at an evening meeting in the Bonner School Library. To get some background before the meeting, a small group convened by the Clark Fork Coalition gathers in the River City Grill. Bob Benson, who often paddles the river, says he's come so "Each time I go upside down in the Clark Fork, I know what I'm breathing." Jean Curtiss, then a candidate for Missoula county commissioner, expresses her concern about groundwater contamination. "If I win the election, it's something my constituents would want me to be informed about," she says.

Geoff Smith of the Clark Fork Coalition explains that the Environmental Protection Agency has outlined seven possible alternatives for proceeding with the reservoir cleanup. Most of the alternatives depend on keeping Milltown Dam in place; others present variations on removing both the sediment and the dam. Doing nothing is another option. It could be argued, says Smith, that leaving the dam in place would help manage the sediment, but in his view, to adequately rid the river of the long-term threat these toxics pose, the reservoir would have to be eliminated. In addition to the problems posed by toxic sediments and their seepage into groundwater, there is the issue of surface-water contamination. "I've always felt that surface-water issues didn't really get a fair shake in the original cleanup plan," says Smith of the 1996 Superfund cleanup plan for the site. Until something is done to clean up what's already in the river, he explains, the contaminated sediments in the reservoir will continually spill into the river and be replaced with still more. And as the reservoir fills with sediment, the volume of water falls, decreasing the power-generating capacity of the dam.

The upper walls of Bonner School Library are decorated with a mural depicting the life cycle of a logging operation, from standing tree to house frame. The room is filled with people of all ages. Words like "focused feasibility study," "total recoverables versus total dissolved," "acute, short-term lethal" and "chronic long-term" are uttered as Russ Forba, EPA's Region 8 representative from Helena, projects a series of charts and outlines onto a screen at the front of the room. There is some shuffling and squinting. At one point an older man wearing a plaid flannel shirt and red suspenders says, "Are we supposed to be able to read that? You're standing right in the way!"

The study presented seems to focus on the catastrophic scouring of sediment during the 1996 ice jam flood, when the levels of toxics in the river skyrocketed. The implication is that acute risks of contamination occur only at times of unusually high river flows. The typical flow, the study concludes, does not represent a significant increased risk of contamination. "I feel there's a little more risk than what's stated in the risk assessment. I think you need to question the data and where they drew the line," comments a Montana Department of Environmental Quality staff member. "The bottom line are the words used to describe the risk—low to moderate and rare event—but it's not low or moderate or a rare event," says Peter Nielsen, of the Missoula City County Health Department, questioning the study's standards.

"Is the sediment going to stay or is it going to go? I think this is the way most folks look at it," says Forba. He explains that this risk assessment was not designed to look at the arsenic plume or specific issues relating to fish. "Why doesn't the risk assessment look at adding to the arsenic plume in the groundwater?" comes a question from the floor, voicing a general frustration. "If you say it's safe to leave sediments in place that are putting arsenic in our groundwater but that if you removed them, you'd have to put sediments in a sanitary landfill," says someone else. "How many times do you have to find 'new data' before you realize we have a serious situation with poison in our groundwater? I don't think anyone is going to change their mind about the fact that we have poison in our water and it needs to be removed," says another community member.

Then the question is raised as to how—or if—the sediment should be removed. If it was removed, where would it go? "Why not run them along the interstate," somebody jokes. "There's enough to raise the interstate by fifteen feet for ten miles." It's then that people begin to realize that discussing sediment removal means talking reservoir and dam removal. At this point a Montana Power Company representative cautions that "surrender of the FERC license does not equate with dam removal. It's very rare that FERC says 'Remove that dam.'" Yet in the cases of the Edwards Dam on the Kennebec and dams on the Elwha River on the Olympic Peninsula in Washington state, it has.

An older woman then rises to her feet and says, "We've always seen the reservoir as an asset to our community. We don't want to see it destroyed." She points out that some people think the arsenic plume is stable. A man who has been monitoring it closely says this is not the case. Another woman shakes her head at the possible prospect of seeing the reservoir and dam go and says it would be a shame to lose the river and see all the water disappear.

A middle-aged man stands and begins to speak with obvious emotion. "I live in this community, too," he says, "and I'd miss the reservoir, too. But I'd feel a thousand times worse if we missed this opportunity to clean this up. It's really pretty, especially in the fall when the leaves are reflected. But it's an emperor's new clothes. What we see isn't really what it is: a toxic waste site. It would be disrespectful of the future not to clean it up. We owe it to ourselves and owe it to the future."

In June 2000, despite hundreds of public comments to the contrary, and the fact that Milltown Reservoir pike are eating endangered native bull trout, the Federal Energy Regulatory

Commission granted the Montana Power Company a third extension on its hydropower license for Milltown Dam. The extension moves the expiration date on the current license—which had originally been due to expire in 1993—from 2004 to 2006. Following that decision, the Clark Fork Coalition and Trout Unlimited filed for a new hearing to examine FERC's ruling on the extension. The conservation groups also filed a sixty-day notice of intent to sue FERC for failure to comply with the Endangered Species Act in allowing the dam to harm endangered bull trout. The request for a new license hearing was denied, but FERC asked the dam owners to conduct a study of the dam's effect on the bull trout.

In late November 2000, ARCO released its assessment of how to deal with the toxic sediments in Milltown Reservoir. Its preferred solution would be to leave the sediments in place but retrofit the dam with a rubber crest. ARCO's Montana manager, Sandy Stash, told the press that the company concluded sediment removal of any kind was too risky. "How the heck could you do something that invasive in a river without having impacts downstream?" Stash said to the *Missoulian*. ARCO's report will be presented for public comments; those comments will be taken into consideration when the Environmental Protection Agency writes its cleanup plan. The U.S. Fish and Wildlife Service and Army Corps of Engineers have already criticized ARCO's cleanup analysis, as have the Montana Department of Fish, Wildlife and Parks and the U.S. Geological Survey. "This is it," says Tracy Stone-Manning of the Clark Fork Coalition in response to ARCO's November 2000 cleanup recommendation. "We are going for it," she says, clearly energized by the work ahead. "We are going to take out billboards, TV ads, newspaper ads, everything."

While they know their task may seem Sisyphean, Stone-Manning and her colleagues at the coalition try to imagine what the river would look like without the dam and reservoir. Part of keeping people engaged in what will be a long task, Stone-Manning explains, is showing them what they're working toward. Helping people create a picture of the restored river, she says, is key. From atop the windy bluff above the dam, we hold our fingers up and squint to block the brick powerhouse from view and attempt to visualize a river channel with riffles and rapids. A few months later I receive a T-shirt with an artist's rendering of Milltown after the dam. "Clean Water, No Dam—A Future for Milltown," it reads.

In a policy announcement coming shortly after the 2000 election, Montana's new governor, Republican Judy Martz, says she will encourage the state to make its environmental regulations more favorable to business. Meanwhile, under the new administration of George W. Bush, FERC is hoping to streamline its process for relicensing dams, a move that environmentalists fear could cut the public—who most often brings environmental concerns into consideration—out of the process. How this will affect Milltown Dam remains to be seen. But the Clark Fork Coalition and the community are not giving up on the cleanup yet, and in January 2001, a coalition of Montana conservation groups went to court to challenge the adequacy of the federal government's protection of bull trout.

"It's exciting to see the community say, 'This can happen,'" says Stone-Manning.

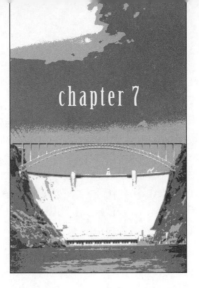

chapter 7

California

"REPLUMBING THE PLUMBING"

On a warm October morning in 2000, in a small pool formed by stream bank boulders along Clear Creek, a few miles southwest of Redding, California, three fall-run chinook salmon flick their tails and wriggle. Water and scales glitter in the hot autumn sun. A sizable crowd peers over the rock ledge to see these fish. People wearing hard hats and orange safety vests, carrying clipboards, notebooks, cell phones, tape recorders and cameras. Many of the safety vests bear the logo of the U.S. Department of the Interior's Bureau of Reclamation, with the words "Dam Busters Tour" around the logo. The salmon are waiting to make their way up the twelve miles of Clear Creek that will soon be reopened to them once Saeltzer Dam is fully removed.

Pieces of large earthmoving machinery are scattered around the site. Rows of folding chairs and wire-bound bales of hay have been brought in to provide seating for the event. Culverts have been laid in place to create a cofferdam through which the creek can temporarily flow as the dam is removed. Water is already rushing downstream, and the salmon swim below a small rush of rapid.

"Make no mistake about it," says Secretary of the Interior Bruce Babbitt to the group gathered to watch him and California Secretary of Resources Mary Nichols take a ceremonial swipe of the backhoe at the soon to be demolished dam. "We are writing water management and conservation history today. We're writing a new chapter in California and American conservation history."

It's probably no exaggeration to say that more than in any other single state, the history of California has been determined by the manipulation of water. In determined ignorance of the natural inclination of their watersheds, California's rivers have been shunted across basins, piped into cavernous culverts and channeled into cement canals. Their groundwater has been pumped and their floodplains and wetlands drained, bermed and diked. Almost every river in the state has been dammed, and approximately 90 percent of the state's waterway miles are diverted in one way or another. The resulting map of California's water projects reminds me of a map of the New York City subway system. "California's very existence is premised on epic liberties taken with water,"[1] wrote Marc Reisner in *Cadillac Desert*, his classic history of water in the American West.

This extensive engineering has facilitated California's economic and population growth, but at great environmental costs that are only now beginning to be fully recognized. Altering the flow of California's rivers has taken a particularly heavy toll on native anadromous fish. Since the 1950s, about 85 percent of California's salmon and steelhead have disappeared. Roughly 95 percent of the spawning habitat for the state's spring-run salmon is gone. Some 90 percent of salmon and steelhead in the Central Valley are now blocked from reaching their natural, historic habitat. Large populations of chinook salmon once thrived in California's Sacramento and San Joaquin Rivers. Most of these runs are now extinct, and others are listed under the Endangered Species Act. Similarly, most of California's chum, pink and sockeye salmon are gone.

Coho, once found throughout northern California, are now extinct in much of that range, and their remaining runs are very small. Dams, water diversion and other development have damaged habitat for the inland runs of California's steelhead, and many of those are now also gone. Of those that remain closer to the coast, many are considered at risk of extinction or of special concern.

In an attempt to repair some of this damage, a number of dams in California are beginning to be rethought. In 1998, four small dams on Butte Creek, an eastern tributary of the Sacramento, were demolished to restore a threatened run of chinook salmon. Other dam removals are planned or are under way on Battle, Clear and Deer Creeks, all tributaries of the Sacramento. Yet because California's economy is so closely tied to the delivery of water, any dam removals in the state remain strongly tied to regional water politics. Even finding out which dams could go is proving difficult. A bill to fund an assessment of the state's dams recently failed to make it through the state legislature. Its supporters have said they will bring it back. It is painfully clear that California's growing consumption of water will increasingly compete with needs of native fish and river restoration.

"We are coming to grips with the past," says Mary Nichols in her remarks at Saeltzer Dam. Removing this dam "shows a lot of changes in the way we do business in California. Without repudiating our past we can learn from it. . . . What we've learned in recent years is that many dams have outlived their usefulness." Saeltzer Dam, Nichols tells me later, is at "the beginning of a long list of outdated dams, of nonfunctioning dams we can remove without sacrificing water supply and flood control."

To acquaint myself with the watershed of which Clear Creek forms a small part, I head south from the Oregon border into California around the base of Mt. Shasta, a 4,300-foot snow-covered peak at the southern end of the Cascade Mountains. There, the ponderosa pine and Douglas fir of the Cascades and Siskiyous give way to long-needled gray pine, oak, manzanita, chinquapin and madrone. The soil turns redder as the elevation and latitude drop toward the huge reservoir created by Shasta Dam. A pivotal point of the state's river redirection, the reservoir collects the Pit River, along with water from the McCloud and Sacramento Rivers, and sends it south with water from the Trinity and Feather Rivers toward the Central Valley, Los Angeles and San Francisco.

Shasta Dam was built between 1938 and 1945, during the heyday of America's large dam construction. A huge concrete dam that arches across the river, rising to over 600 feet high and almost 3,500 feet wide, Shasta Dam was designed to store water for irrigation of the Sacramento and San Joaquin Valleys and to generate hydroelectric power. These days, however, dam operation is modified to allow enough cool water through the system to protect the downstream rivers' threatened chinook salmon.

Slightly further south is the Whiskeytown Dam, located at the very southern end of the Klamath Mountain foothills. It was built between 1960 and 1963 to divert water from the Trinity River—a major tributary of the Klamath—into the Sacramento to irrigate the Central Valley. Clear Creek is the main southern outlet of the Whiskeytown Reservoir.

South of Mt. Shasta and the slopes of the Cascades, the Klamath, Siskiyou and Marble Mountains and the Sierra Nevadas, where the headwaters of California's major rivers rise, give way to irrigated crop fields. Mile after mile of vegetable crops, orchards and vineyards stretch to the horizon, bordered by irrigation ditches. Water spray from countless spigots splits into sparkling prisms. Where the ground is unwatered, its pale brown matches the aqueduct's cement. About 80 percent of the water used in California goes to agriculture, primarily in the Central and San Joaquin Valleys, which is now the world's most productive farming region.

Directing any of this water back into California's rivers is a radical idea, but the predicament of the state's anadromous fish is compelling this to happen. In 1994, the state of California and the federal government announced a jointly sponsored, multibillion-dollar plan known as CalFed to restore the Sacramento–San Joaquin Delta. The plan aims to guarantee water to farmers and the cities of central and southern California, while at the same time restoring upstream habitat and the badly degraded river delta. Removal of some of California's estimated 1,400 dams is an important part of that restoration. "There are so many [dams] that it's a matter of setting priorities and getting the financial resources assembled," says Mary Nichols. "Each dam is unique and presents specific challenges to the communities affected." The Saeltzer Dam removal is a CalFed restoration project, as are the decommissioning of five diversion dams on Battle Creek and removal of the Butte Creek dams.

For over ninety years, the privately owned, sixteen-foot-high, concrete Saeltzer Dam diverted water into the Townsend Flat Ditch to irrigate three ranches and about 400 acres of pastureland. The aging dam was beginning to crack. In the words of the Bureau of Reclamation's project assessment, the dam posed "a dangerous attractive nuisance" to those who used the downstream gorge and pool below the dam for recreation. Instead of using Clear Creek, this property will be irrigated by water from the Sacramento and the Central Valley Project—perhaps an ultimately imperfect solution, but one that will jump-start recovery of a local salmon run.

"It's an obvious choice," Secretary Babbitt tells me the morning of the Saeltzer "dam busting," between "several hundred acres of irrigated pasture versus several thousand spawning salmon . . . a kind of a no-brainer."

Saeltzer Dam blocked Clear Creek's chinook and steelhead populations, which have plummeted in recent years so that all are proposed for listing under the Endangered Species Act. Clear Creek also provides habitat for a number of animals whose numbers have dwindled to a point unhealthy for their survival, among them the white-faced ibis, western burrowing owl, western spadefoot toad, green sturgeon, California red-legged frog, San Joaquin pocket mouse and northwestern pond turtle. Bald eagles, peregrine falcons and Aleutian Canada geese, listed under the Endangered Species Act, use the creek valley. Although their numbers are low, Clear Creek probably still has some of all the wildlife species it used to, so prospects for restoration are encouraging, a California Department of Fish and Game official tells me.

The Clear Creek area was originally settled by Wintu Indians, who hunted in the wooded valleys and hillsides around the Sacramento and fished for steelhead and salmon. Following Jedediah Smith and Peter Ogden's explorations of the Sacramento Valley in the mid-1820s, European settlers and fur trappers began coming to the region. They brought with them diseases that took a disastrous toll on the Native people throughout California's Central and surrounding river valleys.

The discovery of gold in Clear Creek in 1848, about a mile and half upstream from the site of Saeltzer Dam, triggered a great influx of settlers, and by the 1870s, a community was established near Clear Creek. Rudolph Saeltzer and James McCormick, local businessmen who ran a department store, owned land along the creek. There the McCormick-Saeltzer Company began the Redding Land Ditch and Cattle Company, formed the Townsend Flat Water Ditch Company and, in 1902 and 1903, built the McCormick-Saeltzer Dam to divert water for several hundred acres of orchards, alfalfa fields and pasture for local cattle ranches.

During the California Gold Rush of 1848, whole hillsides along the Sacramento River and its tributaries were eroded, sending huge amounts of sediment into the creeks, burying salmon spawning beds and the aquatic insects on which the fish feed. So much soil washed into the streams from the mining that, "by 1884, the bed of the Sacramento River had risen twenty feet at its confluence with the Feather River . . . and was one of the primary causes for the decline of salmon in the Sacramento River,"[2] writes fisheries biologist Jim Lichatowich.

In the early 1900s, gold mining began again in and around Clear Creek and, after World War II, was replaced by gravel mining. Sand and gravel destined for highway and construction projects were dredged from the mine tailings as well as from Clear Creek's channel and floodplain. There's now a working cement and gravel operation not far downstream from the dam site, and the cumulative effect of all this mining and dredging has left what several people tell me is a devastated landscape. "A moonscape," says Steve Evans, conservation director of the California nonprofit group Friends of the River. But below the dam, he says, is a "rugged little gem of a canyon gorge." To restore the natural creek bed, some 25,000 cubic yards of sediment will be removed and the floodplain replanted with willows and cottonwoods.

Since the 1940s, it's been known that Saeltzer Dam blocked upstream spawning habitat for salmon and steelhead. Despite the California law requiring dams to have functioning fish ladders, Saeltzer Dam had none. Removing the dam opens ten to twelve miles of salmon and steelhead habitat, but migrating fish will still be blocked further upstream by Whiskeytown Dam, which also has no fish passage. Removing Saeltzer Dam will also enable more water to be released from Whiskeytown Reservoir into Clear Creek. Increasing the cold-water flows into Clear Creek out of Whiskeytown is a crucial part of this restoration.

"As long as we take away the obstacles that have damaged it rather than simply trying to mitigate, nature has a way of repairing itself," says Steve Evans with cautious optimism about the project.

Buford Holt, an environmental specialist with the Bureau of Reclamation in Redding, has a different perspective but comes to a similar conclusion. "A hundred years ago," says Holt, "we drained swamps and wetlands. We flooded deserts. We kept on doing it past when society wanted it. Now we have a turnaround and it's time to stop flooding deserts and draining marshlands. The same can-do mentality that accomplished those projects makes [the Bureau of] Reclamation the vehicle for getting restoration done more than any other agency."

"It took a long time to plan the removal of Saeltzer Dam, but deconstruction moved quickly once it started," says Mary Nichols. To plan and implement the removal, federal and state agencies worked with the Centerville Community Services Project, the Townsend Water Ditch Company and the McConnell Foundation, a local organization that owns 85 percent of the property served by the dam's water diversion. One of the things that facilitated removal was the fact that the McConnell Foundation, which was a willing participant in the process, was the sole owner of the dam, associated property and water rights. That the Secretary of the Interior would turn out to herald the removal of a small, privately owned dam that provided no drinking water or hydropower and irrigated only a small acreage points to the complexity of such projects.

"I was thinking about how to wax poetic about what's going on here today," says Secretary Babbitt, looking out over the deconstruction site toward Clear Creek. "If you make your way carefully down to the rock ledge and look into this torrent of water, . . . you'll see three large fall-run chinook salmon in their spawning dress, turning scarlet . . . urgently waiting for us to complete this project. . . . In a miracle of God's creation, these salmon spend two to three years in the ocean. They've made their way back through the bay and delta, made their way past the water withdrawal and pumping systems to find the Sacramento River and make their way to the place where they began."

On the way back to Redding, we pass the gravel quarry and cement plant. Adjacent to the quarry is an oblong gravel-ringed pond that has been used by a water-skiing school. Because this pond will lose its water when Saeltzer Dam is gone, the school's proprietor was one of the few who objected to the dam removal. As we drive by, Secretary Babbitt turns and says to me half-jokingly, "Are you taking notes? Now that's going to be a real loss."

Before the diversion of the tributary creeks of the Sacramento for irrigation, before overfishing in the late nineteenth and twentieth centuries, the vigorous nineteenth-century canning industry, erosion from stream-bank development of many kinds and periods of drought, the Sacramento is estimated to have produced some 700,000 spawning salmon each year. The first salmon cannery on the Sacramento River was established in 1864, and the canning reached its peak here in 1882, when about twenty canneries packed some ten million one-pound cans of salmon. But less than forty years later, in 1919, the last Sacramento River cannery closed, after packing merely 150,000 pounds of fish.[3] The numbers of fish then plummeted so severely that Sacramento River winter chinook were the first salmon to be listed under the Endangered Species Act, being declared threatened in 1989 and endangered in 1994.[4]

Ironically, it was salmon from the Sacramento River that were used to start the nation's salmon hatchery program, which many fisheries biologists now believe has contributed to the demise of native wild fish. The hatchery program was initially designed for the Northeast, where, by the 1870s, native fish runs were already in serious decline. Hesitant to fund a program that would not benefit the whole country, Congress asked the U.S. Fish Commissioner to see how the program could be used to augment fish runs in other regions as well. Because it flowed through a region with high summer temperatures, the Sacramento was chosen to be the source of salmon eggs to supplement runs in southern and mid-Atlantic rivers. Thus in 1872, against the better judgment of prominent scientists, the first western hatchery in the United States was established on the McCloud River, a northern tributary of the Sacramento. It is estimated that in the next eleven years, the hatchery took about 30 million eggs from the river's salmon. The politics of salmon hatcheries continues to be controversial, and it is clear that elimination and degradation of habitat combined with years of overfishing have done more damage than artificial propagation could ever make up for.

Now a concerted effort is being made to return salmon to these same waters. As part of this restoration, four diversion dams on Butte Creek have been removed, where in 1987, only fourteen spawning spring-run chinook salmon were found.[5] If these fish had been listed under the Endangered Species Act, it would have meant curtailing downstream water withdrawals. The threat of listing provided an incentive to replace the dams—and a dozen other water diversions that trapped fish—with pumps and pipes that would allow irrigation without blocking fish migration. Wielding his ceremonial sledgehammer at a Butte Creek dam removal in 1998, Secretary Babbitt declared its demise "one small blow for salmon." So far the project has been a success, with 20,000 adult chinook returning in the spring of 1999. But further upstream the Centerville Head Dam continues to block salmon from the full range of their habitat, and Friends of the River and other conservation groups are pushing to have that dam reconsidered as well. "We've only done the bottom half of the watershed," says William Kier, a fisheries consultant who has worked on California fish and water issues since the 1960s, when he headed the California Department of Fish and Game's environmental review staff. "We haven't done the job yet."[6]

Yet in November 1999, the Pacific Gas and Electric Company and the CalFed restoration program agreed to remove five diversion dams from Battle Creek, another northern tributary of the Sacramento, enabling imperiled chinook salmon and steelhead to reach the headwaters of their spawning habitat for the first time in a century. Kier describes Battle Creek as a salmon refuge,[7] one of the only places left for California's most vulnerable fish species to find habitat reliably sheltered from drought. Here, even in mid-summer, cool water comes off of Mt. Lassen and Mt. Shasta, creating ideal conditions for salmon. Many such streams from the southern Cascade Mountains were blocked by Shasta Dam and by dams built for mining a century ago. Kier calls the Battle Creek restoration "the crown jewel of the CalFed program."

Anadromous fish have fared even less well in southern California than they have in the north. When Ed Henke was growing up in Ventura in the 1930s, steelhead were still plentiful in the Ventura River. Each year, large runs of steelhead migrated up the river and into Matilija Creek, which flows out of the San Ynez Mountains not far from the ocean. But in the late 1940s, these steelhead were blocked from reaching vital spawning grounds when the Matilija Dam was built across the creek near the cities of Ojai and Ventura. Because of dams like this and other development, which degraded and eliminated their habitat, steelhead have declined over 90 percent throughout California since the 1950s. In southern California, their numbers are down 99 percent since the early 1900s.

Henke has spent years documenting the effect of the Matilija Dam on the river's steelhead and turned his passion for those fish into something of a crusade. He describes himself as a "longtime advocate for our self-perpetuating native-indigenous cold-water aquatic resources." Henke's goal is to return steelhead to the river by removing the Matilija Dam. In 1998 Henke released a history and analysis of the dam's impact on the river's ecosystem that helped lay the groundwork for what has become a nationally supported endeavor. "When I started I was kind of a lone ranger in this," says Henke. Matilija Dam is now high on the list of dams that local conservation groups like California Trout, Friends of the River and American Rivers would like to see removed. It also made it onto the Clinton administration's agenda of dams to be busted.

Steelhead are big, beautiful fish. Watching them in their spawning dance is mesmerizing. On a damp early spring morning in 1996, I accompanied a crew of volunteers to count spawning steelhead on a river near the northern Oregon coast. We walked the stream banks above the river, training our eyes to spot the gravelly redds where the fish lay their eggs. After several hours, from a high spot above a bend in the river we saw flashes of silver and pink. Several large fish shimmied and looped. These fish have great presence, and it's easy to understand how one could become devoted to their preservation.

The Matilija Dam was built by Ventura County to control downstream flooding and provide a water reservoir for the Ojai Valley. Constructed to retain over 7,000 acre-feet of water, the dam is now so silted that it holds less than 500 acre-feet of water, Henke explains. It traps sand that should flow downstream to naturally replenish the coastal beaches. It is estimated that the dam now impounds enough sand and sediment to extend all of Ventura County's beaches by thirty feet. The 198-foot-high dam was completed in 1948 without effective fish passage, and it has blocked access to upstream spawning grounds ever since. Early on in its history, an attempt was made to trap and truck the fish over the dam, but that effort seems to have been abandoned after moving only seven adult fish in the course of a year.

When the dam was proposed in the late 1930s, some in the community expressed concern about the wisdom, safety and cost of such a project. Despite these questions, a bond issue was passed in 1945 to fund construction of the Matilija and Casitas Dams, part of the Ventura River Water Development Project. There has been concern about the stability of the dam's construction "since the day it was built," says Henke, as well as about what would happen to the narrow canyon and to surrounding communities in case of an accident or flood.

Further complicating conditions for the Ventura River and its tributaries is the Robles Diversion Dam, completed in 1958 just 1.5 miles downstream from Matilija Creek. Its purpose is to divert water from the Ventura River—including water from the Matilija

Dam impoundment—into the headworks of the Robles-Casitas Canal and the Casitas Reservoir. In so doing, it greatly reduces the amount of instream water, which steelhead need to migrate and spawn.

In 1997, southern California steelhead were listed under the Endangered Species Act. This focused attention on obstacles to their recovery like Matilija and Robles Diversion Dams, says Nick DiCroce, board member and chair of California Trout's conservation committee. He believes that a California Trout lawsuit—charging that unscreened diversions and low flows at the Robles Diversion Dam constituted a "take" of the ESA-listed steelhead—pushed the federal government to act. "The suit was an important way to use the ESA to recover imperiled steelhead," he says. The water district responded by putting a fish-passage plan into effect and initiating plans to remove silt impounded by the dam. Now the district is seriously reassessing the Matilija Dam.

Removing the 198-foot-high dam from the narrow canyon will be an enormous undertaking, but local political officials and federal agencies agree that it should go. "It is important to keep the benefits of removing Matilija Dam in the forefront and not let the size of the project discourage us," Ventura County supervisor Kathy Long told the press in 1999. "I feel this project will prove to be not only a wise and sound investment but a visionary one also." Estimates on the cost of removing the dam vary from $20 million to almost ten times that.

DiCroce is surprised at how quickly federal agencies responded to the notion of removing Matilija Dam. "Usually government agencies are known for their slow action," he says. "I'm amazed at how quickly they've responded to Babbitt making this a priority." Money for the first phase of assessing dam removal has been readily available, he says, and all those involved—the county, local water district and federal agencies, including the Bureau of Reclamation and Army Corps of Engineers—have been "wonderfully cooperative up to this point." But where the money will come from for the next phase of feasibility studies, let alone to actually remove the dam and restore the river, has yet to be determined. "We'd like to see it removed in our lifetimes," says DiCroce, alluding to the length of time these projects seem to take.

In October 2000, Secretary Babbitt made the eighth and final stop of his official "Dam Busters Tour" at Matilija Dam. Maneuvering the levers of a crane, Babbitt helped remove an immense block of concrete from the top of Matilija Dam. "We will produce the resources that will bring your plans to a reality. . . . The benefits, in the long run, will far outweigh the costs," Babbitt told the assembled crowd.

"My fantasy is to see abundant schools of steelhead swimming up the Ventura River, past the former Matilija Dam and up into the reaches of the river where they will spawn and continue their life cycle," DiCroce told the *Los Angeles Times* at the October dam-busting event. When I ask him about Matilija Dam, Babbitt says that he tends "to favor taking it down a brick at a time and letting the runoff shape the stream." Lest anyone get too excited about an actual breaching and the prospect of steelhead swimming freely, the block that was removed from the dam is well above the waterline. So for now, the dam will have a gap-toothed smile, but nothing practical has changed for the river's struggling steelhead or the downstream beaches.

Because he has been so influential in setting at least part of the national agenda for river restoration and dam removal, I wanted to speak with Secretary Babbitt. I catch up with him in California on the morning of the "Dam Busters Tour" visit to Saeltzer Dam and have the good fortune of being offered a ride to the dam site with the Dam-Buster-in-Chief himself. I ask him what first sparked his interest in dam removal.

"What got me thinking about it," says Babbitt, "was a long time ago, close to twenty years ago, on a dory boat trip through the Grand Canyon over Memorial Day. The river started to disappear as we got to Tanner Rapid. So we spent Memorial Day at Tanner Creek waiting for the Colorado to be reinstated by the operators at Glen Canyon. I realized then that the river was being manipulated like a giant toilet bowl. It started me thinking about the downstream effects of dams.

"After that I really started noticing things: the dead riparian vegetation along the high-water mark. The dead willows, cottonwoods and mesquite. I thought about the decline of the native fish and the change in the beaches. It got harder to find a beach to camp on," he recalls. "You'd end up putting your sleeping bag on a boulder.

"The downstream effect of dams was not much thought about in the days of Hetch Hetchy and Dinosaur Canyon," says Babbitt of two dams that were bitterly opposed in the early days of the American conservation movement. "Those dams were thought of as flooding the landscape. It was about altering the landscape. It wasn't about altering the life of the river."

How optimistic is he about the prospects of restoring native salmon runs? I ask. "Take down a dam on a small stream and the salmon come back. But salmon have so many challenges," he reflects. "Those salmon are hostage to so many things: fishing on the high seas, to weather. . . . The success of salmon restoration is complex. The economic trade-offs are kind of secondary. It's very real once you can reduce it to a factual discussion not overlain with a lot of psychological perceptions."

Given those complexities, I ask him how tied to politics and policies current river restoration and dam removal efforts are? We have spent so much of our history in this country fragmenting our watersheds, how hard does he think it would be to begin to shift our focus and understanding to thinking about rivers on their own time frame?

"This movement is on its way," Babbitt assures me. "It's no longer dependent on the policies of federal agencies. It's rooted in communities all over the country. We've gone from a concern for landscape early in the century which never really awakened to rivers until the late twentieth century. Not until the late twentieth century did concern for rivers really blossom. Concern for rivers has blossomed with an enormous depth. Communities really respond to rivers and river restoration. A river has such a wonderful and specific place in a community. People get it right away. It's easy for communities to relate to."

"The main thing has been a perceptual change," Babbitt tells me. "We all tend to think of landscapes as we have known them in the past. It's difficult to envision the landscape as it was. We've gone in the last decade from thinking of dam removal as vandalism to an awakening and threshold of an acceptance. Dam removal is but an incident in the life of a watershed."

As I learned more about California's engineered rivers, with their cross-basin diversions shunting mountain stream water into deserts and churning salmon streams through turbines to power countless computer-filled offices and homes and to provide drinking water for the growing millions of Californians—I began to think of the system as a hydrologic push-me-pull-you. A real case of wanting to have one's cake and eat it, too. Or, as William Kier said, summing up the state's dam removal efforts, "We'd like to rearrange the plumbing and show you how it will work better when we're done." I wondered how much more could be taken out of the system before parts began to teeter like a house of cards.

A number of nonfederally owned hydropower dams in California will come up for license renewal within the next decade. Communities will have to ask hard questions about their dams' futures. That some of California's salmon streams are beginning to be freed of unnecessary dams seems an enormously hopeful sign. Still, California must have the courage to look at the entirety of its fragmented watersheds and make difficult decisions about truly putting some of those pieces back together again. Solutions should be sought that will not repair one basin or ecological function at the expense of another.* With the dry winter of 2000–2001, the experience of California's power crisis and an economic downturn, I wonder what priority the state will give CalFed and other river restoration projects. We have seen how quickly a crowded system like California's can be thrown off balance, so it seems more important than ever to begin addressing issues of carrying capacity and the limits to growth. Thinking critically about what we have done to California's rivers with dams is part of that process.

---

*There has been talk in California of "water banking," of storing water from underground aquifers and using it to supplement depleted surface-water systems, but it's not yet been determined how this might affect the ecology of groundwater and the whole aquatic and riparian food chain.

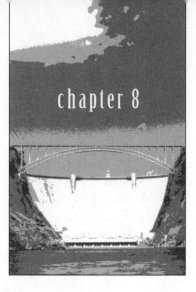

chapter 8

Oregon

SAVAGE RAPIDS DAM AND
THE ROGUE RIVER

The Rogue River begins high in the Sky Lakes Wilderness in Oregon's Cascade Mountains. There are peaks called Venus, Jupiter and Lucifer and places called Crippled Horse Spring, Fool Creek and Bareface Butte. For many miles the Rogue runs through protected wilderness. Significant portions of the Rogue have been designated a National Wild and Scenic River. Throughout the watershed there is old-growth Douglas fir, ponderosa and white pine, madrone, grand and Shasta red fir, live oak, Port Orford cedar, big leaf and vine maple. Along the lower Rogue River stands an old-growth Douglas fir tree that is eight feet in diameter. In places, the Rogue runs through narrow rock canyons, tumbling over boulders in a splash of rapids. The river is a popular choice for whitewater rafting and fishing trips. A current Internet search for information about the Rogue yields a long list of bed-and-breakfasts and rafting and fishing outfitters.

The Rogue is an important spawning ground for salmon and steelhead, including the southern Oregon and northern California coho salmon, which are listed as threatened under the Endangered Species Act. The river's spring-run chinook salmon, Oregon coastal steelhead and sea run–cutthroat trout have also been dwindling in number and are currently under review for possible listing under the ESA. The Rogue's young anadromous fish travel downstream to the ocean in the spring and early summer. Adult fish return upstream to spawn in the fall and winter. Both journeys are impeded by dams.

Between the Cascades and the Pacific Ocean, where the Rogue empties into the sea at the coastal town of Gold Beach thirty-five miles north of the California border, the river and its major tributaries are blocked by a series of dams—Lost Creek Dam, Gold Ray Dam and Savage Rapids Dam are the largest of those on the mainstem. A smaller dam, the Jackson Street Dam on Bear Creek, a tributary of the Rogue that runs through the city of Medford, was removed in the summer of 1998, making it the first sizable dam in the Pacific Northwest to be demolished to protect endangered fish. There are plans to remove two small dams on the Little Applegate, a tributary of the Rogue, but the most controversial of Rogue River dams is Savage Rapids.

That dams block salmon is old news in Oregon. "As early as 1848," writes Jim Lichatowich, "Oregonians included a clause in their territorial constitution mandating that 'rivers and streams . . . in which the salmon are found or to which they resort shall not be obstructed by dams or otherwise, unless such dams or obstructions are so constructed as to allow salmon to pass freely up and down such rivers and streams.' But this law, like most laws intended to protect salmon habitat," comments Lichatowich, has never been fully enforced.[1] Now that Pacific Northwest salmon numbers have dwindled so that over 230 stocks have been lost in the past century and many others are threatened by extinction, anything that might jeopardize their survival is being carefully scrutinized.

Located just east of Grants Pass in southern Oregon, the Savage Rapids Dam is the last dam on the Rogue before the river reaches the ocean. The National Marine Fisheries Service has called the

dam the "biggest fish killer on the Rogue." Built in 1921, it is owned
and operated by the Grants Pass Irrigation District, formed in 1916
for the benefit of local farms. The fate of the dam has generated a
controversy that has been raging for over a decade. At times, the
struggle between those who want to save the dam and those who
want it removed has seemed positively operatic.

Built solely to divert Rogue River water for irrigation, the Savage
Rapids Dam stores no water, generates no hydropower and per-
forms no flood control. The dam lifts water into canals—or ditches
—using gravity and pumps from which individual users take the
water. According to local reports, in the old days, so much water
was taken out of the river onto farm fields that hundreds of salmon
were washed up onto pastures where they were left to die. Because
of inefficient and leaky irrigation canals, only about 20 percent of
the water currently diverted by the dam actually ends up being
used. When the Irrigation District was first established, the area it
served was rural farmland. Today, about half the land parcels in
the Irrigation District are less than half an acre in size, and 70 percent are less than an acre, so overall, the average land parcel
served by Savage Rapids Dam is less than two acres.[2] Clearly, most
of the land in the district is no longer used for agriculture. The water diverted by Savage Rapids Dam is now primarily used to water
lawns, gardens, hobby farms, a cemetery and a golf course.

The three-mile slack water behind the dam is used for waterski-
ing, swimming and summer boating, and this stretch of water has
become a focal point of life for many in the community. But a series of studies by the Grants Pass Irrigation District and the Bureau of Reclamation have recommended that, because of its
inefficiency and hazards to fish, the dam be removed and replaced
with pumps that would provide water for the District's farms and
ranches while allowing safe passage for the river's fish.

Although removing the dam would cost less than making the
improvements that would otherwise be required, there is vocifer-
ous and tenacious support for Savage Rapids Dam. Even the listing of the Rogue's coho salmon under the Endangered Species Act
has failed to persuade supporters that the dam should go. They
view efforts to remove the dam as the thin end of a wedge of government intrusion into local and personal rights. Thus the debate

over Savage Rapids Dam has turned into a political tug-of-war between local custom and the need for conservation. The politicking has been intense, rife with misinformation and accusation, its reach extending to the Oregon state capitol and governor's office.

On a warm sunny morning in May 1999, I drive about five hours south of Portland to meet Bob Hunter, an attorney for Water Watch, an Oregon-based river conservation group that's been active in the effort to remove Savage Rapids Dam. From the freeway I turn off onto old Route 99, the original north-south highway through Oregon that predates the construction of Interstate 5. Along the river are cabins and small houses—some with manicured lawns extending to the water's edge—as well as mobile homes, the Lazy Acres River RV Park, Sawtooth Taxidermy, Circle W Campground, the Rod & Reel Inn and the Steelheader Tavern. Just before the WeAskU Inn, I find the turnoff for Savage Rapids Dam.

There is a dusty parking area and a chain-link fence posted with "No Trespassing" signs. Hunter and I walk down to the dam. I expect to see water gushing through the dam, but there is none. Although the weather is warm and there is a record high snowpack in the mountains, which will mean high river levels, the Irrigation District has not yet begun operating the dam for the season. A river with several Class 4 and 5 rapids, this dammed stretch of the Rogue looks meek and tame. The narrow impoundment is flat and virtually currentless. The thirty-nine-foot-high dam stretches 500 feet across the river. Its concrete spillway and zigzags of cement that now serve as fish ladders are mostly dry. Near where we stand, on the south side of the river, are metal screens at the edges of the dam near the riverbank. These screens are to keep young fish from getting into the irrigation canals. They look like a corridor of cheese graters.

Hunter points out that the cement ladders meant to provide passage when the dam is not diverting water are only on the south side of the dam. The other side has a fish ladder near the dam's turbines, but that works only during irrigation season. This means that for half the year, the north side of the river is virtually impassable for fish. When the dam was completed in 1921, it had a fish ladder on the north side only; the seasonal south bank fish ladder was added in 1934. It wasn't until 1958 that the turbines were screened to prevent fish from getting caught in them. (In the Northwest, where dams and salmon passage are now a subject of some urgency, there has been talk of "fish-friendly turbines." A recent cartoon in *The Oregonian* showed an old turbine and a new, fish-friendly turbine. From the old one, the fish emerged in many tiny pieces; from the new, in two neat halves.) At Savage Rapids, newer screens were added on the south side in 1981. But their mesh, Hunter explains, exceeds the size stipulated by National Marine Fisheries Service regulations, and small fish slip through their holes. The screens over the pump and turbine system are now old and do not meet current standards. Clearly, Savage Rapids Dam is anything but state-of-the-art.

While salmon runs had already fallen from their historic high numbers, by the time construction began on Savage Rapids Dam in 1921, salmon would have seemed anything but endangered. In the late 1800s, one of the Pacific Northwest's leading salmon-canning entrepreneurs, R. D. Hume, had his base of operations on the Rogue River. The success of that business, which peaked around the turn of the twentieth century, would have been fresh in the minds of those who planned Savage Rapids. By 1960, the annual catch of Northwest salmon had shrunk to 5 million pounds, down from 40 million pounds in the 1920s. By the 1980s, the salmon population in the Rogue River was a quarter of what it had been less than ten years before, and hatchery, rather than wild salmon, made up nearly half of all adult salmonids in the river. The scientific and political discussions about the cause of these declines are the subject of multimillion-dollar studies covering countless reams of paper. Yet no matter how the numbers are crunched, the fact is, on the Rogue—as elsewhere in the range of the Pacific salmon—current fish populations are the tiniest fraction of what they were less than a generation ago.

As dams like Savage Rapids proliferated throughout the Pacific Northwest, salmon populations plummeted. In the first decades of European settlement in Oregon, hundreds of dams were built in the Rogue River basin. Around 1900, two dams went up on the main stem of the Rogue near where Savage Rapids Dam now blocks the river. One, built by the Grants Pass Power Supply Company, although only a twelve-foot-high log dam, blocked most of the river's salmon run. That dam washed out in a flood but was replaced by another, which gradually deteriorated until it became defunct around 1940. In 1905, an additional dam was built about three miles upstream from Grants Pass. That dam completely blocked salmon from swimming up or downstream. It was destroyed—story has it by a load of dynamite floated into the dam.

As Hunter and I stand at the dam, some other visitors arrive. A pair of retirement-age men wearing mesh ball caps—one has a gold watch inscribed with "20 Years Safe Driver"—stop to chat with us about the fishing. "We used to go down to Gold Beach," says the Safe Driver, "but the fishing's no good anymore. So I brought my buddy up here. But it's not fair. The fish are all stacked up below the dam. People are just picking 'em off." Hunter explains that by the Bureau of Reclamation's reckoning, if the dam wasn't here, there would be nearly 100,000 more adult salmon and steelhead being produced in the Rogue. "Is that right," says the angler whose fishing this dam is destroying.

The reach of the Rogue spanned by Savage Rapids Dam is important habitat for five runs of salmon and steelhead, including southern Oregon and northern California coho salmon now listed as threatened under the ESA. Once found throughout the Pacific Northwest from Alaska to northern California, coho are now extinct in half their historic range. Some local populations of southern Oregon coho are now extinct; others are classified as at risk of extinction. Before migrating to the ocean to mature, juvenile coho spend a year or so in freshwater, so they are particularly sensitive to anything—like Savage Rapids Dam—that might harm their time in the river. Not only do the dam's ineffective fish ladders and inadequate screens impede the passage of fish to and from the sea, its seasonal impoundments also destroy important spawning grounds, conditions that many fish cannot survive.

Bob Hunter explains that on the south side of the dam, while some juvenile fish traveling downstream slip through the screens into the irrigation canals, some adult fish leap over the sides of the ladders and become stranded on the rocks below. Some get trapped in the dam's turbines while others become disoriented and vulnerable to predators. "The dam prevents fish from getting upstream to spawn," says Hunter. "This limits their chance of successful spawning."

None of this seems to have impressed many in the Grants Pass Irrigation District. While it is cost-effective to replace Savage Rapids Dam with pumps, District officials have until recently staunchly opposed dam removal. In 1998, the district spent $280,000 of its $1 million annual budget on legal fees in the campaign to save the dam. With remarkable obstinacy it has defied state and federal actions requiring it to comply with environmental regulations and protect the endangered fish by removing the dam. In November 1998, when the Irrigation District failed to comply with the conditions of its water-withdrawal permit—that the district move toward removal of the dam—the Oregon Water Resources Commission took the extraordinary step of canceling one of the District's two water rights.

The Grants Pass Irrigation District has refused to cooperate, even though the Bureau of Reclamation calculates that Savage Rapids Dam reduces salmon and steelhead runs on the Rogue by 22 percent—a decline, wrote Hunter in a recent article for the *Journal of Western Water Law,* that "translated into approximately $5 million in economic losses each year to the region's sport and commercial fishing industries and related businesses." The Irrigation District has defended the dam even though the National Marine Fisheries Service has declared the Savage Rapids Dam a significant source of incidental "taking" of coho salmon, meaning that if no remedial action is taken, the dam would be declared in violation of the Endangered Species Act. The District has even fought for the dam when the federal government said it would pay to remove and replace the dam with environmentally appropriate, electric-powered pumps.

Supporters consider Savage Rapids Dam a mainstay of their community and local culture and regard any effort to remove it as unwanted government interference. Or as a former Irrigation District board member put it, "The dam is a symbol of man's triumph over nature. It's a symbol of the strength of the country, the strength of the West."

"This is what built the West, building dams," says Hunter, citing sentiments of the dam's defenders. "To have the government come in, or some outside person come in and tell us to remove it, that's just un-American."

As at other impoundments and reservoirs, those who have chosen to live around Savage Rapids Dam and its slow-moving water find life without the reservoir almost unthinkable. Without the dam, the Rogue would fall back to a narrower channel, backyards facing the reservoir would change and flat-water recreation would give way to moving-water pursuits. "For the illusion of lakeside living, the Rogue River's anadromous fish pay a terrible price," a National Sportfishing Industry Association board member and sporting goods salesman wrote in a 1999 op-ed piece in the Medford, Oregon, *Mail Tribune*. Like commercial fishing, sportfishing has suffered with the decline of Oregon's salmon and steelhead, and in the struggle to restore Northwest salmon runs, fishermen and environmentalists have become allies.

Opposition to removal has been so adamant that facts have occasionally become irrelevant. "In its 77-year history, Savage Rapids Dam has never blocked upstream migration of salmon or steelhead," wrote former Grants Pass Irrigation District board chairman Dennis Becklin in a November 1998 op-ed piece in *The Oregonian,* even though two weeks before, he had received a letter from the National Marine Fisheries Service stating that the dam "remains a major juvenile and adult salmonid fish passage impediment in the Rogue River due to poor juvenile screens, spill, predation and poor adult fishways. As NMFS has stated previously, dam removal will permanently resolve these fish passage problems."

At one point, Becklin even compared his position in the crusade to save the dam to that of "the guy in front of the tanks at Tian-an-men Square." Under his leadership, the Grants Pass Irrigation District convinced local and state politicians to oppose dam removal. Among their numbers has been Grants Pass's Oregon state senator, who, in the late 1990s, was Senate president. With this representation, a number of bills that would have blocked or hindered removal of Savage Rapids Dam were introduced and won support of the entire legislature. Governor John Kitzhaber, an outspoken advocate of salmon restoration, vetoed them all.

Following the politics around Savage Rapids Dam has been like watching a Ping-Pong match. Back in 1929, the state of Oregon issued the Grants Pass Irrigation District a water permit for the irrigation of over 18,000 acres. Oregon law requires this water to be used without waste, and the permit holder to prove that the water is being put to beneficial use. It wasn't until 1982, more than half a century later, that Grants Pass Irrigation District completed a survey documenting its use of permitted water. The survey showed that the District had only 7,738 acres under irrigation. In response, the state's Water Resources Department issued the District a permit for the corresponding smaller amount of water. In a 1988 attempt to obtain the additional water—that would coincide with the original 18,000-acre permit—the District applied for a new permit. This application was challenged by conservation organizations, local fly-fishers and fisheries scientists, who maintained that it wasn't in the public interest to allow the District to waste water needed in the river, especially while Savage Rapids Dam continued to kill fish. A settlement was reached allowing the Irrigation District to divert the larger amount of water on a temporary basis but on condition that a plan be developed to conserve water and address public concerns about the effects of the dam, namely its impediment to salmon passage. The temporary permit, granted in 1990, was set to expire in 1994.

From those four years of planning emerged the recommendation that Savage Rapids Dam be removed and replaced with pumps. Dam removal was the cheapest, most beneficial and only permanent way to adequately improve conditions for the river and its fish, concluded a study conducted by the Irrigation District, along with the Bureau of Reclamation, U.S. Fish and Wildlife Service and Oregon Department of Fish and Wildlife. Under the proposed plan, however, during the irrigation season water levels in the reach of the Rogue downstream from Savage Rapids Dam—a stretch designated as a State Scenic Waterway—would still be too low to meet the instream flows required by the Oregon Scenic Waterway Act. Despite this failing, the state agreed to grant the additional water right on the condition that the Irrigation District proceed with conservation measures and work toward dam removal.

So, in the fall of 1994, the Grants Pass Irrigation District agreed to move forward with plans to remove the dam. Then, although all signs pointed in the direction of dam removal and Oregon Senator Mark Hatfield was ready to work for federal funding, local opponents dug in their heels. In 1995, new pro-dam members were elected to the Irrigation District board, the cooperative agreement collapsed and the opportunity to obtain federal funding for dam removal was lost. Thus, the Ping-Pong match continued. In 1996, because of a 1995 Oregon Senate bill, a Savage Rapids Dam task force was formed. The group met over the course of a year but by 1997 had reached no consensus.

"Make no mistake about it. Savage Rapids Dam is bad for fish," wrote Governor Kitzhaber, in a 1997 op-ed piece in the *Medford Mail Tribune*. "Adult fish die in the outmoded fish ladders and juvenile fish die at turbine intakes and in passing over the dam. It has been estimated that more than 20 percent more salmon would spawn in the Rogue above Savage Rapids if these problems could be solved." Kitzhaber also pointed out that, according to the U.S. Bureau of Reclamation, saving Savage Rapids Dam would cost about $2.4 million more than removing it.

Meanwhile fish conditions in the region continued to deteriorate. Because Rogue River coho salmon were listed in 1997 as threatened under the Endangered Species Act, federal law required the Grants Pass Irrigation District to solve Savage Rapids Dam's fish passage problems, and so, the district board decided to move forward with dam removal. But, in yet another about-face, at the end of 1997, the Irrigation District elected a new board of directors, which then defied the state's order and refused to submit a plan for dam removal, putting the District in violation of its water permit. Because of the District's new refusal, in 1998, the Oregon Water Resources Commission canceled the second water permit.

At the same time, the National Marine Fisheries Service (NMFS) determined that Savage Rapids Dam constituted a significant "take" of threatened Rogue River coho salmon. Under the Endangered Species Act, anything that would harm, harass, pursue, hunt, shoot, wound, kill, trap, capture or collect a threatened species constitutes a "take" and is prohibited without a special permit. In the case of salmon, such a permit would be issued by NMFS. To obtain a permit allowing for the incidental take, the Grants Pass Irrigation District would have to produce a habitat conservation plan showing that all possible efforts were being made to minimize and mitigate for the harm being done to the threatened salmon. However, according to NMFS, the best and only way to improve conditions for coho and meet the requirements of the Endangered Species Act is to remove Savage Rapids Dam.

At this point the Irrigation District failed to submit such a plan. So in April 1998, NMFS sued the Irrigation District to block water diversions at the dam until juvenile coho had completed their seasonal downstream migration. The National Marine Fisheries Service and the Irrigation District reached a settlement but only for 1998. This required that the dam be shut down for a short period in the spring and early summer to allow the young salmon to pass safely downstream. By January 1999, the Irrigation District was back in court appealing the Oregon Water Resources Board decision to cancel the district's request for additional water. A November 1999 Irrigation District press release asserted that the "District continues to believe, based on the advice of its consulting biologists, that removal of Savage Rapids Dam is not necessary to protect salmon and steelhead runs in the Rogue River." Between 1998 and 2000, the Irrigation District had spent about half a million dollars on legal fees, largely in pursuit of preserving the dam, but the district has also sued some of its own patrons, who, unhappy over rising costs, have attempted to leave the district by canceling their water rights. The Irrigation District has long linked its fate to that of Savage Rapids Dam and has described dam removal as threatening the survival of the District—even of the community itself.

In the next turn of events, in January 2000, Grants Pass Irrigation District board chairman Dennis Becklin stepped down, and 60 percent of the Irrigation District's patrons voted in favor of dam removal. Later that spring, members of the Oregon congressional delegation met with both sides in the debate to craft a bill that would provide funding to keep the Irrigation District in business while enabling dam removal to proceed. Toward the end of the 106th Congress, U.S. Senators Gordon Smith and Ron Wyden introduced such a bill, but too late in the session for any action to be taken. The assumption was, Bob Hunter told me, that such a bill would be reintroduced the following year. Meanwhile the migrating salmon and steelhead, who do not vote, continue their struggles in negotiating the dam.

After immersing myself in the saga of Savage Rapids Dam, Bob Hunter suggests that I might like to see an example of successful dam removal. So we drive into the city of Medford to view the remnants of the Jackson Street Dam, removed in July 1998. We walk down to Bear Creek, where chunks of concrete on the banks are the only remaining evidence of the 120-foot-wide dam that once blocked the creek's flow. Like Savage Rapids Dam, Jackson Street Dam was built to divert water for irrigation. And like Savage Rapids, because of poorly constructed fish passage, the dam blocked migrating fish. Among these fish are the threatened coho salmon.

The dam was built in 1960, impounding a stretch of shallow, slow-moving water. The dam exacerbated already poor water conditions on the creek, water sullied by heavy use of the surrounding urban, suburban and rural communities. In the late 1990s, after over ten years of discussions within the community, with state, federal and local agencies and conservation groups, a solution was reached. With funding from the state of Oregon, the Bureau of Reclamation and the Medford Urban Renewal Agency, among others, the dam was replaced with a more environmentally friendly system of water diversion. The new configuration creates some slackwater, but it is at least 90 percent smaller than the old one. A removable three-foot-high structure has taken the place of the eleven-foot-high dam. By the time I saw it, the old streambed had begun to be restored, and coho had already been sighted in the newly flowing channel. One of the great benefits for the local human community has been an approachable, aesthetically appealing waterway in a downtown park, in place of a dirty, stagnant pond. Jackson Street was a small dam, but its demise occasioned a visit from Secretary Babbitt, who proudly listed the dam among the stops of the Department of the Interior's "Dam Busters Tour." "It's a little dam," said Babbitt, "but it's a big win for this community."

On my way home, I follow a bit of the Rogue upstream from Savage Rapids, to find Elk Creek where what looks like the beginnings of a cement pyramid towers over the creek bed. Installed by the Army Corps of Engineers between 1986 and 1987, these massive blocks of concrete represent some $100 million and only a third of the would-be dam's height. *The Oregonian* newspaper has called the dam "Oregon's biggest boondoggle." The dam was intended for flood control as part of the Rogue Basin Project, but two other dams on the Rogue obviated the need for Elk Creek Dam, so this hulk of cement sits useless in the creek. The Army Corps of Engineers has been trapping and hauling Elk Creek's steelhead and coho salmon around the structure, but conservation groups and fishermen say the handling is harming the fish. In 1997, the Corps agreed and recommended breaching Elk Creek Dam to allow fish passage. Three years later, in March 2000, with no such action taken, environmental and fishing groups sued the Corps for the dam's "take" of threatened coho. Funding to dismantle or notch the uncompleted dam and restore Elk Creek would have to be authorized by Congress. So far this has not happened. Meanwhile the fish wait.

As for Savage Rapids, as of October 2000, the state of Oregon's cancellation of the Grants Pass Irrigation District water permit remained under appeal, so the district continued to draw water. The permit would allow the dam to harm the river's threatened coho but only if that harm is mitigated to the fullest extent possible. The best way for Savage Rapids Dam to make up for the take of the endangered fish has not changed: The dam should be removed.

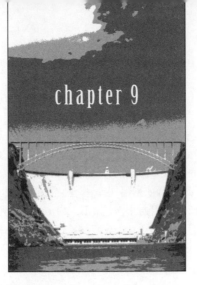

chapter 9

Washington

THE OLYMPIC PENINSULA

AND THE ELWHA RIVER DAMS:

"THE FISH IN THE TREES"

On an April afternoon, Port Angeles is a wet
and windy place. Its main streets lie close to the waterfront on the
north coast of the Olympic Peninsula in the northwestern corner
of Washington State. A narrow spit of land known as Ediz Hook
barely shelters Port Angeles's harbor from the Strait of Juan de
Fuca. Across the strait is Vancouver Island, off the southwest
coast of British Columbia. A ferry runs regularly between Port Angeles and the Canadian city of Victoria. A short drive inland from
Port Angeles are the snow-covered peaks of the Olympic Mountains. Olympic National Park is less than five miles from town. On
a clear day, the luminous, snowy tops of the Olympics can be seen
from downtown Seattle across the bay on the eastern shore of
Puget Sound. Not so long ago, Port Angeles was a busy mill town,

but on a chilly, rain-spitting day in 2000, the city has a lonely feel to it.

There's a newly refurbished path along the harbor front planted with trees and decorated with flowerbeds. Many of these bear commemorative plaques honoring loved ones lost at sea. Seagulls, terns and ravens squawk and bounce around the damp grass. In the water, cormorants dive and bob. There's a new playground at the harbor and a cluster of eateries that run the gamut from white tablecloths to those shouting, "Lottery tickets sold here." The Thai restaurant I pick for dinner turns out to be quite good.

First settled in the mid-1800s and incorporated in 1890, Port Angeles is now a city of nearly 19,000 residents. In 1912, it was home to the world's largest sawmill. The recessions of the 1970s hit the local timber business hard. Timber industry downturns followed in the 1980s, and the 1990s brought pressure from declining markets in Asia as well as environmental considerations at home. Port Angeles and surrounding Clallam County are geographically isolated from the high-tech boom on the Seattle side of Puget Sound, and the county's average annual wage runs about 20 percent lower than that of Washington state. While Port Angeles has a first-rate bookstore, several coffee shops pulling espresso and outdoor shops carrying the latest assortment of Gore-Tex and Polypro, as I walk the streets, I have the sense of a town struggling to turn a corner.

To reach Port Angeles from the south, you skirt a series of bays and inlets, actually western fingers of Puget Sound, then follow the Hood Canal. Along the road are shuttered sheds with hand-painted signs saying POTLATCH, BIG SKY CHIEF, ROARING DRAGON FIREWORKS, FRIED OYSTERS, SMOKED SALMON, HALIBUT. In summer, wild sweetpeas in intensities of pink, magenta and white bloom on the steep waterfront hillsides. There are small farms and vacation cabins. Near the canal, I see two bald eagles cruising above the treetops. Later I will be told this is good luck. There is lots of water. Almost countless creeks run into the bays and rivers, among them the Skokomish, Duckabush, Dosewallips, Quilcene, Dungeness and the Elwha.

The Elwha River was once one of the most productive salmon streams of its size in the region. Its waters nurtured spring, summer and fall chinook salmon, coho, steelhead, cutthroat trout, Dolly Varden and sockeye salmon, among others. Its prolific fish runs were well known to the coastal tribes from the south, in what is now Oregon, and from the north in present-day British Columbia. Before it was blocked by dams, the Elwha was unique in that it provided a wide range of habitat for all its fish species, from the sandy mouth of the river where it meets the salt water, to the high mountainside channels running with snowmelt. As it descends from the glacial Olympic Mountains to the ocean at the Strait of Juan de Fuca in a relatively short distance, the Elwha has been an ideal salmon incubator. The river was famous for its hundred-pound chinooks known as June hogs, and until the 1940s and 1950s, fish as large as seventy and eighty pounds were regularly found in the Elwha. The biggest chinook now caught there, I am told, are about thirty pounds.

Given its geography, topography and climate, the Elwha is considered one of the best places to begin what is hoped will be a significant recovery of the Northwest's endangered wild salmon. To boost the prospects for the Elwha's salmon, in February 2000—in a prelude to decommission and deconstruction—the federal government acquired two hydroelectric dams, the Elwha and Glines Canyon Dams, that block the river's flow and the migration of its native fish. A vast amount of political maneuvering and work lies ahead before either of these dams will actually come down. Yet, after years of contentious debate, Congress allocated the funding required to purchase the dams from their private owner, the Fort James Corporation, and begin the long task of river restoration.

The Elwha's corner of the Olympic Peninsula was one of the last parts of Washington state settled by European Americans. As recently as 1900, this country seemed like the edge of the world. The roads were bad. There was no railroad. The only real way in was by boat. Archaeologists estimate that the Olympic Peninsula was inhabited by Indians who migrated there from Asia at least twelve thousand years before the 1890s, when the first party of white people crossed the Olympics. Initially, the area's remoteness was a benefit to the native fish as the rivers remained sequestered from pressures imposed by development until comparatively recent times. But early in the twentieth century, with the building of the lower Elwha dam and Glines Canyon dam, conditions changed quickly for the river. The dams almost immediately blocked all passage of the Elwha's anadromous fish. Today, nine of the river's ten native fish runs are in serious decline—its chinook salmon and bull trout are now listed under the ESA—and the Elwha's sockeye may have entirely disappeared.

When looked at today, the whole history of the Elwha dams seems precarious. Although the first Washington state legislature passed a bill in 1890 requiring fish passage at all dams,[1] construction of the 105-foot-high Elwha Dam began in 1910 with no plans for fish passage. In 1912, a year after the dam was completed, its foundation gave way as the reservoir was filling. The hole in the foundation was filled with tree limbs, rock and dirt and patched over with concrete. The patching is still visible. Covered with clumps of moss, with water springing out from chinks in the jury-rigged concrete, spilling down rocks and trickling from a hodge-podge of pipes, the Elwha Dam looks more like a Rube Goldberg contraption than an example of deliberate engineering. It is a gravity dam, which is designed to be built on bedrock, but the Elwha Dam rests on loose alluvial gravel in a location vulnerable to seismic activity. The dam's spillways are inadequate for the flood-level flows, and ever since it was built, the Elwha Dam has posed significant safety concerns. "Basically, it's on roller skates," says Shawn Cantrell, of Friends of the Earth, who has driven over from Seattle with his colleague Lisa Ramirez to give me a tour of the two Elwha dams.

Before setting out for the river, we look at a relief map of the Olympic Peninsula in the visitors center of Olympic National Park. The steep forest, snow-covered peaks and deep river valleys of the Olympics are laid out for us in three-dimensional, molded, colored plastic. Shawn says he likes to show people this map because it gives such a vivid presentation of the Elwha's watershed. Over 80 percent of the Elwha watershed is in the National Park. This is significant, Shawn explains, because it has made consideration of dam removal much easier than if more substantial amounts of private land were involved.

The highest of the mountains in the park is Mt. Olympus, which at nearly 8,000 feet towers over the surrounding, low-lying, temperate rainforest and subalpine slopes. Western redcedar, Douglas fir, yellow cedar, sitka spruce and mountain hemlock grow out of the moss and fern-carpeted forest floor, festooned with great beards of celadon and jade green lichen. There are black bear, cougar and black-tailed deer. High up are glacial lakes and meadows that in summer fill with wildflowers: paintbrush, lupine, Turk's head lilies, columbine, larkspur, rhododendron and penstemon. The views from these slopes can be breathtaking. Ribbons of vibrant blue shine between sky-high trees, with glimpses of snow-topped peaks, islands, straits of glinting water and shaded rivers tumbling to the sea. In a curiosity of geography and topography, the coastal plain of this part of the peninsula is located in the rain shadow of the Olympic Mountains, and so, the city of Port Angeles receives only twenty-six inches of rain a year, while sixty miles inland, the forest is soaked by 140 inches. Thus, the upper reaches of the Elwha are within the coastal temperate rainforest, but its mouth is in a comparatively dry climate.

The mouth and delta of the river are where the Lower Elwha Klallam Tribe now live, having been relocated from their homelands on the Olympic Peninsula. Some Klallam families have lived near the mouth of the Elwha since the 1870s; the Elwhas were moved there in the 1930s. The Lower Elwha Klallam reservation itself was not formed until 1968, and its location in the floodplain has long been fraught with difficulties. Tribal elders still remember the sound of the flooding river ripping tree trunks as it roared down the canyon when the Elwha Dam's foundation failed in 1912. The manipulation of water levels at the dams has exacerbated flooding in the lower river, causing chronic problems for the tribal homes in the floodplain. It was not until the 1970s and 1980s that federal funding was made available to improve housing on the reservation. To this day, safety problems at the dams have not been fully addressed, and the fish—the mainstay of life for the Indians of the Olympic Peninsula—continue to dwindle in number.

A few miles north of the National Park boundary, we stand on the walkway that crosses the dam. Below us is the sound of rushing water where the river, released from the dam, sluices down a big cement chute and tumbles into the lower canyon. Swallows swoop and dart in the steep narrow canyon below. It's a cool morning, and there is mist above the water. Fingers of cloud float through the slopes above. The dam has a curious arrangement of pipe and ductwork. Shawn explains that these were added in various attempts to improve the dam's operation, not always successfully. The reservoir above the dam is wide and shallow. Fir-covered slopes rise on all sides. I am told that when the dam blew out during construction, after the wall of water came through, people picked fish out of the trees.

As we stand on the edge of the Elwha River canyon, surveying the several stories' worth of cement that now block its path, it is astounding to imagine that anyone could have not realized the problems the dam would cause. Looking at the Elwha Dam, it is also easy to understand the complexity of safely removing such a structure. While the old dam is being removed, a temporary dam will have to be built to shunt the water out of the reservoir to prevent sudden flooding below.

The Elwha Dam was conceived of by Thomas Aldwell, who owned a tract of land along this stretch of river. Aldwell's Olympic Power Company built the dam into the vee of a rock canyon at river mile 4.9. His idea was to dam the river, capture the falling water and sell the hydropower to Port Angeles, thereby bringing electricity to the northern part of the Olympic Peninsula. A representative for the Port Angeles Chamber of Commerce, Aldwell was actively involved in promoting the sale of timber from the Olympic Forest Reserve—which the precursor to the national park was then called. Although this reserve was set aside in 1897, and what became Olympic National Park in 1938 was proclaimed a national monument in 1909, industrial-strength logging continued there until the 1950s. Electricity generated by the Elwha Dam helped expand the lumber mills in Port Angeles, which increased revenue for timber companies like Crown Zellerbach, with which Aldwell worked closely and to which he would sell the dam in 1919.[2]

As early as 1911, it became clear that the Elwha Dam was blocking the river's fish. That first fall, when salmon should have been returning upstream to spawn, hundreds were observed downstream at the base of the dam, but none in the river or its tributaries above. In an attempt to make up for this loss, despite a

Washington law prohibiting blockage of salmon streams for any purpose other than collecting eggs for propagation, the state allowed construction of a hatchery on the lower Elwha. The hatchery opened in 1915, but it was not a success and was abandoned in 1922. Using the hatchery to make up for the lack of fish passage at the Elwha Dam, wrote Northwest fisheries biologist Jim Lichatowich, "set a critical precedent that linked dams and hatcheries. . . . The merger allowed the industrial development of the water by substituting hatcheries for wild fish and reservoirs for free-flowing rivers."[3]

Between the Elwha Dam and Glines Canyon Dam upriver, a two-lane park road climbs along a free-flowing stretch of the Elwha, through tall firs and pines. The river splashes and tumbles over boulders and downed trees, creating white-water riffles and rapids with touches of glacial aqua in between. Glines Canyon Dam is a towering 210 feet. Its arc of moss-covered concrete is wedged in between steep canyon riverbanks. We walk through the damp woods and scramble over some slippery rocks to approach the dam. The snow-covered peaks of the Olympic Mountains rise above the flat water of the reservoir called Lake Mills. Shawn points out a long light vertical place on the face of the dam where the moss is thinner than elsewhere. That's the spot, he says, where, some years ago, dam-protesting activists painted a crack.

The Northwestern Power and Light Company built Glines Canyon Dam from 1925 and 1927. When Olympic National Park was created in 1938, the dam was included within its boundaries. Located at river mile 13.5 in an otherwise beautiful section of the park, Glines Canyon Dam is twice as high as the Elwha Dam and looms over the natural riverbed. Like the Elwha Dam, Glines Canyon Dam was built without fish passage. No attempt was made to make up for the loss of the salmon runs here until the 1970s and 1980s, when the Washington State Department of Fisheries and the Elwha Tribe compelled the dams' owner, Crown Zellerbach, to confront the issue of fish restoration.

Until the late 1950s, there was heavy logging in the Elwha valley backcountry of Olympic National Park. Some of these logs ended up floating in the water of Lake Mills. The logging, and the roads built to get equipment in and bring logs out, would have sent unnaturally large loads of sediment into the streams that feed the Elwha and crushed and removed streamside vegetation that shades the water and keeps temperatures cool. None of this can have been healthy for the Elwha's salmon and steelhead.

When the Elwha dams were built, electricity was scarce and salmon were plentiful. Apart from the Klallam and Elwha Tribes, few opposed blocking passage of the Elwha's anadromous fish. With dams lacking fish passage just five and ten miles from the mouth of the Elwha, 90 percent of the river's salmon habitat was completely blocked. The dams' impoundments trap sediment and gravel that would otherwise wash down the river. Under natural conditions, this gravel, as it's deposited along the riverbanks and particularly at the mouth of the river, creates a vital nursery ground for young fish. Without this flow of sediment, the mouth of the river and the normally sandy, silty fan of its delta become deprived of gravel, and the whole structure of the riparian food web is thrown off balance. But when Elwha and Glines Canyon Dams were built, powering generators, running saw blades and cutting boards generally took precedence over nurturing fish. "The Department of Fisheries tended to approach the Elwha situation like the death of a distant relative," wrote Bruce Brown in his book about Pacific salmon, *Mountain in the Clouds*, "it was all somewhat sad, but there was nothing they could do about the outcome."[4]

In 1919, the Crown Zellerbach Company bought the Elwha Dam from Aldwell's Olympic Power Company and in 1936 acquired the Glines Canyon Dam from Northwestern Power and Light. Because the Elwha Dam was built before creation of the Federal Power Commission—which predated the Federal Energy Regulatory Commission—it was built without a license. Although the Glines Canyon Dam received a fifty-year license from the Federal Power Commission in 1926, Crown Zellerbach did not apply for the Elwha Dam's license until 1968. Given the contested licensing and the tangle of ownership in the years that followed, the Elwha Dam has never been licensed.

The power from Elwha and Glines Canyon Dams originally went to the cities of Port Angeles and Bremerton, and subsequently to the Crown Zellerbach paper mill in Port Angeles. The mill is now owned by the Japanese company Daishowa, which purchased it—but not the two dams—from Crown Zellerbach's successor, James River, Inc. With about three hundred jobs, Daishowa is one of the biggest private employers in Clallam County. While the mill is no longer dependent on hydropower from the Elwha River dams, Port Angeles has a long history of linking the dams to local jobs. Electrical power now moves through the West on a huge grid of transmission lines, but in many communities where the dam and mill were the economic hub, the equation of dams and jobs persists.

When Glines Canyon Dam was due for relicensing in the mid-1970s, the Washington State Department of Fisheries asked for and received a financial contribution from Crown Zellerbach for Elwha River fish restoration efforts. A spawning channel was created in the river and some flows were modified to benefit fish, but the majority of the problems caused by the dams remained. As Glines Canyon Dam's relicensing process inched forward, Crown Zellerbach again applied to the Federal Energy Regulatory Commission for a license for the Elwha Dam. Granting such a license, FERC replied, would be contingent on various repairs as well as improved plans to deal with emergencies that might occur at the dam. These proceedings continued throughout the 1970s, with the Elwha's fish runs remaining blocked.

The earliest real advance toward removal of the Elwha dams came in 1986 with passage of the Electric Consumers Protection Act. This amendment to the Federal Power Act requires federally licensed dams to assess the costs of their environmental impacts along with the benefits of power generation. To qualify for a new license, dam owners must prove that hydropower operations would not unduly harm fish and wildlife. Consequently, federal agencies began to require fish passage at hydropower dams licensed by FERC, a requirement Crown Zellerbach fought at the Elwha dams.

Adding impetus to this move, at about this time, the Lower Elwha Klallam Tribe filed a motion with FERC requesting that a fish-restoration plan for the Elwha include dam removal. The proposal met with opposition. "This is America," was the comment from one congressional aide. "We're about building things up, not tearing things down."[5]

With Glines Canyon Dam's license renewal under negotiation and the lower Elwha dam lacking license or fish passage, conservation groups began to rally to the idea of intervening in the relicensing process and working toward dam removal. It was at this point, Shawn Cantrell explains, that Friends of the Earth, the Olympic Park Association, Seattle Audubon Society and the Sierra Club became involved. The tribes and conservation groups wanted a formal environmental impact statement to be conducted before any new licenses were granted for either of the Elwha dams. Several years of legal, political and technical back-and-forth ensued among FERC, Crown Zellerbach, the National Marine Fisheries Service, other federal agencies, the tribes and the conservation community. With its conflicted history of promoting—or failing adequately to promote—the Olympic National Park's conservation mission, the National Park Service initially opposed the notion of removing the Elwha dams, even suggesting that the cost of transporting fish over the dams be shared with Crown Zellerbach.[6] But, in 1990, the Park Service changed its position and came out in favor of restoring the Elwha by removing the dams.

The year 1991 saw major progress toward removal. FERC released a draft Environmental Impact Statement declaring that only removal of the Elwha and Glines Canyon Dams could bring about full restoration of the Elwha's ecosystem and its anadromous fish. The report concluded that dam removal was feasible and that the price of making the improvements necessary to save the dams would equal or exceed the cost of obtaining the power they generated elsewhere. The General Accounting Office concurred. The U.S. Fish and Wildlife Service determined that restored salmon runs in the Elwha would be worth more than the power the dams would ever produce. Taken together, these developments were, in the words of Shawn Cantrell, a "huge, huge victory" for conservation.

The next year, President Bush signed the Elwha River Ecosystem and Fisheries Restoration Act, which mandated restoration of the river and halted any further licensing proceedings on either of the dams. The act further required that if the Department of the Interior officially determined that dam removal was the best way to restore the Elwha, the federal government should acquire and remove both dams. Thus, in 1996, it was decided that removing both dams over a two-year period would be ideal and that the federal government would acquire the dams from the Fort James Corporation. With the dams sold for the purpose of removal, the Port Angeles mill would instead buy electricity from the Bonneville Power Administration. In early 2000, after over twenty years of legal maneuvering around the licensing process, the federal government bought Elwha and Glines Canyon Dams.

Over $37 million in federal funding has been secured, but additional federal funds are needed before Elwha River restoration and removal of the Glines Canyon and Elwha Dams can proceed. Until his defeat in the 2000 election, Washington's senior senator, Republican Slade Gorton, an adamant opponent of dam removal, was chairman of the Senate Interior Appropriations Committee and therefore a key figure in the appropriation of any funding for removal and restoration. Initially opposed to any Elwha dam removal, Gorton later made his reluctant support for the project contingent on legislative assurance that none of the lower Snake River dams ever be breached. Part of Gorton's intransigence stems from his tenure as Washington state attorney general, during which the U.S. Supreme Court ruled against the state in the 1974 landmark Boldt decision. That ruling affirmed tribal treaty rights and guaranteed Northwest tribes 50 percent of fish caught at their usual and accustomed fishing grounds. Dams' destruction of Indian fishing grounds throughout the Pacific and inland Northwest remains a subject of bitter contention, and, in some parts of Washington, hostility toward Indians remains.

Thus far, the federal government has spent $29.5 million acquiring the two dams. For fiscal year 2000, the federal budget appropriated $22 million for the project; another $15 million was appropriated for FY 2001. Whatever happens next in the way of appropriations, first on the decommissioning agenda is a new water treatment plant for Port Angeles. The plant is needed to cope with the sediment that will be released when the dams are removed. Exactly how much such a facility will cost has been a sticking point in negotiations between the city of Port Angeles and the federal government. Designing and engineering the actual removal cannot proceed until that problem is solved.

After leaving Olympic National Park, I drive downhill toward the coast and the Elwha's floodplain to the Elwha Klallam Tribal Center, to see Michael Langland, the tribe's river restoration director. The road passes modest farms and houses set amid low-lying fields shaded by tall trees. The tribal center is close to the water.

The tribes, Langland tells me, have been involved in the dam removal effort longer than anyone else, but their role has been underplayed in the press. The Elwha River valley has been the "stomping grounds for the Klallams for thousands of years." Traditionally, Langland explains, there were twelve bands of the tribe, but only three remain. The tribe had seasonal camps all up and down the valley. Along the river are spiritual cleansing sites. The Elwha Dam is located "where we believe we were created," Langland tells me. "It's a very sacred site."

Since the lower Elwha dam went in, the tribe has been concerned about its safety. "It's very uncomfortable to work and live below the dam, knowing how unstable it is," says Langland. When the dam's spillway gates are opened during high water flows, the downstream flooding is artificially increased. This creates problems on the reservation, for housing, farming and fishing.

"My people have lost the most and suffered the most" with the construction of this dam, says Langland. "We had a birthright taken away," he says of the once rich salmon runs. "The dam totally destroyed the ecosystem, and we're doing everything we can to help by not fishing and we will not do any fishing until the numbers return." Langland takes me on a tour of the Elwha Klallam Tribal Center. We stroll through the airy halls. The walls are covered with posters about language classes, tribal dancing, bus schedules, social services, Head Start and day care.

I'm curious to see the mouth of the river itself, so Langland guides me down a short dirt road to where the Elwha empties into the sea. We stand on the edge of the wide and sandy stream channel. Langland tells me how it has changed over the years. He shows me where, because of the sediment trapped by the dams, there are large rocks at the mouth of the river instead of the fine gravel young fish prefer. We walk onto the beach where a sign indicates that without tribal permission, I would not be welcome. A dead gull is lying in the sand. The bay laps gently at the shore. There used to be good shellfishing here, Langland says, but that's gone now, too. A 1981 Supreme Court decision ruled that the 1974 Boldt decision affirming the tribal treaty right to fisheries implied protection of that habitat. A 1994 court decision extended that right to guarantee the western Washington tribes half the harvestable shellfish in their usual and accustomed salmon fishing areas.

Langland tells me that tribal fisherman have been able to fish commercially—meaning that there were enough fish to sell—within the past ten years. Before the Boldt Decision in 1974, whenever Native American fishermen fished, they were "quickly arrested and jailed doing what many had spent their lifetime doing.

"We're not fishing now," he reminds me. There aren't enough fish.

To say what will happen in the Bush-Cheney administration is "like reading tea leaves," says Shawn Cantrell, when I check back with him shortly after the 2000 election, in which Slade Gorton lost his seat to Democrat Maria Cantwell. Despite Gorton's vocal opposition to dam removal, without him in the Senate, says Cantrell, Washington will have lost a senior senator who, when he chose, could really bring home the bacon.

But in the summer of 2001, Cantrell describes the year's appropriation process for the Elwha as "very encouraging," with support coming from both the Bush administration and the Republican-controlled House. Perhaps the Elwha will prove that a major dam removal can indeed progress on the merits of its restoration regardless of party politics.

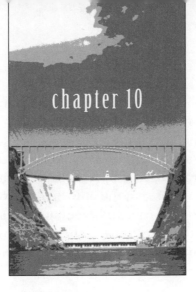

chapter 10

The Lower
Snake River Dams

"SAVE OUR
WILD SALMON"

The hills above the lower Snake River in eastern Washington are a deep mustard yellow. Sumac and maples
have begun to turn red. The flat water of the river reflects the
solid blue sky. It is early October 1999, and I have come to see the
four lower Snake River dams, the breaching of which is now being
discussed by the very government agencies that built them just a
generation ago. Under the Endangered Species Act, which now
protects what's left of Snake River salmon and steelhead runs, the
federal government must ensure that the lower Snake River dams
do not put these fish in jeopardy of extinction.

Due to the cumulative effect of degraded habitat, overfishing at
the turn of the twentieth century and changing ocean conditions,

Snake River salmon have been dwindling in number for well over a century. Their numbers dipped precipitously in the 1970s after construction of the last of the four lower Snake River dams, and all Snake River salmon are now listed as threatened or endangered under the Endangered Species Act. Snake River coho were declared extinct in 1986, and the only Snake River sockeye salmon remaining survive in a captive-breeding program. Breaching, by removal of the earthen sections of the four dams to restore a free flowing river, is one of the ways to help recover the imperiled stocks. This prospect is exhilarating to some, but to others it is threatening.

The fate of these dams and the recovery of the region's wild salmon have thrown the Pacific Northwest into a protracted political, scientific and emotional debate. To many, the dams represent the lifeline of the region's twentieth-century prosperity. Salmon are the Northwest's ecological and spiritual heart and soul.

The four dams of the lower Snake River are, in downstream to upstream order—moving west to east—Ice Harbor, Lower Monumental, Little Goose and Lower Granite, built in 1962, 1969, 1970 and 1975, respectively, by the Army Corps of Engineers. Constructed in the final years of the United States' big dam-building era that began in the 1930s with dams like Grand Coulee on the upper Columbia River, the four lower Snake River dams create a 465-mile slackwater navigation channel that extends from Lewiston, Idaho, to the mouth of the Columbia. They complete the navigation corridor begun with construction of Bonneville, The Dalles, John Day and McNary Dams on the lower Columbia that allows products from the inland Northwest to be transported by barge to Pacific Coast ports, namely Portland, Oregon, and Vancouver, Kalama and Longview, Washington. These ports—which are about eighty to ninety miles from the ocean itself—represent a huge volume of business for the region, not just for exports but for incoming products as well.

The lower Snake River dams are run-of-the-river hydroelectric dams, which means they capture high winter and spring flows that will be used later in the dry season to generate power and to supply water for irrigation. They retain no drinking water and perform no flood control. The four dams now generate about 5 percent of the Northwest's electricity, which is fed into the grid managed by the Bonneville Power Administration. They currently provide irrigation primarily for thirteen large farms, not by creating storage reservoirs but by raising the level of water in their slackwater pools so that it may be more easily pumped to crop fields, orchards and vineyards.

The headwaters of the Snake and Columbia trickle off mountainsides in seven western states—Washington, Oregon, Idaho, Montana, Wyoming, Nevada and Utah—and the Canadian province of British Columbia. Snowmelt from the Wallowas, the Blue Mountains, the Cascades, the western flank of the northern Rockies, the Sawtooths, the Boulder White Clouds, Bitterroots and Tetons flows westward across the Palouse, the sagebrush steppe, scablands and canyons of the central Columbia Basin toward the coastal rainforest. The whole watershed drains close to 260,000 square miles, about 40,000 of which are in British Columbia. Dams have turned the powerful Columbia into a series of impoundments that stretch from central British Columbia to the Pacific and east into Idaho and Montana.

Before 1930, there was no dam in Oregon, Washington or Idaho that impounded more than a million acre-feet of water. By 1965, there were seven, and by 1998, there were ten. The same period of time saw the construction of about thirty dams impounding between 250,000 and a million acre-feet of water.[1] There are now at least forty such large dams in the Columbia Basin and many more if dams on smaller tributary rivers are included in the count. Some of these dams—Grand Coulee Dam on the upper Columbia and the Hells Canyon* complex of dams on the Snake—were built without fish passage. The huge impoundments slow the natural river flow and have flooded riverbanks for miles, eliminating gravel beds used for spawning that also provide important habitat for the aquatic insects on which fish feed. The impoundments' banks have also been straightened and reinforced with riprap, further altering natural streamside and wetland habitat.

---

*The Hells Canyon dams owned and operated by Idaho Power are due for relicensing. Endangered fish runs there are creating a fight between conservation and power generation.

Along the Columbia and Snake, damming inundated traditional Indian fishing grounds, the loss of which has been bitterly disputed for over fifty years. Since the building of the dams on the lower Columbia in the 1930s, 1940s and 1950s, the federal government has promised Columbia River tribes replacement of flooded fishing sites. Even after decades of litigation and Supreme Court rulings affirming the tribal right to fish, these sites have not been fully replaced. Now salmon numbers are so low that Columbia and Snake River fishing is extremely limited.*

Failure to recover these salmon runs may jeopardize the federal government's 1855 treaty with Northwest tribes in which the tribes ceded their ancestral lands to the United States. The treaty guarantees the tribes a right to fish at their usual and accustomed fishing places—places known since time immemorial. Today, 95 percent of the historic salmon population is gone and with it "what was left of the trust between federal river managers and the tribal people," says Charles Hudson of the Columbia River Inter-Tribal Fish Commission. So as salmon numbers dwindle, the question arises: What happens to the treaty if there are no fish to catch?

The Columbia Basin dams were built to electrify the Northwest and irrigate the naturally arid lands of the Columbia Basin. Their electricity, provided at heavily subsidized rates, was destined largely for the Oregon and Washington aluminum smelters that produced metal to furnish the wherewithal for the U.S. and Allied victory in World War II. Northwest residents benefit from this subsidy and pay far less for their electricity than do other regions. Built on the assumption that there would always be more than enough water to satisfy all demands, these dams helped foster what historian of the Grand Coulee Dam Paul Pitzer calls "a myth of plenty."[2]

During the dry years of 2000 and 2001, the competition between water for hydropower dams and water for the river's fish intensi-

---

*A lawsuit was also filed in federal district court on May 3, 2001, challenging the entire federal Columbia Basin salmon recovery plan, charging that it is inadequate in its restoration measures and sets too low a threshold for extinction.

fied. "Salmon did not create the current crisis, and the Columbia River cannot continue to be run on their backs," said Antone Minthorn, chairman of the board of the Confederated Tribes of the Umatilla, to the Western Governors Association in February 2001, when the group met to discuss the allocation of basin water.

That dams kill salmon not even the Army Corps of Engineers can deny. On the lower Snake, the dams raise summer water temperatures to levels unhealthy for salmon. The dams' spillways elevate the level of dissolved gases in the river water in ways that can seriously harm fish. The dams block the passage of young fish on their way to the ocean and the return of adult fish to upstream spawning grounds. Many fish are transported around the dams by barge and truck but often suffer physical distress in the process, which can kill them,* and when dumped back in the river, fish become vulnerable to predators. For fish that swim the river, the dams' turbines create a potentially lethal hazard to negotiate. Some emerge stressed but intact; others become trapped. Overall, the dams have been documented as the biggest threat to salmon on their way to the ocean.†

The catch of salmon in the Columbia River Basin has declined steadily since records were first kept in the second half of the nineteenth century. In the mid-1800s, between ten and sixteen million salmon returned to the Columbia River each year. In the late 1970s, the average returning runs contained between two and three million fish. Today, the current average run of salmon returning to the Columbia is only one million fish. Of those, some 80 percent are hatchery—rather than wild—salmon. Twelve other Columbia Basin chinook, chum salmon and steelhead stocks are now listed under the Endangered Species Act as either threatened or endangered. "We really have a serious risk of extinction for spring and summer chinook in the Snake River," said National Marine Fisheries Service regional administrator Will Stelle in

---

*The federal agencies refer to this as "delayed mortality."
†"The highest [salmon] mortality en route to the ocean . . . now happens 'at the concrete,' as a result of passage through the turbines or elsewhere," reports the *Columbia Basin Bulletin,* citing National Marine Fisheries Service researcher Bill Muir.

February 2000. "Those risks are now and we have to be prepared to do something quickly." The federal government's current salmon recovery plan focuses on four stocks of chinook, chum and steelhead, but one way or another, these dams affect all anadromous fish that swim the mainstem of the Snake.

Since completion of the four lower Snake River dams, only one free-flowing stretch of either the lower Columbia or lower Snake River remains. Called the Hanford Reach, this fifty-one-mile bend of the Columbia, just upstream from its confluence with the Snake, was proclaimed a National Monument in the summer of 2000. It flows through land sequestered by the Department of Energy's Hanford Nuclear Reservation and thus has been curiously protected from other development. Today, some 80 percent of upper Columbia River Basin fall chinook salmon spawn in the Hanford Reach, providing proof of how a free-flowing river benefits fish. But even this stretch of river is not immune to dams' manipulation of water levels.

While in the ocean, Columbia Basin salmon may migrate as far north as Alaska, swimming the currents along the Pacific Coast off Oregon, Washington and British Columbia. The fate of these salmon is affected by wildlife policies of all the states in the watershed, as well as the U.S. and Canadian governments. Today, nearly all commercial salmon fishing takes place in ocean waters and is controlled by international treaty as well as domestic regulations. What happens to salmon in eastern Washington and Idaho directly influences the livelihood of commercial fishermen in Alaska.

The loss of Snake River salmon did not come as a sudden surprise. The lower Snake River dams were built with full knowledge that they would seriously harm salmon. In 1947, the U.S. Fish and Wildlife Service warned that construction "of the Dalles and five planned Snake River dams would wipe out the salmon runs." Their fears were dismissed by Warner G. Gardner, assistant secretary of the Columbia Basin Inter-Agency, who maintained that overall "benefits [of the dams] to the Pacific Northwest are such that the present salmon runs must if necessary be sacrificed."[3] Nearly fifty years later with salmon's survival now truly in question, we have barely begun to act on that knowledge.

Young salmon and steelhead are collected at Lower Granite Dam and transported by fish truck to the Columbia River below Bonneville Dam. Thus, their journey to the ocean is uninterrupted by the dams and the fish mortality problems of nitrogen supersaturation and generators are diminished," reads an explanatory placard at the Lower Granite Dam visitors center.

At Little Goose Dam, steelhead fishermen have set up their campers, RVs and lawn chairs on the shore along the slack water on either side of the dam. A sign warns anglers not to entangle their lines in the wires strung across the river, which are draped with what looks like Christmas tinsel, to deter birds from preying on fish in the slow water.

Ahead of me on the highway is a pressurized steel tanker truck emblazoned with the legend "Fish for the Future." It is part of the Army Corps of Engineers' juvenile fish transport fleet. Miles of colored pipes, bearing a close architectural resemblance to the exterior of the Beaubourg museum in Paris, twist around what are described as juvenile fish passage facilities. Fish ladders resembling steel washboards and amusement park waterslides zigzag and loop alongside the dams' shoreline structures. "Which is the dam with the loop-de-loop?" jokes a friend who has toured these dams. "Little Goose," I say, recalling the hairpin turn of steel runway that rises high over the visitors parking area.

Salmon run deep in the culture of the Northwest. From the Columbia Basin headwaters to the Pacific Ocean, north to Alaska and south to California, salmon are a cultural icon. Salmon are sacred to Northwest tribes. "Our culture, tradition and ceremonies all center around the river and salmon. I cannot overstate its cultural importance," one tribal leader told me.

Even for those in the Northwest who are not tribal members and do not fish commercially or for sport, salmon are central to the region's identity. Salmon are part of the biological fabric of life in the Pacific Northwest. They are nourished by the ecology of the coastal temperate rainforest, with its mild, long rainy season. A web of mosses, lichens, mollusks, ferns and trees creates the environment that enables salmon—and the creatures that feed on them—to thrive. Salmon are wild creatures that are part of every-day life in this region. Endangered salmon swim right through the cities of Seattle and Portland. If you live in the Northwest, where you wash your car or how your house's downspouts are configured means thinking about salmon.

Salmon are an indicator species for the region. Their health depends on clean, cold water in the streams where they spawn. To see a salmon swim upstream or leap up a rapid is astounding. Their biological homing instinct and spawning dance inspire awe. In 1999, the Northwest bishops of the Catholic Church issued a pastoral letter that described the Columbia and Snake Rivers as a "sacred commons." Their letter called for policies that would recognize tribal treaty rights and the need for a sound economy, and honor the existence of salmon and steelhead as creatures of God.

But development conspires against salmon. Logging, road building and construction send large volumes of silt into rivers and streams. Contaminated water running off agricultural fields, lawns and roads, coming through storm drains and from industrial sites, creates damaging pollution. Removing vegetation from stream banks eliminates the shade that keeps water cool. Intensive livestock grazing degrades stream banks and contributes to damaging erosion. Water diversions reduce stream levels, leaving fish to struggle. All of these activities, combined with the effect of dams, have led to the distinct possibility that wild salmon will disappear within our lifetime.[4]

Because so many factors affect the life cycle of salmon, their recovery and restoration are particularly complex—allowing people in one part of the watershed to point fingers at those in another and say "your fault." Is it the logging in the uplands, grazing, agricultural irrigation, industrial pollution or urban and suburban development that is to blame for the salmon's precipitous decline? Some people point out to the sea and blame terns and sea lions for eating too many fish. Others say that changing ocean conditions are responsible for the downturn in salmon numbers. Still others blame the hatchery program, which some consider a solution. Although the dams on the lower Snake are not the one and only source of wild salmon's decline, many—including hundreds of scientists—believe these four dams to be the proverbial straw that broke the camel's back.

In February 2000, a retired fisheries biologist wheeled a five-foot-high stack of studies documenting this damage into a public hearing held by the Army Corps of Engineers, National Marine Fisheries Service and other federal agencies. "We have here a never-ending process of study," said the biologist. "We're studying the old studies and designing new studies but I'm not sure we're going to have any fish left to study."

In December 2000, after a lengthy round of public hearings, held in communities from Alaska to Montana, to gather comments on its proposal to recover the Columbia Basin salmonids affected by federal hydropower dams, the federal government released its plan. While it stops short of recommending breaching the lower Snake dams as the preferred course of action, the plan includes that option if other efforts fall short of the goals set for restoring fish runs. To forestall the need for breaching, the plan calls for restoration of habitat in the watershed's upstream tributaries and in the Columbia estuary, changes in management of salmon hatcheries, continued limitations on harvest (catching fish) and some alteration of current dam operations.

Despite the apparent obstacles, salmon advocates and hundreds of scientists maintain that breaching the four lower Snake River dams is essential to any effective salmon recovery plan. Because congressional authorization is needed to allocate the funding necessary to implement restoration, let alone dam breaching, Snake River salmon recovery will inevitably remain political.

Throughout the Columbia Basin, development, agriculture and logging have degraded river conditions, but the dams on the Columbia's mainstem and on the Snake have physically altered that environment the most. Driving north from Hermiston, Oregon, toward the Columbia, then east along the stretch of river canyon called the Wallula Gap, I pass a series of irrigation pumps and a marina where some handsome sailboats are moored. Here the river used to begin its descent toward Celilo Falls, the great rapids fished by Columbia River Indians for ages before it was drowned by The Dalles Dam in 1957. The dark rock outcrops on the river-banks are so striking, it's hard to remember what I'm seeing is only a remnant of what this river was.

Further upstream above the Snake are great swooping hillside fields, planted or plowed for grain. The slopes become steeper and the earth darker as I enter the Palouse, with its rich deep soil laid down eons ago in the wake of retreating inland seas. Some of the hills are plowed at what looks to be a precariously vertical pitch. A few old homestead farms nestle in the clefts of hillside. Continuing east, irrigated fields of potatoes and vegetables, orchards and vineyards give way to dryland crops of wheat, soybeans, barley and lentils. After the huge industrial storage sheds and processing plants along the mid-Columbia, the cottonwood plantations and pulp mills clustered at the confluence of the Snake and Columbia, the roads above the lower Snake stretch out in rural isolation.

Towns like Windust, Kahlotus, Almota, Dusty, Starbuck and Washtucna are marked by little more than their grain elevators. It seems clear that as the roads improved—and agribusiness grew—the distances between these small towns and the cities of Kennewick, Richland, Pasco, Clarkston, Lewiston, Walla Walla, Pullman and Colefax shrank, eventually eliminating the demand for local car dealerships and supermarkets. Pomeroy's storefronts sport signs announcing antiques and collectibles, but in towns that still have viable commercial centers, the predominance of John Deere and other heavy farm equipment dealers indicates that espresso-sipping tourists are a scarcity. There is little evidence of what these communities were like before the dams, and it's difficult to imagine this broad flat stretch of river surging with whitewater and waterfalls.

At Ice Harbor, I follow a road uphill above the dam. It leads to a high spot with a long view of the river, where a low wall surrounds a large brick-red chunk of what must have been river canyon wall. The rock is emblazoned with petroglyphs. This, says a brass plaque, is "A Memorial to the Ancestors of the Indians Now Known as Colville, Nez Perce, Umatilla, Warm Springs and Yakima. They lie near 'Where the Two Rivers Meet.'" The plaque is dated 1965. I squint in the sun and sketch the petroglyphs in my notebook. On another plaque I read:

"A Memorial: Indians once came to the river to fish for salmon. Here they met friends, traded, played games, danced and sang. After drying their fish they moved back to their villages. But some were not destined to return home. They lie in burial grounds along the river. Now they rest undisturbed beneath the waters of Lake Sacajawea. This great boulder carved with petroglyphs by earlier Indians was taken from near the riverbank and here commemorates the flood burial sites. By this act we bind together the generations."

The flood refers to the rising of the thirty-two-mile long impoundment called Lake Sacajawea created when Ice Harbor Dam was constructed. I wonder about the binding of generations.

In the parking lot on the north side of Lower Monumental Dam is a pickup with a "Save Our Dams" bumper sticker. In a corner behind some metal tanks outside the building housing the dam's works, near a fish ladder stands a semi-abstract sculpture of an Indian holding a salmon and a fishing spear. In Clarkston, Washington, I pass an alley where a "Save Our Dams" display parade float is lodged. In the "Comments" section of the sign-in book in the visitors center—as at all the lower Snake dams—are messages from dozens of schoolchildren saying, "Save Our Dams!" I wonder if they have been coached. In October 2000, a week before the presidential election, signs shouting "Save Our Dams" pepper the roadsides, boosting the state's slate of Republican candidates along with Bush and Cheney.

In February 2000, I go to Pasco, Washington, to sit in on a public meeting held by the agencies of the Federal Caucus* to gather comments on their draft plan for recovering Columbia Basin salmon and steelhead, a document called "The Draft Lower Snake River Juvenile Salmon Migration Feasibility Report and Environ-

---

*The Federal Caucus consists of the Army Corps of Engineers, Bonneville Power Administration, Bureau of Indian Affairs, Bureau of Land Management, Bureau of Reclamation, Environmental Protection Agency, Fish and Wildlife Service, Forest Service and National Marine Fisheries Service.

mental Impact Statement and the Federal Caucus All-H Paper." Located at the confluence of the Snake and Columbia, Pasco, Richland and Kennewick are known as the Tri-Cities. Many people here work for the Department of Energy at Hanford or are farmers whose fields are irrigated by the dams and shipped out through their locks. Others work at food-processing plants and at the local chip and paper mills. Many families moved to the area when the first dams were built; others arrived recently from Mexico and Central America to work at area farms. Politically, it is a generally conservative community, and feelings run high about the dams in this part of the Columbia Basin. Over the past thirty-five to forty years, the region's economy has relied on what the dams provide, and far from everyone is convinced that removing the dams is the way to save salmon.

Outside the hotel where the meeting is taking place are a number of Boise Cascade* employees with signs that say "Save Our Jobs—Save Our Dams," "Fish and Jobs—We Can Have Both!" "Don't Breach Our Economy!" "Dams Equal Jobs" and "Get the Nets Out of the River!" The nets refer to Indian fishing. The Boise Cascade workers have been given the day off to come to the hearing. A group of tribal members stand on the sidewalk drumming. Their signs say "Save the Salmon." The fact is that the federal dams are allowed to kill up to 90 percent of endangered juvenile salmon and up to 40 percent of adult salmon, while in 2000, tribal fishers were allowed to catch only 8.5 percent of listed salmon.

I speak with several older men who are milling about. One says he is a farmer from Moses Lake, Washington, a town whose farms are irrigated by the Columbia Basin Project. "It's not about the fish," he says. "It's more about control of the water and the money tree." He then describes a UN plot to take over the National Parks and says he worries that if the lower Snake River dams come out his property will be flooded. This is utterly impossible, but I keep that thought to myself. One of his comrades, a longshoreman from the southern Oregon coast town of Coos Bay, laments the state of the timber industry, informing me that "some hippie rode

---

*Boise Cascade is one of the nation's largest paper and wood products manufacturers.

into town on a flatbed yelling 'spotted owl' and we haven't shipped much timber ever since." They then make derogatory remarks about the Native Americans standing nearby.

Inside the lobby knots of people are waiting to put their names on speaking rosters. There are elected officials from Umatilla and Hermiston, Oregon, from the Tri-Cities—mayors, county and port commissioners and local businesspeople. The crowd is largely male. Representatives of the Columbia River Inter-Tribal Fish Commission are here along with many tribal members. There are representatives of regional fishing groups, federal agencies and a few environmental organizations, the Sierra Club and the Save Our Wild Salmon coalition among them. The atmosphere is notably tense. "This is not a voting contest," remarks a fellow from the Department of the Interior's Washington, D.C., office. That point, it seems to me, would be hard to impress on most of those assembled.

The tribes, conservation and fishing groups, irrigators and the Army Corps of Engineers all have leaflets and fact sheets spread out on folding tables and are ready to engage anyone who wanders by in conversation. "What I don't understand is the problem with the salmon. I mean they're not rationed. You can buy them in the supermarket," says an older woman in a neat navy pantsuit to a man from the sport fishermen's association.

The Pasco High School's agricultural science class is at the hearing on a field trip. As students step off the school bus, "Save Our Dams" supporters hand them yellow ribbons. I ask a couple of girls about the yellow ribbons and about saving the dams. "I don't really know. I think it's for jobs, but I want to make up my own mind," says one.

I see a large man wearing a T-shirt that says "Eat the Terns—Barbecue a Tern." Caspian terns have been flocking to an island made of dredge spoils at the mouth of the Columbia and eating lots of juvenile salmon, posing a knotty problem as wildlife regulations protect both salmon and terns. "The best thing to do about the terns," says the man with the shirt, "is to turn a bunch of pigs loose on Rice Island. They'd eat them, they'd get fat and then you'd butcher them." He seems to be at least half-serious. Committees of respected scientists will spend months trying to solve the problem. Just when things are heating up with lawsuits from conservation groups and a crisis in humane tern relocation, the terns fly off and settle somewhere less bothersome.

I speak with a county commissioner from Union County in northeastern Oregon. "It's not about fish," she tells me. "It's about being able to control land. It's about removing people's ability to manage their own lifestyles. It's being done in Washington, D.C., not here. They're taking people's ability to control their own lives. We seek balance. I want to save the salmon but also the amenities of being able to live and work here. The dams brought electricity to this region in this century. It's no different than wilderness areas, where we want to protect livelihoods as well as wilderness. The further you are from the area, the more you want to protect it," she says of the rural-versus-urban divide that characterizes Oregon and Washington. I ask how she would respond if someone pointed out that it was the federal government that built the dams. "Well, the federal government has changed since they put the dams in," she says.

"Whatever we do is going to affect thousands of people in the region and we're going to have to live with those decisions and each other," says Colonel Eric T. Mogren, deputy commander of the Northwest Division of the Army Corps of Engineers, opening the meeting. "We must look for common ground in our legal and moral obligations for protection of the environment, in respect for the treaty rights of the tribes and in respect for the economy of the region."

"There are no silver bullets," cautions Will Stelle, National Marine Fisheries Service regional administrator.

The meeting begins with testimony from elected officials and tribal leaders. When the first tribal leader rises to speak, there is audible muttering in the room. "Who elected those people?" a man near me says.

"My work is to oversee the continued existence of the salmon of the Columbia River. There is a power much greater than any of us here. . . . We need to open up our minds and our hearts and very seriously consider breaching the four lower Snake River dams," declares a chief of the Confederated Tribes of the Umatilla. "We stand firm in our belief that the four lower Snake River dams should be breached," says Thomas Morning-Owl, general counsel for the Confederated Tribes of the Umatilla. "My kids have to listen to slurs. 'Go back to where you came from. Spear chucker. Wagon burner.' We're foreigners in our homeland," says a member of the Umatilla Indian Reservation board of trustees. "We're like the salmon. We have to fight every day for where we live. We're going to have to work together. Money can't bring these fish back when they're gone," he says somberly.

"We need a plan to recover salmon and preserve the economy. Our area predominantly opposes dam breaching. Our jobs and way of life are at stake," says the commissioner of the Port of Walla Walla to applause. "Removal of the Snake River dams would have a devastating effect on everyone in the region, on the barging of agricultural products to the Pacific Coast ports. Why are we studying these dams when salmon spend most of their lives in the ocean?" says the Garfield County commissioner. Stating his opposition to dam breaching, the mayor of Umatilla asserts that "if these dams were not in place this winter, Portland would be experiencing devastating flooding." This is simply not true.

Several middle-aged men from Lewiston, Idaho, lament the loss of salmon and steelhead and cite statistics showing the heavy taxpayer subsidy for Snake River barging. Barging here receives an annual federal subsidy of $10 million. When several tribal elder women speak, many in the audience ignore them, carrying on their own conversations, and have to be quieted by the moderator.

"Not so many years ago, the Corps came to sell us the dams," says a man from Clarkston, Washington. "Now, due to lawsuits and extremists you're trying to take them away and change our way of life. It's your responsibility," he says to the panel of federal agency representatives, "to take care of what you sold us and to take care of us." Voicing an unpleasant undercurrent that ran through the day's proceedings, another man says, "It's time to stop fishing. Time to stop netting. Time to revisit the tribes' agreements."

Two weeks before the Pasco hearing, about 250 people fill a meeting room at the Portland Airport Holiday Inn to deliver their oral comments on the same federal salmon recovery plan. This crowd is notably different from the one in Pasco. It is mostly urban, outdoorsy and professional. In the Pacific Northwest this is not an oxymoron. Portland and Seattle are known for their quality of life, for their proximity to rivers, mountains, the ocean and salmon streams. Many at the Portland hearing are members of regional conservation groups. Many have brought their children with them. In three hours of testimony about four dozen people speak. Only one speaker favors saving the dams.

In the official press packet is a list of those who've formally endorsed the retirement of the lower Snake River dams. It includes the Idaho Statesman, the Columbia River Inter-Tribal Fish Commission, the Nez Perce Tribe, the Yakama Nation, the Sierra Club, Friends of the Earth, National Wildlife Federation, the Wilderness Society, Trout Unlimited, Zero Population Growth, American Rivers, Republicans for Environmental Protection, Physicians for Social Responsibility, the Center for Marine Conservation and Taxpayers for Common Sense, along with dozens of commercial fishermen based in southeastern Alaska and western Washington. The evening feels like a groundswell of support for salmon. Similar reports come back from the hearings in Spokane, Astoria, Lewiston and Seattle.

It is simply irresponsible to call the dams 'a killing field' for salmon and focus the entire debate on dams when . . . there are myriad causes to this problem—including over fishing, possibly by Alaskans," said Representative George Nethercutt, a Washington Republican, in a press release in the fall of 1999.

"The fact that it's safer to transfer them by truck than let them loose in the rivers says it all," said Alaska Governor Tony Knowles to reporters asking for his position on breaching the four lower Snake Dams at an October 25, 1999, press briefing in Juneau.

Knowles's and Nethercutt's comments came amidst the latest volley of reports, studies and statements debating the fate of the four lower Snake River dams and the fight to save Pacific salmon—a debate that at times seems headed for a showdown between federal agencies. Among the barrage of government-commissioned reports is one released in 1998, known as PATH—Plan for Analyzing and Testing Hypotheses—by a team of

scientists from the National Marine Fisheries Service, other federal and state agencies, tribes and universities. This study concluded that breaching the dams is the surest way to recover Snake
River salmon.

Following the PATH report came the December 1998 release of
the Army Corps of Engineers' draft Environmental Impact Statement assessing the effects of the hydropower system on Snake
River salmon and steelhead. Buried in a key appendix to the report is the finding that dam removal alone could be sufficient to
recover Snake River stocks of fall chinook and steelhead and
therefore must be included in any recovery plan.

Then, in a move ripe for cynical interpretation, NMFS commissioned another study using a whole new team of scientists. Rather
than concentrating restoration efforts in the mainstem where the
dams are, the new study—called Cumulative Risk Initiative
(CRI)—emphasizes restoration of upstream tributaries and the
Columbia River estuary downstream. In setting parameters for
salmon recovery, the CRI study places the threshold for extinction
as one fish or less—meaning that any fish (salmon or steelhead),
anywhere in its life cycle or migration pattern, would be counted.

"Where are the fish, man?" a Umatilla tribal member asked his
neighbor during the press conference announcing the study.

Seriously criticized during its review by an independent panel
of scientists, the CRI study caused disagreement among the federal agencies responsible for protecting and managing salmon.
Critics note the study's failure to consider habitat restoration that
includes dam breaching, and for omitting many biological and environmental factors from its analysis. Tribal members, commercial
fishermen, conservationists and many scientists fear that current
salmon recovery plans based on this study place the bar too low—
way below fishable numbers. The goal is to have wild salmon on
the dinner table, not just in the zoo.

Despite these apparent shortcomings, the CRI study became
the basis of a subsequent report released by the Federal Caucus in
December 1999 called the All-H Paper, which would form the
foundation of the federal Columbia Basin salmon recovery plan.
(The H's in "All-H" stand for the Habitat, Harvest, Hatcheries and
Hydropower that affect salmon survival.) Like the CRI study, the

All-H Paper recommends beginning restoration efforts in up-stream tributaries and in the Columbia River estuary. It thus places a substantial burden of recovery on private lands where farmers, ranchers and loggers say they have already done more than their fair share of restoration efforts. And the fishing com-munity—commercial, sport and tribal—has borne the hardships of reduced harvests for many years now.

Preliminary estimates indicate that the All-H Paper's recom-mendations may well cost more than dam breaching. But the pa-per does not include an economic analysis, nor does it say how federal agencies would coordinate their restoration work with lo-cal efforts on private land. Tribal leaders criticize the All-H Paper for not adequately assessing the impact of its proposal on tribal economies. They, along with the paper's Independent Scientific Advisory Board, American Rivers, the Federation of Pacific Coast Federation of Fishermen's Associations, Save Our Wild Salmon and other conservation groups, call the paper a delaying tactic. "We are not comfortable with the apparent drift toward delay of the actual decision about the management decisions bearing on hydrosystem operations, possible dam breaching, and other inter-ventions as well," wrote the Advisory Board in November 1999.

Criticism also came from biologists with the U.S. Fish and Wildlife Service, Oregon Department of Fish and Wildlife, Idaho Department of Fish and Game, Columbia River Inter-tribal Fish Commission and Columbia Basin Fish and Wildlife Authority, who wrote that "given the dangerously low level of these [Snake River salmon and steelhead] populations, we do not believe it prudent to make management decisions on the configuration and opera-tion of the Snake and Columbia hydrosystem for the next 5 to 20 years based solely on one optimistic assumption [by NMFS] about the effectiveness of past and current hydrosystem operations."

But Northwest Republicans welcomed the All-H Paper, as did those business interests that took it to mean that dam breaching was off the table, at least for the moment. This feeling was further confirmed in July 2000, when NMFS announced that it would not make any recommendations concerning dam breaching until the end of 2000—when the Biological Opinion on the effect of Co-lumbia Basin dams on endangered salmon was due. It was also a strategy clearly aimed at postponing any such decisions until after the 2000 presidential election. During the campaign, George W. Bush stated his general opposition to dam breaching, while Al Gore skirted a direct commitment by promising, if elected, to hold a "salmon summit" in the Northwest. If saving salmon were simply a matter of voting demographics, Maria Cantwell's slim victory over Slade Gorton would be instructive, for she won the Senate seat largely on her strength in the more populous, liberal, urbanized districts west of the Cascades, including Seattle, whose city council passed a resolution calling for dam breaching.

In November 2000, shortly before the Federal Caucus released its final Columbia Basin salmon recovery plan, an article based on the National Marine Fisheries Service's Cumulative Risk Initiative study was published in the journal *Science*.[5] The article showed—amid an impressive array of peer-reviewed mathematical modeling—that if dam breaching was the only restoration action undertaken, Snake River salmon runs might not be restored. This finding was hailed by opponents of dam breaching while critics of the study argued that it set too low a threshold for a survivable population and failed to take into account all causes of habitat degradation. Advocates of dam breaching, meanwhile, reminded *their* critics that they have never said breaching alone would recover salmon.

Fascinated at the apparent about-face in federally commissioned studies—the PATH studies that recommended breaching and CRI that did not—I looked at the article in *Science*. Read closely, it states clearly that its models rely on the successful transport of salmon around not only the four lower Snake River dams but the four on the lower Columbia as well. "Breaching the lower Snake River dams would mean the end of fish transportation operations and would therefore eliminate any delayed mortality from transportation. Additionally, the removal of four of the eight dams encountered by Snake River salmon might increase the physiological vigor of salmon that swim downriver, thus improving survival during the critical estuarine phase,"[6] write the authors, noting that transported fish survive at 70 percent the rate of those that are not.

The article's publication provoked a blast from the Western

Division and Oregon and Idaho chapters of the American Fisheries Society, the country's oldest and largest organization of professional fisheries biologists and scientists. In their view, although dam breaching "is not a panacea" (and must be accompanied by restoration of upland and estuary habitat and changes in fishing and hatchery practices), breaching must be an essential element of Snake River salmon restoration. "If improving spawning habitat were the silver bullet," wrote the Oregon chapter of the American Fisheries Society, "there would be healthy salmon populations where there is good habitat. In reality there are miles of excellent habitat in the Snake River basin without salmon. What's declined is not first-year survival, but survival after juvenile salmon negotiate the eight dams standing between them and the ocean. . . . Restoration to fishable levels, not just avoiding extinction, is the appropriate goal."

There is still a contingent of scientists who, unlike the American Fisheries Society, believe that easing fish passage through the dams is key to salmon recovery. A hi-tech mechanical fish has been devised to test "salmon-friendly" turbines. Others suggest fancy underwater lights and guiding devices to steer fish away from the most damaging parts of the dam apparatus. "Although these techniques have improved the direct survival of fish around or through the dams over the years," wrote the American Fisheries Society's Western Division, "Snake River stocks have continued to decline. Many fisheries scientists have concluded there is no feasible technological solution that will recover Snake River salmon and steelhead. Alternatively, there are indications that a more normative and free-flowing river ecosystem is required to facilitate salmon recovery."

While NMFS had its Northwest Fisheries Science Center in Seattle running new sets of fish numbers, the state of Oregon was busy filing an amicus brief in a lawsuit charging that the four lower Snake dams violate the Clean Water Act by elevating water temperature and levels of dissolved gas. The suit was filed in the spring of 1999 against the Army Corps of Engineers by the National Wildlife Federation and a coalition of other conservation groups in Federal District Court in Oregon, with the Nez Perce Tribe intervening on the plaintiff's side. Oregon's brief expressed concern about whether the federal government would work to bring the four dams into compliance with the Clean Water Act.

Having federal dams comply with the Clean Water Act is new, explains attorney Nicole Cordan, policy and legal director of Save Our Wild Salmon in Portland, Oregon. "Privately owned dams have to comply with Clean Water Act standards and need a certificate of compliance," she tells me. Extraordinary as it may seem for an entity with access to so much concrete, federally built and operated dams, like those on the lower Snake, do not need to go through this permitting process. "We are looking for the federal government to be treated like all other polluters," says Eric Bloch, one of Oregon's representatives on the Northwest Power Planning Council* and adviser to Governor John Kitzhaber on Columbia Basin issues.

The details of the suit are technical, but its principles are not. Water impounded behind the dams heats up. When water comes crashing over the dams' spillways, it increases the levels of dissolved gas in the waters below. The suit is asking the federal government and the Army Corps of Engineers to comply with Clean Water Act standards rather than, as Bloch puts it, "self diagnose and self prescribe" solutions to the problem. Bloch fears that if they do, the burden of the remedy will fall on the states and private entities. "We've been working for years with ranchers, farmers and other private entities who are all contributors to pollution." It would "not be fair," he says, to have the federal government treated separately.

"We are in discussions with many constituencies throughout the state, including industry, municipalities, agriculture and forestry, exhorting them to shoulder their share of the burden of returning our waters to standards compliance," wrote Governor Kitzhaber to Environmental Protection Agency administrator

---

*Authorized by Congress in 1980, the Northwest Power Planning Council is a compact among the states of Idaho, Montana, Oregon and Washington charged with balancing the region's need for power with development of a plan to "protect, mitigate and enhance" fish and wildlife populations affected by Columbia Basin power dams.

Carol Browner in August 1999. "To have the federal government argue that it should not have to shoulder its share would seriously prejudice our efforts."

While the terms of this lawsuit were being laid out, the Environmental Protection Agency, as part of an ongoing project, was studying the temperature of the Snake and Columbia Rivers. The resulting assessment, completed in August 1999, says that the Snake River is "the most significant tributary to the Columbia River, with the potential to make the biggest difference in temperature modulation," and that "measured results on the Snake River . . . show that temperatures are above state temperature standards during certain periods within the months of July, August and September." Or, as an expert at EPA told me, "The temperature standard for the Columbia is sixty-eight [degrees], and even if you get the tributaries down to sixty-four, you can't get the mainstem temperature down to standard."

"In general," the EPA report concludes, "removal of the dams, as compared to increasing even the coolest water inputs from tributaries would be the most effective in bringing down temperatures in the Columbia-Snake system . . . removing the lower Snake River dams would significantly reduce average temperatures along the lower stretch of the Snake." There is simply not enough water in the tributaries alone to adequately lower the mainstem temperature, explained a source at EPA.

In February 2001, Federal District Court Judge Helen Frye in Portland, Oregon, ruled that current operation of the four lower Snake River dams does violate the Clean Water Act. She ordered the U.S. Army Corps of Engineers to produce a decision within sixty days that would bring the dams and their reservoirs into compliance and protect threatened and endangered salmon and steelhead. The implications of this decision will likely send ripples throughout the federal hydropower system.

"Taking out the dams is one way to comply," says Cordan, almost slyly.

We are here today because salmon are on the verge of extinction," says Antone Minthorn, chairman of the board of the Confederated Tribes of the Umatilla, speaking with the cadence of a sermon. "We are confronted with the unthinkable. Will we allow this fish which has so captivated people for thousands of years to go extinct? We are here today because the development of the Columbia has been so overwhelming that it has squashed the river. We are here today to enact the changes necessary to save salmon. We must give up some of our development. We must make choices that implicate moral and ethical values. . . . I pray we are not too late."

It is a fall day in 1998, and about 350 people representing the many groups whose life and livelihoods rely on the Columbia fill a hotel ballroom in Portland, Oregon, to listen to panels addressing the future of the Columbia and Snake River system. The day's discussions seem to characterize the terms of the debate. The conference could be called "Stakeholders R Us," as it is clear everyone is here to mark river turf in the fight to save Columbia Basin salmon.

Assembled are consultants, systems, financial and power analysts, directors of public utility and irrigation districts, port managers, industry association representatives, foresters, decorated members of the Army Corps of Engineers, members of the Yakama, Salish and Kootenai, Spokane, Coeur d'Alene, Confederated Tribes of both Umatilla and Warm Springs, Shoshone-Bannock, Nez Perce and Kalispell Tribes, county commissioners, city councilors, attorneys, U.S. and state senators, a mayor, bureaucrats from the Department of the Interior, the Forest Service, the Environmental Protection Agency and the Bonneville Power Administration, a U.S. congresswoman and the governor of Oregon. To an observer, it seems a curious exercise in display—pissing in the sand, someone I later talk to says—but clearly something big is afoot, to make all of these principals turn out. But what is in play? Are the dams of the Snake River really on the table? As Warm Springs tribal elders in Pendleton vests and braids answer calls on their cell phones, port managers take notes on their leather clipboards, and representatives of non-governmental organizations scurry around conferring with key participants.

"I think we've heard from more panelists today than there may be fish left in the river," quips Portland Metro chief executive

Mike Burton toward the end of the afternoon, as the audience laughs nervously. Clearly I am not the only one picturing large-shouldered men—and it is mostly men—sitting around talking while fish die off.

Oregon's Republican Senator Gordon Smith speaks emphatically of states' rights to determine water allocation and says that dam removal could have dire and destructive consequences for the Northwest. In 1999 and 2000 Smith was chairman of the water and power subcommittee of Energy and Natural Resources, a key position in controlling any legislation involving the dams. Oregon Governor John Kitzhaber says it is a "no-brainer, that fish would rather swim than be barged." But he adds, "Are we as a region willing to pay for it? We must be willing to put these issues on the table and put the price tag on it. Effective salmon recovery will cost somebody something."

"We need to do what's right for salmon, not repeat mistakes, and need to economically compensate those who will incur losses from dam removal," says Representative Elizabeth Furse, representing Oregon's first congressional district, a largely urbanized district west of the Cascades that includes part of Portland.

But empathy for salmon is not the motivating factor for most gathered in that room. Dams mean business. The Columbia Snake River Marketing Group estimates that the total value of the system's riverborne cargo in 1997 was $3.1 billion. Thanks to the Columbia and Snake River dams, Portland, Oregon, is now the country's largest wheat-exporting port and the world's second largest grain-exporting port. The Columbia and Snake now transport 23 percent of all U.S. grain exports. This business is so powerful that wheat was excluded from the 1998 U.S. sanctions against Pakistan for detonation of a nuclear device. Because of the dams, the Northwest Food Processors' Association represents the largest manufacturing industry in Idaho, and second largest in Washington and Oregon. Think McDonald's French fries and the agribusiness of the Simplot company.

Commercial salmon fishing used to be a big business on the Northwest Coast, but it has plummeted since the mid-1980s. In 1988, what Glen Spain, northwest regional director of Pacific

Coast Federation of Fishermen's Associations, calls the "last reasonably good year" for Northwest fisheries, commercial, sport and tribal fishing contributed about $1.25 billion to the regional economy.[7] Spain tells me that in 2000, the Northwest's commercial catch was worth only 15 percent of what it was in 1988, before the ESA listings for Columbia and Snake River salmon began. According to the Northwest Sportfishing Industry Association, that industry alone lost 10,000 jobs between 1984 and 1994 due to declining salmon populations.

For a long time it was believed that hatcheries, with their industrial-strength propagation of fish, could make up for the loss of native fish runs. The Columbia and Snake River dams were built assuming this to be true. "As the total number of wild salmon in the Columbia Basin declined, salmon from the hatchery program began to make up a larger and larger percentage of the total run. Today, as proof of their success, hatchery advocates note that artificially propagated salmon make up 80 percent of the total number of salmon on the Columbia, but they fail to mention that the total run has crashed to less than 5 percent of its historical abundance," writes Northwest fisheries biologist Jim Lichatowich.[8]

"Our people have been affected by the dams all up and down the river, from the mouth to the headwaters, from Canada to the Snake," Donald Sampson, executive director of the Columbia River Inter-Tribal Fish Commission, tells a Senate Energy Subcommittee on Water and Power in the spring of 2000. "We believe artificial propagation must be part of restoration. . . . We must protect the habitat and we must restore habitat. The tribes believe breaching the four lower Snake River dams is the cornerstone to recovery of salmon in connection with other activity," says Sampson. While hatcheries will continue to play a role in salmon restoration, it's clear that what their champions initially hoped for has been a dismal failure.

"Who's going to pay for all of these changes?" asks irrigation consultant Fred Ziari. "What is the most cost effective? Without direct involvement of farmers and ranchers in the Northwest, there will not be any meaningful salmon recovery," he cautions. Like others wary of dam removal and spending additional money on studies—several billion dollars have already been spent—Ziari points to habitat restoration projects in the Umatilla Basin and Okanagan valley that are showing signs of success.

"The biggest risk is uncertainty," says Craig Smith, vice president of the Northwest Food Processors Association, which, in Smith's words, produces "basically 80 percent of all the French fries made in the United States."

What goes on the barges, Smith explains when I ask about transportation, is almost entirely produce traveling west for export to the Pacific Rim and Asia. Shipping east is mainly by rail or truck. One Columbia Basin farmer I spoke with, whose operation grows organic vegetables for the Cascadian Farms and other labels, ships some 40 percent of his produce to Asia. This is not unusual. Much has been made of the cost-effectiveness of barging. According to Smith, one of the reasons for shipping by barge is that it's less expensive to load products once into a container that goes directly from the barge onto the oceangoing vessel, rather than reloading from truck or train. "Transportation," Smith says, "is important to our industry but not as important as it is to pulp, paper and wheat." Of the goods that travel the Snake, 18 percent are woodchips and logs; 75 percent is grain, primarily from Washington state. Smith does not mention that, by some accounts, Columbia and Snake River barging is the country's most heavily subsidized transportation.

If the lower Snake dams are removed, commercial barge navigation would stop at the Tri-Cities and be eliminated from the Snake between there and Lewiston. In a report prepared for American Rivers, Trout Unlimited and other nonprofit conservation groups, Dr. G. Edward Dickey, formerly the chief of the Planning Division for the Army Corps of Engineers and acting assistant secretary of the Army during the first Bush administration, writes that it would cost the federal government at most $162.5 million—and the states, $108.5 million—to augment the existing surface transportation infrastructure to make up for the cargo capacity that would be lost if all four lower Snake dams were removed. Boosters of the existing system cite statistics to show that barges create fewer carbon monoxide and hydrocarbon emissions than the trucks and trains required to carry the same amount of cargo. But could that be improved upon, I wonder.

While some are investigating salmon-friendly alternatives for transporting goods along the Snake and Columbia, plans are under way to expand the existing system by deepening the Columbia River shipping channel from the river's mouth to Portland to accommodate deeper-draft vessels. The channel-deepening project has caused an uproar among conservationists and others who fear it will harm endangered salmon in the very estuary where federal agencies have said restoration must occur. Communities at the mouth of the Columbia are also concerned that the additional dredging would damage the local commercial shellfishing industry. The National Marine Fisheries Service initially supported the project but has since declared its opposition on ecological grounds. But the Port of Portland—the public entity that oversees all operations at the city's port and Portland International Airport and over 3,000 acres of industrial real estate—and a number of Northwest businesses and lawmakers continue to push for the project, citing its importance to the regional economy.

And what about the hydropower? The financing of electric power generation through the Columbia-Snake hydropower system is enormously complex. It involves a grid that shuttles power throughout the western states, including California, and provides electricity at highly subsidized rates to select northwestern industries. This scheme has been further complicated by deregulation, power production by individual utility companies and industries themselves. Built on the assumption that water would be plentiful and demand would not exceed supply, this system is being tested by endangered salmon, the dry winter of 2000–2001 and escalating consumer and industrial demand.

According to the Army Corps of Engineers, the four lower Snake River dams have a "peaking output of nearly 3.5 million kilowatts . . . more than enough generating capacity to supply the electrical . . . needs of three cities the size of Seattle." Peaking output means the rare occasions when water flows are at their very highest. In practice, the dams typically run at far below this level, producing about 5 percent of the region's total power. If the

Pacific Northwest were to lose this electricity, costs to residential ratepayers would not rise dramatically; according to some calculations, individual monthly electrical bills would increase only $4 or $5.[9] According to the Northwest Energy Coalition and other conservation groups, with taxpayer subsidies, the huge price of fish protection measures and other environmental impacts of dams figured in, generating power from the lower Snake River dams actually costs the region money.

Electric power, being invisible—unlike barges, wheat fields and fish—is not an easy concept for some of us to grasp. Since the lower Snake dams are run-of-the-river projects, they produce more energy in wet years than they do in dry. This means that the value and quantity of the energy vary. Coming on the heels of California's energy crisis in the winter of 2000, the dry spring of 2001 is challenging the premise on which this industry is built and calling into question the Bonneville Power Administration's commitment to protecting salmon.

Changes in the well-entrenched systems provided by the lower Snake River dams cannot be made by flipping a switch. Changing the commercial transportation system from Lewiston, Idaho, to Pasco, Washington, would involve rearranging many of the nearly 5,000 jobs the Columbia Snake River Marketing Group says are influenced by the ports of Lewiston, Clarkston and Whitman County, Washington. Although it does not provide details, Dickey's plan calls for funding economic development to support communities that would be affected by such a transition. The federal government's recovery plan doesn't delve into such scenarios. The Army Corps' assessment also fails, says American Rivers, to fully reflect the economic benefits of dam removal.[10] The Corps, however, does estimate that breaching the dams could create almost as many full-time jobs as elimination of the dams would cause. The full costs of the federal plan, with its emphasis on upland tributary and estuary restoration, have yet to be calculated. Over the long term, conservationists contend, dam removal would be less expensive.

When considering the social implications of removing the lower Snake River dams or significantly altering their operations, it's worth remembering that Lower Granite Dam was completed in 1975. So it is not long ago that Lewiston and Clarkston had their lives changed dramatically. Nor is it surprising that talk of dam breaching would be met with resistance or skepticism. These cities, like the farming towns in Washington's Columbia Basin, do not look as if they're populated by Microsoft or dot.com millionaires. Their circumstances are clearly influenced by the fate of the growing season, demand for produce, their pulp mills, factories and ports. If dam operations were significantly altered or the lower Snake were to become a free-flowing river again, life would again have to change for these communities. And those who would likely feel the first impacts of any such change are probably not those who've profited most from the dams.

"The Snake River discussion is, I think, manageable in economic terms," says Secretary of the Interior Bruce Babbitt in October 2000, when I ask for his view on the politics of Snake River salmon. "I think it's become less contentious. At first it was a shock of disbelief that this could ever happen but now we've gotten past this psychological stuff," Babbitt observes. "It's the cost of exporting grain versus the potential benefits of restoring salmon."

"Science and the law have to drive the agency, not policy. Politics cannot play the primary role, and currently there is no political support for dam removal," says National Marine Fisheries Service spokesman Brian Gorman in November 2000. "That will happen," Gorman tells me, "only when there's overwhelming scientific evidence, and it would be embarrassing to say otherwise. When it would be like standing at the school door saying segregation now, segregation forever." Despite what many would say is overwhelming scientific evidence pointing to the dams' destructive effect on salmon, the political harangue continues over which vision of salmon restoration will prevail.

On December 18, 2000, over two hundred scientists signed a letter to President Clinton urging the federal government to include a commitment to dam breaching in its plan to recover

Snake River salmon. Three days later, the Save Our Wild Salmon coalition issued a press release criticizing the federal government's plan for its lax timeline and failure to focus recovery efforts in the river's mainstem, where the dams are killing fish. "Salmon are going to live or die on the Bush administration's watch, and we will do whatever is necessary, including taking this to court, to hold their feet to the fire," says Bill Arthur of the Sierra Club.

From my vantage point in the Pacific Northwest, this tug-of-war does not look as if it will flag anytime soon. Even with our knowledge about the importance of considering the health of an entire watershed, the big questions of restoring Columbia Basin salmon are still being dodged. Will it work to restore the estuary and upland tributaries without returning any natural conditions to the rivers' mainstems? Will the politics ever be moved by the science? Can the region ever be persuaded to alter any of its practices of consumption and conventional economic growth? There are difficult decisions to be made and no absolute guarantees of success. But the longer we wait, the fewer fish there will be, and that cannot bode well for anyone or anything in the region.

On my way home to Portland, I visit McNary Dam on the Columbia. On the south side of the dam is the Pacific Salmon Visitor Information Center. Several stories of glass and metal walkways overlook the dam's Juvenile Bypass Facility. The center looks sleek and chic. Inside are imposing fish models and lots of glossy brochures. I walk outside to look at the fish ladders and see an apparently dead steelhead slide by.

"Salmon smolts are loaded onto barges at the rate of 5000 per minute," says an information card. "How long would it take to fill an average barge-load of 450,000 salmon?" I try to take a picture of the steelhead, but it is gone. "Raceway ponds hold the fish until they are ready to be transported downstream," reads another card. "At that time they flow through pipes to a barge. Imagine riding with the fish down the river until they are released below Bonneville Dam." Steerage, I think, and leave to find the fish-viewing room at the other end of the parking lot.

Inside the small cement building, the light is greenish, reflecting the water behind the glass. There are no shiny leaflets, educational exhibits or informational displays of any kind. The room looks to have been cast aside in favor of the new facility with its videos and fiberglass models. Behind the cloudy glass, an eel and a carp struggle by in the current.

Afterword

"ENVIRONMENTALISTS EAT ENDANGERED SPECIES"

Where does dam removal go from here? The winter of 2000–2001 buffeted the East Coast with blizzards, but the Pacific Northwest had its driest winter in many years. As winter warmed to spring in early 2001, the snowpack, rivers and reservoirs in Montana, Idaho, Washington, Oregon and California were at near-record lows. The region's hydropower system relies on winter rains and snowmelt to course through the turbines of Columbia Basin dams. With low water and increasing demands for electricity, dam operation will more than ever determine the fate of Northwest salmon.

The new year also ushered in a presidential administration hostile to promoting conservation over ever-increasing production. What will this mean for communities engaged in river restoration that entails dismantling edifices of industry and power generation? How will recent power crises affect the nation's approach to removing hydropower dams whose environmental costs exceed their economic benefit? In May 2001, in the name of streamlining the process, the Federal Energy Regulatory Commission proposed a new set of regulations for licensing hydropower dams. If enacted, these rules could significantly undermine other government agencies' and communities' ability to protect rivers, fish and wildlife from environmentally harmful dams. Whether these proposals survive remains to be seen, but they are indicative of a political climate unfriendly to dam removal and river restoration. Clearly, there are many challenges ahead, not least among them continuing to educate people to think for the very long term—that is, in river time.

In April 2001, the Bonneville Power Administration, which operates eight dams on the Columbia and Snake Rivers, declared an emergency, allowing it to send water through the dams' turbines rather than spill it to aid spring migration of salmon. Although these fish are protected by the Endangered Species Act, a provision of the National Marine Fisheries Service's December 2000 Biological Opinion allows the BPA to give hydropower production precedence over salmon recovery. "This is a loophole the size of Grand Coulee Dam," said Kristin Boyles, an attorney with the Earthjustice Legal Defense Fund, a nonprofit public-interest law firm that has been working on behalf of salmon advocates. The National Marine Fisheries Service acknowledges the lack of spills could increase salmon mortality by 15 percent. Trout Unlimited cites state and tribal scientists who fear the loss could be as high as 95 percent for the year's migrating salmon.

In May 2001, Pacific Northwest conservation and fishing groups filed suit against the National Marine Fisheries Service, challenging the basis of the December 2000 NMFS Biological Opinion, charging that it violates the Endangered Species Act by failing to adequately protect the imperiled fish. The federal budget proposed for 2002 provides funding for the initial steps toward removal of the Elwha Dam on the Olympic Peninsula but not even six months' funding for projects required to implement the federal Columbia-Snake salmon recovery plan. If currently proposed restoration measures fail, the necessity of dam removal will increase. Whatever the ultimate decisions, in 2001, fish are being sacrificed to hydropower and irrigation. Whether these endangered species survive the impacts of this drought may well depend on conserving electricity, raising the price of a beer can and forgoing a government-subsidized alfalfa and potato crop.

But there is some good news. In the fall of 2000, near Augusta, Maine, salmon redds were spotted in the Kennebec above the Edwards Dam site, and in early 2001, wild baby salmon hatched and swam in a stretch of the Kennebec that is flowing freely for the first time in over 160 years. In July 2001, a settlement was finally reached that will, if implemented, ensure removal of the Savage Rapids Dam from Oregon's Rogue River by 2006. And in Wisconsin as well as in many other communities around the country, old and defunct dams continue to come down. With the removal of the Linen Mills Dam in October 2001, the entire Baraboo River now runs free, making it the longest mainstem of an American river to be restored to free-flowing conditions through dam removal.

Revived native fish runs in Wisconsin, North Carolina, Maine and other states where dams have come out provide evidence of the ecological benefits of removing dams. The longer we wait to remove dams that have outlived their usefulness, the more difficult the problems plaguing those rivers may become. We have made enormous progress in the past several decades at restoring our rivers. To continue that progress will require great vigilance and patience, take time and cost money, and there will be many obstacles, but we cannot afford to do otherwise. And none of this would be happening without the dedicated, courageous and often audacious work of countless individuals and organizations who have committed themselves to protecting and restoring the rivers that shape our lives. They deserve our support.

It's a beautiful spring evening. Bluebells and rhododendrons are blooming, the dog is lounging in the grass and the grill is unwrapped for the first time this season. Friends have invited me to dine on wild chinook salmon caught by and purchased from tribal fishers in the Columbia River Gorge. It may be the light or soft air, but this is probably the best fish I have ever tasted. "Quick, get the camera," a friend jokes. "Environmentalists eat endangered species!"

Thanks to the past few years' heavy snowfall, chinook are relatively plentiful in the Columbia this year. So, under the guidelines of its Biological Opinion, the National Marine Fisheries Service has increased the harvest level of the river's listed salmon to 13 percent from last year's 8.5 percent. Of this year's returning chinook, as few as 10 percent—or as many as 20 percent—of these fish may be wild. The rest are hatchery fish. For a limited time, tribal, commercial and sportfishing are allowed. Tribal fishers sell their catch directly to the salmon-hungry from coolers in the back of pickups at specified locations along the lower Columbia.

Most hatchery fish are marked by a clipped adipose fin. Our fish's fin was whole, so it most likely began life in stream-bottom gravel rather than in a cement pond. I wondered what its journey to the ocean was like. Our fish was caught near The Dalles Dam so it had to negotiate at least one dam on its way to and from the sea. But had it traveled downstream by barge or truck? Had it climbed fish ladders or dodged churning turbines? Or had it swum freely downstream in a push of spilled water?

Should we be eating this fish at all? In this time of industrially processed and manipulated food, virulent bacteria and marauding parasites, there's a good argument to be made for eating wild fish. A Native American friend assures me that a "harvestable surplus" is the tribal goal for restored salmon runs and that the tribes consider harvest a completion of the salmon's life cycle. I thought about how good this fish tasted. If we forget what wild fish taste like, what it's like to wait for their season, if we allow our rivers to disappear and degrade so we can no longer eat their fish, we will have choked off one of the continent's life forces.

Americans believe more than ever that environmental protection must take precedence over environmentally destructive development. We have learned, from their loss, the importance of open spaces, wild places, intact landscapes and free-flowing rivers. In this age of global interconnection, we understand the interdependence of ecological systems and have learned the intricate workings of each of their pieces. To ignore that knowledge and refuse to restore our rivers would be to cheat ourselves and the future. We can no longer say we didn't know.

Elizabeth Grossman
Portland, Oregon
August 2001

notes

Introduction

1. Jack A. Stanford, J. V. Ward, William J. Liss, Christopher A. Frissell, Richard N. Williams, James A. Lichatowich, Charles C. Coutant, "A General Protocol for Restoration of Regulated Rivers," *Regulated Rivers: Research & Management,* Vol. 12, No. 405, 1996, pp. 391–413.

2. World Commission on Dams, *Dams and Dam Development: A New Framework for Decision-Making, The Report of the World Commission on Dams* (London: Earthscan Publications, 2000), p. 10.

3. This according to American Rivers' tabulation of data in the U.S. Army Corps of Engineers' National Inventory of Dams.

4. Created by the Federal Water Power Act, passed by Congress in 1920.

5. This according to American Rivers, Friends of the Earth and Trout Unlimited, "Dam Removal Success Stories," December 1999, the most comprehensive reporting on recorded dam removals to date.

6. With thanks to Bill Oliver (Mr.Habitat@aol.com), who was kind enough to send me a tape.

Chapter 1

1. Henry David Thoreau, *The Maine Woods* (Boston: Ticknor & Fields, 1864), pp. 3–4.

2. Louise Dickinson Rich, *The Coast of Maine: An Informal History* (New York: Thomas Y. Crowell, 1956), p. 190.

3. Friends of Merrymeeting Bay: http://www.mltn.org/trusts.FMB.htm.

4. Anthony Netboy, *The Atlantic Salmon: A Vanishing Species* (Boston: Houghton Mifflin, 1968), p. 330.

5. Friends of Kennebec Salmon: http://www.gwi.net/~fks/ksalmon.html.

6. Rioux's column appears in the *Kennebec Journal* and Waterville's *Morning Sentinel.*

7. Netboy, *Atlantic Salmon,* p. 315.

8. Ibid.

9. John M. Anderson, Frederick G. Whoriskey and Andrew Goode, "Marine Matters: Atlantic Salmon on the Brink," *Endangered Species Update,* Vol. 17, No. 1 (2000), p. 15.

10. Ibid.; also Netboy, *Atlantic Salmon,* p. 326.

11. Netboy, *Atlantic Salmon,* p. 326.

12. Ibid., p. 328.

13. Atlantic Salmon Federation, "State of the Wild Atlantic Salmon Populations in North America 2001," May 31, 2001, http://www.asf.ca/.

Chapter 2

1. Through the EPA's National Estuary Program website or http://h20.enr.state.nc.us/nep/ap_region.htm.

2. Environmental Defense: www.environmentaldefense.org.

3. USFWS citing Hugh Smith, *The Fishes of North Carolina* (Raleigh, NC: E. M. Uzzell and Company, 1907).

4. Mike Wicker, in "Nonpoint Source News Notes," No. 54, November 1998.

5. U.S. Fish and Wildlife Service Coastal Program, "Success on the North Carolina Coast," citing S. G. Worth, the North Carolina Fish Commissioner in 1881.

6. James Eli Shiffer, "Demolition Sets the Neuse Free: Quaker Neck Dam Crumbles into History," *Raleigh News & Observer,* December 18, 1997.

7. John Hightower personal communication, November 9, 2000.

8. Mike Wicker, U.S. Fish and Wildlife Service, May 24, 2000.

Chapter 3

1. Archie Carr, "The Bird and the Behemoth," in Jeff Ripple and Susan Cerulean, eds., *The Wild Heart of Florida: Florida Writers on Florida's Wildlands* (Gainesville: University of Florida Press, 1999), pp. 40–41.

2. Al Burt, Jr., *Al Burt's Florida: Snowbirds, Sand Castles and Self-Rising Crackers* (Gainesville: University Press of Florida, 1997), pp. 18–19.

3. Debbie Drake, Foreword, *Wild Heart of Florida,* p. x.

4. Bill Belleville, *River of Lakes: A Journey on Florida's St. Johns River* (Athens: University of Georgia Press, 1999), p. xvii.

5. Florida Defenders of the Environment; also Belleville, *River of Lakes.*

6. Bill Belleville, *River of Lakes,* p. xvii.

7. Sidney Lanier, "Florida: Its Scenery, Climate, and History" (1875), as quoted by Belleville, *River of Lakes,* p. 125.

8. Work Projects Administration, *Florida: A Guide to the Southernmost State, Compiled and Written by the Federal Writers' Project of the Work Projects Administration for the State of Florida* (New York: Oxford University Press, 1939), pp. 526–527.

9. Florida Defenders of the Environment: http://www.fladefenders. org/publications/history.html.

10. Doug Martin, "Environmentalist Marjorie Harris Carr Dies Friday at 82," *Gainesville Sun,* October 11, 1997.

11. Joe Hutto, "River of Dreams," in *Wild Heart of Florida,* p. 106.

Chapter 4

1. In the summer of 2001, Stephanie Lindloff became the River Restoration Coordinator for the New Hampshire Department of Environmental Services, coordinating a public-private effort to identify and remove dams in order to improve public safety and restore natural resources.

2. Tracy Will, *Compass American Guides: Wisconsin* (Oakland, CA: Fodor's Travel Publications, 1994), p. 93.

3. Ibid., p. 41.

4. The University of Wisconsin and Wisconsin Department of Natural Resources are doing extensive studies on the effects of dam removal on the Baraboo. Their work will probably add significantly to the scientific literature on the biological and physical impacts of dam removal.

5. Wisconsin Department of Natural Resources, "Lower Wisconsin River Water Quality Management Plan," January 1994.

6. Aldo Leopold, *A Sand County Almanac with Essays on Conservation from Round River* (New York: Oxford University Press; Ballantine Books, Random House, 1966), p. 104.

7. John Exo, University of Wisconsin Extension Service, personal communication.

8. Will, *Compass American Guides: Wisconsin,* p. 175.

9. John Exo, "Restoration of the Baraboo River Through Dam Removal: A Summary," http://www.dnr.state.wi.us/org/gmu/lowerwis/baraboo.htm.

10. State of Wisconsin, Division of Hearings and Appeals, Case No. 30 NO-98-1030.

11. Wisconsin Department of Natural Resources, "Environmental Analysis and Decision on the Need for an Environmental Impact Statement, Ward Mill Dam," p. 5.

12. This is the site of one of the only published studies of a fishery's response to a dam removal. See P. Kanehl, J. Lyons and J. Nelson, "Changes in the Habitat and Fish Community of the Milwaukee River, Wisconsin, Following Removal of the Woolen Mills Dam," *North American Journal of Fisheries Management*, Vol. 17 (1997), pp. 387–400.

13. Leopold, *Sand County Almanac*, p. 124.

Chapter 5

1. David Brower, quoted in Michelle Cole, "Oregon Conservationists Mourned the Death of David Brower on Monday, Calling Him an Inspiration," *Oregonian*, November 2, 2000.

2. Eliot Porter, *The Place No One Knew: Glen Canyon on the Colorado*. Foreword by David Brower (Layton, UT: Gibbs Smith, 1988; originally published by Sierra Club Books, 1963), p. 8.

3. Edward Abbey, *Desert Solitaire* (New York: Ballantine Books, Random House, 1968), p. 173.

4. Steven W. Carothers and Bryan T. Brown, *The Colorado River Through Grand Canyon: Natural History and Human Change* (Tucson: University of Arizona Press, 1991), p. 15.

5. Michael Kowalewski, Guillermo E. Avila Serrano, Kari W. Flessa and Glenn A. Goodfriend, "Dead Delta's Former Productivity: Two Trillion Shells at the Mouth of the Colorado River," *Geology*, Vol. 28, No. 12 (December 2000), pp. 1059–1062.

6. Studies by the Bureau of Reclamation and Glen Canyon Institute.

7. Scott K. Miller, "Undamming Glen Canyon: Lunacy, Rationality or Prophecy," *Stanford Environmental Law Journal*, Vol. 19 (January 2000), p. 121.

8. Russell Martin, *A Story That Stands Like a Dam: Glen Canyon and the Struggle for the Soul of the West* (Salt Lake City: University of Utah Press, 1999), p. 72.

9. Richard J. Ingebretsen, "Foreword," *Stanford Environmental Law Journal*, Vol. 19, No. 1 (January 2000), p. xi.

10. Martin, *A Story That Stands Like a Dam*, p. 325.

Chapter 6

1. Richard Manning, *One Round River* (New York: Henry Holt, 1997), p. 14.

Chapter 7

1. Marc Reisner, *Cadillac Desert: The American West and Its Disappearing Water* (New York: Viking Penguin, 1986), p. 9.

2. Jim Lichatowich, *Salmon Without Rivers* (Washington, DC, and Covelo, CA: Island Press, 1999), p. 58.

3. Ibid., p. 85.

4. Ibid., pp. 202, 123–124.

5. According to American Rivers and Trout Unlimited.

6. His consulting firm, William M. Kier Associates, is based in Sausalito, California.

7. See the work of Charles Dewberry, Jim Lichatowich et al.

Chapter 8

1. Jim Lichatowich, *Salmon Without Rivers* (Washington, DC, and Covelo, CA: Island Press, 1999).

2. Robert Hunter, Staff Attorney of WaterWatch of Oregon, personal communication, May 1999.

Chapter 9

1. Lichatowich, *Salmon Without Rivers*, p. 77.

2. Carsten Lien, *Olympic Battleground: The Power Politics of Timber Preservation* (San Francisco: Sierra Club Books, 1991), p. 206.

3. Lichatowich, *Salmon Without Rivers*, p. 135.

4. Bruce Brown, *Mountain in the Clouds: A Search for the Wild Salmon* (New York: Simon & Schuster, 1982), p. 94.

5. Shawn Cantrell, Friends of the Earth, personal communication.

6. Lien, *Olympic Battleground*, p. 348.

Chapter 10

1. Ecotrust, *Salmon Nation: People and Fish at the Edge* (Portland, OR: Ecotrust, 1999), p. 24.

2. Paul C. Pitzer, *Grand Coulee Dam: Harnessing a Dream* (Pullman: Washington State University Press, 1994), p. 389.

3. Roberta Ulrich, *Empty Nets: Indians, Dams, and the Columbia River* (Corvallis: Oregon State University Press, 1999), pp. 57–58.

4. See Trout Unlimited's "Doomsday Clock," which predicts that Pacific Northwest salmon could become extinct by 2016. See www.tu.org.

5. Peter Kareiva, Michelle Marvier and Michelle McClure, "Recovery and Management Options for Spring/Summer Chinook Salmon in the Columbia River Basin," *Science*, Vol. 290 (November 2000), pp. 977–979.

6. Ibid.

7. Pacific Rivers Council, "The Economic Imperative of Protecting Riverine Habitat in the Pacific Northwest," Research Report No. V, January 1992, p. 10.

8. Lichatowich, *Salmon Without Rivers*, p. 198.

9. This is a 1998–2000 calculation from a 1999 report prepared for the Northwest Energy Coalition.

10. A study analyzing the economic impact of bypassing the dams using data collected by the Army Corps of Engineers has been released by University of Oregon professor Dr. Ed Whitelaw and his group ECO-Northwest. The study concludes that the Corps's own analyses have seriously underestimated the economic benefits of dam breaching. "This study delivers much needed perspective on the overall benefits of restoring healthy salmon runs," said Donald Sampson, executive director of the Columbia River Inter-Tribal Fish Commission, praising the report in a press statement.

bibliography

Abbey, Edward. *Desert Solitaire*. New York: Ballantine Books, Random House, 1968.

Adams, Glenn. "Alewives Swarm Up Open River." *Central Maine Newspapers*, Associated Press, May 15, 2000.

———. "Maine Challenges Salmon Listing," Associated Press, December 8, 2000.

Alden, Peter, Richard B. Cech, Gil Nelson et al. *National Audubon Society Field Guide to Florida*. New York: Chanticleer Press, Alfred A. Knopf, 1998.

American Fisheries Society. "Resolution of the Oregon Chapter of the American Fisheries Society on Snake River Salmon and Steelhead Recovery," adopted February 17, 2000.

American Rivers. "Irrigation After Partial Removal of the Four Lower Snake River Dams—A Position Paper," November 1999.

———. Friends of the Earth and Trout Unlimited. "Dam Removal Success Stories—Restoring Rivers Through Selective Removal of Dams That Don't Make Sense," December 1999.

American Sportfishing Association. Press Release, November 9, 2000. info@asafishing.org.

Anderson, John M., Frederick G. Whoriskey and Andrew Goode. "Marine Matters—Atlantic Salmon on the Brink," *Endangered Species Update*, Vol. 17, No. 1 (2000), p. 15.

Associated Press. "Dam Breaching Called Best Option, Western Chapter of Fisheries Biologists Passes Resolution," *Spokesman-Review* (Spokane), July 15, 1999.

———. "Panel Delays Decision on Water Draw," *The Oregonian* (Portland), August 28, 1999.

———. "Gorton Moves to Block Study of Dam Removal," *The Olympian* (Olympia, WA), September 19, 2000.

———. "Babbitt Helps Breach California Dam," *Seattle Daily Journal of Commerce*, October 13, 2000.

Babbitt, Bruce. "A River Runs Against It: America's Evolving View of Dams," *Open Spaces Quarterly*, Fall 1998, Vol. 1, No. 4, pp. 8–13.

Baraboo Range Preservation Association. "The Area We Preserve." http://www.baraboorange.org/wepreserve.html.

Barnard, Jeff. "With Fish Dying Out, Dam's Function Is Reconsidered," *Statesman Journal* (Salem, OR), Associated Press, August 23, 1998.

Bartram, William. *Travels*. Penguin Nature Library. Introduction by James Dickey. New York: Penguin Books USA, 1988.

Becklin, Dennis. "Guest Opinion: Savage Rapids Haters Wage Holy War," *Mail Tribune* (Medford, OR), November 15, 1998.

———. "Op-Ed: Metro Area to Learn Why Grants Pass Is Fighting," *The Oregonian* (Portland), November 17, 1998.

Belleville, Bill. *River of Lakes—A Journey on Florida's St. Johns River*. Athens: University of Georgia Press, 1999.

Bernton, Hal. "Ruling Hisses at Snake River Dams," *Seattle Times*, March 25, 2000.

Blumm, Michael C., Laird J. Lucas, Don B. Miller, Daniel J. Rohlf and Glen H. Spain. "Saving Snake River Water and Salmon Simultaneously: The Biological, Economic, and Legal Case for Breaching the Lower Snake River Dams, Lowering John Day Reservoir and Restoring Natural River Flows," *Environmental Law*, Vol. 28, No. 4 (1998).

Bolling, David. *How to Save a River: A Handbook for Citizen Action*. Washington, DC, and Covelo, CA: Island Press, 1994.

Bonin, Gordon. "Agreement Sets Deadline for Salmon Listing," *Bangor Daily News* (ME), June 13, 2000.

Brandes, Kathleen M. *Maine Handbook*. Chico, CA: Moon Publications, 1998.

Brown, Bruce. *Mountain in the Clouds: A Search for the Wild Salmon*. New York: Simon & Schuster, 1982.

Burt, Al, Jr. *Al Burt's Florida—Snowbirds, Sand Castles, and Self-Rising Crackers*. Gainesville: University Press of Florida, 1997.

California Department of Fish and Game, U.S. Bureau of Reclamation. "Saeltzer Dam—Fish Passage and Flow Protection Project." Joint Environmental Assessment/Initial Study, Public Draft, June 2000. Redding, CA, Shasta Lake, CA, North State Resources, Inc.

Carothers, Steven W., and Bryan T. Brown. *The Colorado River Through the Grand Canyon—Natural History and Human Change*. Tucson: University of Arizona Press, 1991.

Carr, Archie. "The Bird and the Behemoth," in Jeff Ripple and Susan Cerulean, eds., *The Wild Heart of Florida: Florida Writers on Florida's Wildlands* (Gainesville: University Press of Florida, 1999), pp. 40–41.

Carson, Rachel. *Silent Spring*. New York: Fawcett World Library, 1962.

Clark Fork Coalition. *Currents,* www.clarkfork.org.

Coastal America. www.coastalamerica.gov.

Cole, Jeff. "Citizens Launch New Effort to Save Waubeka Dam," *Journal Sentinel,* May 20, 1999.

Collins, Kristin. "Riverkeeper Fights to Save Endangered Neuse," *Free Press* (Kinston, NC), August 2, 1998.

Columbia Basin Bulletin. Bend, OR: Intermountain Communications, www.cbbulletin.com.

Columbia Snake Current. A joint publication of the Columbia and Snake Rivers Campaign and Trout Unlimited, 1999–2001.

Columbia Snake River Marketing Group. "The Great Waterway—The Guide to Marine Facilities and Industrial Properties on the Columbia and Snake River System." Portland, OR: Merchants Exchange and the Columbia Snake River Marketing Group, 1999.

Cone, Joseph. *Common Fate: Endangered Salmon and the People of the Pacific Northwest.* Corvallis: Oregon State University Press, 1995.

Connelly, Joel. "Babbitt Puffs a Bit, Sees Two Dams Gone," *Seattle Post-Intelligencer,* February 11, 2000.

Cox, J. "King of the Rogue," *Rogue River Press,* March 14, 1999.

Cronin, John, and Robert F. Kennedy, Jr. *The Riverkeepers.* New York: Touchstone/Simon and Schuster, 1997, 1999.

Curtis, Wayne. "The Coast Is Clear—of Salmon," *Grist Magazine,* Earth Day Network, April 12, 2000.

Davenport, Don. *Natural Wonders of Wisconsin: Exploring Wild and Scenic Places.* Chicago: Country Roads Press, 1999.

Devlin, Sherry. "MPC, ARCO Want Cleanup, Not Removal," *The Missoulian,* May 3, 2000.

———. "Milltown Extension Granted by Feds," *The Missoulian,* June 20, 2000.

———. "FERC Won't Reconsider Licensing of Milltown," *The Missoulian,* September 27, 2000.

———. "Company: Sediments Must Stay," *The Missoulian,* November 29, 2000.

Dickey, Dr. G. Edward. "Grain Transportation After Partial Removal of the Four Lower Snake River Dams: An Affordable and Efficient Transition Plan," prepared for American Rivers, September 1999. www.amrivers.org.

Duncan, David James. "Salmon's Second Coming," *Sierra,* March/April 2000, pp. 31–41.

Duncan, Roger C. *Coastal Maine: A Maritime History.* New York: W. W. Norton and Company, 1992.

Earthjustice Legal Defense Fund. www.earthjustice.org.

Ecotrust. *Salmon Nation: People and Fish at the Edge.* Portland, OR: Ecotrust, 1999.

Environmental Defense. "Florida: Nixon Halts Canal Project, Cites Environment," *Newsletter,* Vol. 2, March 1971. www.edf.org/pubs/newsletter/1971/Mar/n_nixonhalt.htmlf_column.html.

———. "Bottomland Hardwood Forests: A Wetland Resource Worth

Preserving," *Newsletter,* Vol. 10, No. 4 (July 1979). www.environmental defense.org/pubs/EDF-letter/1979/Jul/f_column.html.

Environmental Protection Agency. EPA's National Estuary Program website, http://h2o.enr.state.nc.us/nep/ap_region.htm.

Exo, John. "Restoration of the Baraboo River Through Dam Removal: A Summary." http://www.dnr.state.wi.us/org/gmu/lowerwis/baraboo.htm.

Farmer, Jared. *Glen Canyon Dammed: Inventing Lake Powell and the Canyon Country.* Tucson: University of Arizona Press, 1999.

Federal Caucus. "Conservation of Columbia Basin Fish: Final Recommendation for a Basinwide 'All-H' Salmon Recovery Strategy." Winter 2000, Issue 5.

Federal Caucus News. National Marine Fisheries Service. www.Salmon Recovery.gov.

Florida Atlas & Gazetteer. Yarmouth, ME: DeLorme, 1997.

Florida Defenders of the Environment, www.fladefenders.org.

Fradkin, Philip. *A River No More: The Colorado River and the West.* Berkeley and Los Angeles: University of California Press, 1995.

Friends of Kennebec Salmon. www.gwi.net/~fks/ksalmon.html.

Friends of Lake Powell. www.lakepowell.org.

Friends of Merrymeeting Bay, and information available through http://knox.link75.org/mmb/welcome.html.

Friends of the River. *Rivers Reborn: Removing Dams and Restoring Rivers in California.* www.friendsoftheriver.org.

Glen Canyon Action Network. www.drainit.org.

Glen Canyon Institute. "Citizens' Environmental Assessment (CEA) on the Decommissioning of Glen Canyon Dam: Interim Report Fall 2000," Flagstaff, AZ.

————. *Hidden Passage: The Journal of Glen Canyon Institute.* Summer, Fall and Winter 1999 issues. www.glencanyon.org.

Gove, Judy, and Richard Michelon. "Guest Opinion: Vote for Those Who Put GPID Water First," *Mail Tribune* (Medford, OR), October 30, 1998.

Gregory, Gordon. "From a Dam on the Rouge, a Wider Debate Is Rippling Out," *The Oregonian* (Portland), May 11, 1998.

Henke, Ed. "A Case for Removal of the Matilija Dam," July 8, 1998, Ashland, OR. Unpublished paper.

Hog Watch. www.hogwatch.org.

Hollenbach, Margaret, and Jill Ory. "Protecting and Restoring Watersheds: A Tribal Approach to Salmon Recovery." Portland, OR: Columbia River Inter-Tribal Fish Commission, 1999.

Hughes, John. "House Panel Votes Down Breaching Snake Dams," *Seattle-Post Intelligencer,* Associated Press, July 22, 1999.

Hunter, Robert G. "Water Diversion and Salmon: Pressure Mounts to Remove Savage Rapids Dam," *Western Water Law & Policy Reporter,* December 1998.

Hydropower Reform Coalition. www.amrivers.org.

Idaho Water Users Association, Inc. "Testimony Before the Subcommittee on Water and Power of the Senate Energy and Natural Resources Committee," April 18, 2000.

Ilgenfritz, Ric. "Testimony of Ric Ilgenfritz, Columbia Basin Coordinator, National Marine Fisheries Service—Northwest Region, National Oceanic and Atmospheric Administration, U.S. Commerce Department, Before the Subcommittee on Water and Power of the Senate Energy and Natural Resources Committee," April 18, 2000.

Ingebretsen, Richard J. "Foreword," *Stanford Environmental Law Journal*, Vol. 19, No. 1 (January 2000), pp. xi–xiv.

Jewett, Joan Laatz. "Grants Pass Water Permit Is on Endangered List," *The Oregonian* (Portland), April 1, 1998.

Kanehl, P., J. Lyons and J. Nelson. "Changes in the Habitat and Fish Community of the Milwaukee River, Wisconsin, Following Removal of the Woolen Mills Dam," *North American Journal of Fisheries Management*, Vol. 17 (1977), pp. 387–400.

Kareiva, Peter, Michelle Marvier and Michelle McClure. "Recovery and Management Options for Spring/Summer Chinook Salmon in the Columbia River Basin," *Science*, Vol. 290 (November 3, 2000), pp. 977–979.

Kennebec Coalition. "A River Reborn: Benefits for People and Wildlife of the Kennebec River Following the Removal of Edwards Dam." The Kennebec Coalition, c/o Natural Resources Council of Maine, Augusta, ME.

Kitzhaber, John. "Remove Savage Rapids Dam," *Mail Tribune* (Medford, OR), September 26, 1997.

Kohl, Herbert, Senator. "Funding for Baraboo River Study Included in Appropriations Bill, Kohl, Baldwin Announce." http://kohl.senate.gov/press/092800a.html.

Kowaleswksi, Michael, Guillermo E. Avila Serrano, Kari W. Flessa and Glenn A. Goodfriend. "Dead Delta's Former Productivity: Two Trillion Shells at the Mouth of the Colorado River," *Geology*, Vol. 28, No. 12 (December 2000), pp. 1059–1062.

Landers, Dixon. "Willamette River Main Corridor Restoration: What Is Important to Salmon?" *Salmon at the Millennium*. Portland: Oregon Trout, 2000.

Lawson, John. *A New Voyage to Carolina*. Chapel Hill: University of North Carolina Press, 1967.

Lee, Mike. "Hastings' Breaching Resolution Approved," *Tri-City Herald*, July 22, 1999.

Leopold, Aldo. *A Sand County Almanac with Essays on Conservation from Round River*. New York: Oxford University Press; Ballantine Books, Random House, 1966.

Lichatowich, Jim. *Salmon Without Rivers: A History of the Pacific Salmon Crisis.* Washington, DC, and Covelo, CA: Island Press, 1999.

Lien, Carsten. *Olympic Battleground: The Power Politics of Timber Preservation.* San Francisco: Sierra Club Books, 1991.

Long, Cindy. "County Could Step In If Irrigation District Meets Its Demise," *Daily Courier* (Grants Pass, OR), May 2, 1998.

Lower Elwha Klallam Tribe. www.elwha.org.

Luczkovich, Joseph J., and David Knowles. "Environments and Ecosystems of North Carolina." Department of Biology, East Carolina University, Institute for Coastal and Marine Resources and Department of Biology.

Lundeen, Dan, and Allen Pinkham. *Salmon and His People: Fish and Fishing in Nez Perce Culture.* Lewiston, ID: Confluence Press, 1999.

Mail Tribune (Medford, OR). Editorial: "Enough, Already," August 14, 1998.

Maine Atlas & Gazetteer. Yarmouth, ME: DeLorme, 2000.

Maine State Legislative Document (LD) 2136, as cited on page 1–1 of the Draft Capital Riverfront Improvement District Master Plan Report, July 2000.

Manning, Richard. *One Round River: The Curse of Gold and the Fight for the Big Blackfoot.* New York: Henry Holt, 1997.

Mapes, Lynda V. "Chorus of Boos Greets Salmon Strategy," *Seattle Times,* July 28, 2000.

———. "Another Potential Lightning Boldt," *Seattle Times,* January 17, 2001.

Martin, Doug. "Environmentalist Marjorie Harris Carr Dies Friday at 82," *Gainesville Sun,* October 11, 1997.

Martin, Russell. *A Story That Stands Like a Dam: Glen Canyon and the Struggle for the Soul of the West.* Salt Lake City: University of Utah Press, 1999.

McCully, Patrick. *Silenced Rivers: The Ecology and Politics of Large Dams.* London: Zed Books, 1996.

McPhee, John. *Encounters with the Archdruid.* New York: Noonday Press/Farrar, Straus and Giroux, 1971.

———. *The Control of Nature.* New York: Noonday Press/Farrar, Straus and Giroux, 1989.

McRae, W. C., and Judy Jewell. *Montana Handbook.* Chico, CA: Moon Publications, 1992.

Merrill, WI, City of. www.ci.merrill.wi.us/general/history_frame.html.

Miller, Scott K. "Undamming Glen Canyon: Lunacy, Rationality or Prophecy?" *Stanford Environmental Law Journal,* Vol. 19, No. 1 (2000), pp. 121–221.

Montana Atlas & Gazetteer. Yarmouth, ME: DeLorme, 1999.

Montgomery, Keith. "The Baraboo Ranges and Devil's Lake Gorge: A

Geological Tour." Department of Geography-Geology, University of Wisconsin, Marathon County. http://www.uwmc.uwc.edu/geography/baraboo/baraboo.htm.

Mulick, Chris. "Tri-Citians Get Chance to Question Locke," *Tri-City Herald,* July 22, 1999.

National Audubon Society Field Guide to the Southeastern States, The. New York: Chanticleer Press, Alfred A. Knopf, 1999.

National Marine Fisheries Service. "Review of the National Marine Fisheries Service Draft Cumulative Risk Analysis Addendum, Independent Scientific Advisory Board, Northwest Power Planning Council, ISAB Report 99-7," November 8, 1999.

———. "Anadramous Fish Appendix to the DEIS, U.S. Army Corps of Engineers; National Marine Fisheries Service (A-fish appendix biological analysis) Lower Snake River Juvenile Salmon Migration Feasibility Study DEIS," December 16, 1999.

National Wildlife Federation. www.nwf.org.

Natural Resources Council of Maine. www.maineenvironment.org.

Netboy, Anthony. *The Atlantic Salmon: A Vanishing Species?* Boston: Houghton Mifflin, 1968.

Neuberger, Richard. *Our Promised Land.* New York: Macmillan, 1938.

Nichols, Mike. "Waubeka May Be Losing Dam That Defined It," *Journal [WI] Sentinel,* December 2, 1998.

North Carolina Atlas & Gazetteer. Yarmouth, ME: DeLorme, 2000.

North Carolina Department of Environment and Natural Resources. http://www.enr.state.nc.us; and http://h2o.enr.nc.us./nep/neuse-river-basin.htm.

Northern California Atlas & Gazetteer. Yarmouth, ME: DeLorme, 1998.

NW Energy Coalition, Seattle. www.nwenergy.org/nwec.

"NW Fishletter." Energy NewsData Corporation, September 3, 1999. www.newsdata.com/enernet.fishletter.

Oregon Atlas & Gazetteer. Freeport, ME: DeLorme, 1991.

Oregon Natural Resources Council, www.onrc.org.

Oregon Trout. "Testimony Before the Subcommittee on Water and Power of the Senate Energy and Natural Resources Committee," April 18, 2000.

Oregon Water Resources Commission, State of. Final Order, "In the Matter of the Cancellation of Permit No. 50957 and the Denial of the Request for Modification of Implementation Schedules."

Oregonian, The (Portland). Editorial: "Elk Creek Dam: Get Over It," July 12, 1999.

Pacific Rivers Council. "The Economic Imperative of Protecting Riverine Habitat in the Pacific Northwest," Research Report No. V, January 1992, p. 10.

Page, Lawrence M., and Brooks M. Burr. *A Field Guide to Freshwater*

Fishes: North American North of Mexico. The Peterson Field Guide Series, Boston and New York: Houghton Mifflin Company, 1991.

Palmer, Tim. *Endangered Rivers and the Conservation Movement.* Berkeley and Los Angeles, CA: University of California Press, 1986.

———. *America by Rivers.* Washington, DC, and Covelo, CA: Island Press, 1996.

Paulson, Michael. "Deal Clears Way to Buy Elwha Dams," *Seattle Post-Intelligencer,* October 20, 1999.

Perry, Bill. *A Sierra Club Naturalist's Guide: The Middle Atlantic Coast: Cape Hatteras to Cape Cod.* San Francisco: Sierra Club Books, 1985.

Petersen, Keith C. *River of Life Channel of Death: Fish and Dams on the Lower Snake.* Lewiston, ID: Confluence Press, 1995.

Pittman, Craig. "Governor Sounds the Death Knell for Dam at Rodman," *St. Petersburg Times,* July 15, 2000.

Pitzer, Paul C. *Grand Coulee Dam: Harnessing a Dream.* Pullman, WA: Washington State University Press, 1994.

Porter, Eliot. *The Place No One Knew: Glen Canyon on the Colorado.* Introduction by David Brower. Layton, UT: Gibbs Smith, Inc., 1988. Originally published by Sierra Club Books, 1963.

Power, Stephen. Gannett News Service, "Kitzhaber Seeks Dam Breaching Support," *Statesman Journal* (Salem, OR), March 1, 2000.

Quinn, Beth. "Dam Fight Costs GPID a Third of Its Water," *Mail Tribune* (Medford, OR), November 7, 1998.

Ragland, Jenifer. "Begins Demolition of Silt-Choked Matilija Dam," *Los Angeles Times,* October 13, 2000.

Reisner, Marc. *Cadillac Desert: The American West and Its Disappearing Water.* New York: Viking Penguin, 1986.

Rich, Louise Dickinson. *The Coast of Maine: An Informal History.* New York: Thomas Y. Crowell, 1956.

Rioux, Dwayne. "Maine Lore: Feeding Frenzy—Striped Bass Action Phenomenal on Lower Kennebec," *Central Maine Newspapers,* June 21, 2000. outdoors@centralmaine.com.

Ripple, Jeff, and Susan Cerulean, eds. *The Wild Heart of Florida: Florida Writers on Florida's Wildlands.* Gainesville: University of Florida Press, 1999.

River Alliance of Wisconsin. www.wisconsinrivers.org.

Sampson, Donald. "Columbia River Inter-Tribal Fish Commission, Donald Sampson, Executive Director, Testimony Before the Subcommittee on Water and Power of the Senate Energy and Natural Resources Committee, April 18, 2000."

Save Our Wild Salmon Coalition. www.removedams.org.

Schoenherr, Allan A. *A Natural History of California.* Berkeley and Los Angeles: University of California Press, 1992.

Shaw, Robinson. "California Dams Failing to Aid Salmon," *Environmental News Network,* November 9, 1999. www.enn.com.

Shiffer, James Eli. "Demolition Sets the Neuse Free: Quaker Neck Dam Crumbles into History," *Raleigh News & Observer,* December 18, 1997.

Smith, Senator Gordon. "Opening Statement of Senator Gordon Smith, Subcommittee on Water and Power of the Senate Energy and Natural Resources Committee," April 18, 2000.

Southern & Central California Atlas & Gazetteer. Yarmouth, ME: De-Lorme, 1998.

Spickler, Marjorie. "Guest Opinion: Dam Supporters Fight for Our Rights, Too," *Mail Tribune* (Medford, OR), May 7, 1998.

Stanford, Jack A. "Rivers in the Landscape: Introduction to the Special Issue on Riparian and Groundwater Ecology," *Freshwater Biology,* Vol. 40 (1998), pp. 402–406.

Stanford, Jack A., J. V. Ward, William J. Liss, Christopher A. Frissell, Richard N. Williams, James A. Lichatowich and Charles C. Coutant. "A General Protocol for Restoration of Regulated Rivers," *Regulated Rivers: Research & Management,* Vol. 12, No. 405 (1996), pp. 391–413.

Star (Ventura, CA). Editorial: "Bringing Balance to Water System," May 24, 2000.

Tekiela, Stan. *Wildflowers of Wisconsin: Field Guide.* Cambridge, MN: Adventure Publications, 2000.

Thoreau, Henry David. *The Maine Woods.* Boston: Ticknor & Fields, 1864.

Topping, Gary. *Glen Canyon and the San Juan Country.* Moscow: University of Idaho Press, 1997.

Ulrich, Roberta. *Empty Nets: Indians, Dams, and the Columbia River.* Corvallis: Oregon State University Press, 1999.

U.S. Army Corps of Engineers. "Draft Lower Snake River Juvenile Salmon Migration Feasibility Report and Environmental Impact Statement with Federal Caucus Conservation of Columbia Basin Fish 'All-H Paper,'" February 3, 2000.

———. Walla Walla District. McNary Lock and Dam, Pacific Salmon Visitor Information System. "Fish of the Snake and Columbia Rivers," "Columbia-Snake River Transportation System," and "Lower Granite Lock and Dam, Pertinent Data."

U.S. Bureau of Reclamation Central Valley Project—Shasta/Trinity Divisions. www.usbr.gov/dams/ca10186.htm and http://datawed.usbr.gov/html/shasta.html.

U.S. Department of Commerce. "Federal Fisheries Agency Adds Nine West Coast Salmon to Endangered Species List," March 16, 1999.

———. "Federal Agencies Release Four-H 'Working Paper' on Salmon Recovery in Pacific Northwest," November 16, 1999.

———. "Federal Agency Unveils Innovative E.S.A. Salmon Rules," June 20, 2000.

U.S. Department of the Interior. "Interior Secretary Signs Landmark Conservation Agreement to Remove Edwards Dam," May 26, 1998.

———. "Dams Are Instruments, Not Monuments: We Evaluate Them by the Health of the Watersheds to Which They Belong." Remarks of Interior Secretary Bruce Babbitt, FERC Distinguished Speakers Series, Washington, DC, July 8, 1998.

———. "Dams Are Not Forever." Remarks of Interior Secretary Bruce Babbitt, Ecological Society of America, August 4, 1998, Baltimore.

———. Media Advisory, "Babbitt Releases Plan to Overhaul Hydro Project, Restore Salmon," November 9, 1999.

———. Media Advisory, February 8, 2000.

———. "Secretary of the Interior Bruce Babbitt to Host Dam Removal Events," October 4, 2000.

U.S. Fish and Wildlife Service. http://nc-es.fws.gov/coastal/coastalindex.html.

———. USFWS Coastal Program. "Success on the North Carolina Coast," citing S. G. Worth, the North Carolina Fish Commissioner in 1881. http://nc-es.fws.gov/coastal/quaker.html and www.fws.gov/cep/northcar.pdf.

———. USFWS citing Smith, Hugh. *The Fishes of North Carolina* (Raleigh, NC: E. M. Uzzell and Company, 1907).

Wisconsin Department of Natural Resources. www.dnr.state.wi.us/org/land/er/factsheets/etlist1.htm#FISH and www.dnr.state.wi.us/org/gmu/lowerwis/baraboo.htm.

Washington Atlas & Gazetteer. Freeport, ME: DeLorme, 1995.

WaterWatch of Oregon, Portland. www.waterwatch.org.

Western Environmental Law Center. "Elle Creek Dam Found in Violation of Endangered Species Act." Media Advisory, February 1, 2001. www.welc.org.

White, Richard. *The Organic Machine: The Remaking of the Columbia River*. New York: Hill and Wang/Farrar, Straus and Giroux, 1995.

Wicker, Mike. *Nonpoint Source News Notes*, Issue #54, November 1998. www.epa.gov/owow/info/NewsNotes/issue54/nna54.html.

Wild Salmon Resource Center. Downeast Salmon Federation, Columbia Falls, ME. www.mainesalmonrivers.org.

Wildman, Laura A. S. "Sediment Transport Relating to Dam Removal: A Literature Search of Current Methods Used for Analyzing Sediment Transport," December 10, 1997.

Wiley, John K. "No Breaching of Dams, Bush Vows, as 2000 Welcome His Spokane Stopover," *Seattle Times*, Associated Press, September 25, 2000.

Will, Tracy. *Compass American Guides: Wisconsin*. Oakland, CA: Fodor's Travel Publications, 1994.

Wisconsin Atlas & Gazetteer. Freeport, ME: DeLorme, 1995.

Wisconsin, State of, Division of Hearings and Appeals. "Case No. 3-NO-98-1030, Application of International Paper Company to Abandon the Ward Paper Company Dam, City and Town of Merrill, Lincoln County, Wisconsin, Findings of Fact, Conclusions of Law and Permit.

Wisconsin, State of, Wisconsin Department of Natural Resources. "Lower Wisconsin River Water Quality Management Plan," January 1994.

———. "Environmental Analysis and Decision on the Need for an Environmental Impact Statement, Ward Mill Dam," August 5, 1998.

———. "Environmental Analysis and Decision on the Need for an Environmental Impact Statement (EIS) Wisconsin Department of Natural Resources—International Paper Company, Application for a Permit to Abandon Ward Paper Company Dam, City and Town of Merrill, Lincoln County, Wisconsin," September 11, 1998.

———. "Supplement to August 5, 1998, Environmental Assessment for the Proposed Abandonment and Partial Removal of the Ward Paper Company Dam," February 2, 1999.

———. "Fish References." http://www.dnr.state.wi.us/org/land/er/factsheets/etlist1.htm#FISH.

Witt, Bradley, Secretary-Treasurer for Oregon AFL-CIO. "Statement, Before the Subcommittee on Water and Power of the Senate Energy and Natural Resources Committee," April 18, 2000.

Wood, Robert L. *The Land That Slept Late: The Olympic Mountains in Legend and History*. Seattle: The Mountaineers, 1995.

Work Projects Administration. *Florida: A Guide to the Southernmost State, Compiled and Written by the Federal Writers' Project of the Work Projects Administration for the State of Florida*. New York: Oxford University Press, 1939.

World Commission on Dams. *Dams and Dam Development: A New Framework for Decision-Making: The Report of the World Commission on Dams*. London: Earthscan Publications, 2000.

WRAL 5 OnLine. "Dam Destroyed as Fish Wish Comes True," May 30, 1998. www.ural-tv.com/news/ural/1988/0530-dam-destroyed-as/Reporter/Photographer:BrianBowman.

acknowledgments

Everywhere I have gone in the course of writing this book, people have been extremely generous with their time, information and expertise. My thanks to everyone who shared with me their interest in the issues, knowledge, love of rivers and enthusiasm for the project. First, special thanks to Shawn Cantrell, Steve Evans, Betsy Ham, Charles Hudson, Bob Hunter, Pam Hyde, Stephanie Lindloff, Tracy Stone-Manning and Mike Wicker for reviewing the manuscript and helping me get the facts right. My sincerest thanks also to: Frank and Maggie Allen for the loan of a rental car, Bruce Babbitt, Joe Bakker, Judith Bashore, Eric Bloch, Kristen Boyles, Steve Brooke, Matt Brown, Rick Brown, Leah Cohn, Nicole Cordan, Dave Courtemanch, Kathy Crist, Laura Rose Day, Jan and Jeff DeBlieu, Nick DiCroce, Rick Dove, Rick Emerlen, John Exo, Ellen Fagg, Andy Goode, Brian Gorman, Ben Green, to my family—Alvin and Sari Grossman, Emily Grossman, Jane, Olivia and Philip Zisman, Robert Hass, Ed Henke, James Hepworth and Tanya Gonzales, Steve Hannon, Tim Hester, John Hightower, Buford Holt, Ric Ilgenfritz, Dr. Richard Ingebretsen, Kristina Jackson, Jan Hasselman, Bruce Keller, Andy Kerr, William Kier, Paul Koberstein and *Cascadia Times*, Hank Lacey, Michael Langland, Pete Lavigne, Jeri Ledbetter, Ester Lev, Gilly Lyons, Sam Mace and Ken Olsen, Richard Manning, Rob Masonis, Ellen Meloy, Christopher, Hannah and Lisa Merrill, Karen and Ralf Meyer, Joan Moody and her colleagues on Secretary Babbitt's staff, Carla and Jeff Moore and sons Bradley and Fred, Jim Myron, Peter Nielsen, Matt O'Donnell, Bill Oliver, David Orr, Felice Pace, Lisa Ramirez, Evan Richert, Douglas Robison, Gordon Russell, Mark Salvo, Matt Sicchio, Kathie Schmiechen, Dwayne Shaw, Jack Shoemaker, Trish

Hoard, Keltie Hawkins, Heather McLeod and all their colleagues at Counterpoint Press, Craig Smith, Geoff Smith, Mary Lou Soscia, Glen Spain, Dr. Jack Stanford, Leslie Straub, Robert Stubblefield, Ed Taylor, Margot and George Thompson, Laird Townsend, Todd True, Diane Valentine, Doug Watts, Heather Weiner, Amie Wexler, Wendell Wood, James Workman, Fred Ziati and Chris Zimmer. And thanks to Brooke Williams, Logan Hebner and Bob Helmes, who first got me to paddle a river.

index